What's Wrong With Dorfman ?

What's Wrong With Dorfman?

A Novel

By

John Blumenthal

FARMER STREET PRESS   CALIFORNIA

4

Cover and book design by Pete Masterson,
Aeonix Publishing Group, www.aeonix.com

Cover image: "The Anatomy Lecture of Dr. Nicolaes Tulp"
by Rembrandt © CORBIS

This is a work of fiction. With the exception of historic facts, places
and persons, all names, places, characters, and incidents are entirely
imaginary, and any resemblance to actual events or to persons living
or dead, is coincidental. The opinions expressed are those of the characters and should not be confused with those of the author.

Publisher's Cataloguing in Publication Data
(Provided by Quality Books, Inc.)

Blumenthal, John 1949 —
    What's wrong with Dorfman? : a novel / by John
Blumenthal. — 1st ed.
      p. cm.
      LCCN: 00-101031
      ISBN: 0-9679444-0-6

    1. Motion picture industry—Fiction.
2. Screenwriters—Fiction.   I. Title.

PS3552.L8485W53 2000   813'.6
        QBI00-277

00 01 02 10 9 8 7 6 5 4 3 2 1

Published by
Farmer Street Press
2060-D Ave. De Los Arboles #497
Thousand Oaks, CA 91362
Printed in the United States of America

He who laughs has not yet heard the bad news.

—*Bertolt Brecht*

If I could drop dead right now, I'd be the happiest man alive.

—*Attributed to Samuel Goldwyn*

Part One

CHAPTER

I diotic as this may sound, I have never been entirely convinced that one day I, Martin Dorfman, will actually be a dead person, that I will truly shuffle off this mortal coil, that I will, like billions of poor saps before me, perish, expire, croak, give up the ghost, pass away, breathe my last, kick the bucket. Sure, I've *worried* about death often enough, I've even obsessed on the subject, but not with any sense of realistic urgency. Why? Because in my heart of hearts I always figure the Grim Reaper will somehow skip over me, that Modern Science will find a cure, that I will never actually *expire*, not me, no way. If I could argue my way out of sixth period gym class at Rimbaldi Junior High, a feat requiring more than a little finesse, I can certainly wrangle my way out of something as pedestrian as death. In a pinch, my special relationship with God — the one in which I implore Him for mercy when I'm really desperate and then deny His very existence the following week — will cause Him to overlook my poor, pitiful self when my time comes to meet my Maker *i.e.* Him. Or my name will get lost in the mammoth filing system that surely must exist in His Heavenly Bureaucracy. Mine, you see, will be the missing card in the Cosmic Rolodex.

Part of the problem is that, having spent most of my life in a state of aliveness (opinions may differ), I simply can not picture myself as a dead person. Me, a corpse, forget it! It's just not my look folks. On some people cadaverhood works, but not me. What would I wear?

How could I keep a straight face with all those mourners looking so grim?

The fact is, I've only been to two funerals in my lifetime, but I just can't seem to make myself believe that there is really anybody *in the box*. It's a prank, you see, they've actually just left town for awhile or they've become part of the government's witness protection program. Somewhere, in some whitebread Midwestern town, these so-called "dead people" are actually still alive with bogus names, menial jobs and some plastic surgery. We are standing here weeping over an empty box, folks, I'm certain of it. We are eulogizing thin air!

And then the stark reality of it all suddenly hits me: I, Martin Dorfman, could develop colon cancer or Crohn's Disease or some other malignant horror and die by early next week and guess what would happen? Nada. Sure, my friends would weep and moan and say nice things about me, such as how generous and caring and optimistic I always was, all of it bunk. A rabbi I had never met in my life would utter a few generically pertinent words, a sort of Mad Lib Funeral Speech, a fill in the blanks panegyric. *Martin Dorfman was a blank man, a man of blank and blank. A man who felt blank for his fellow man.* Sure, my wife Ursula would grieve for awhile, shed some tears, soak a few hankies, but eventually she would remarry someone handsomer, wittier and more romantically inclined than me and live happily ever after in a larger house in a better part of town, one with a quieter dishwasher and a larger walk-in closet. The kids would be sad, but the promise of a frozen yogurt on a waffle cone with two toppings would snap them out of it with stunning alacrity.

All of which is going through my mind on this day — April 10, 1992 — as I hold in my hand two Little Pink Pills which, I am assured, will cure me of a mysterious disease that has plagued me for two solid years. Two years! One hundred and four weeks of nausea! Seven-hundred and thirty days of anguish! Seventeen thousand, five hundred and twenty hours of despair. One million, fifty one thousand, two hundred seconds of grief.

The point is, will these Little Pink Pills save me from another inept sojourn in the garage with the motor running and the door closed, a bungled attempt to do away with myself? Perhaps next time I should try hanging. Cleaner than bullets. No mess to clean up. On the other hand, I must say, the guillotine does have its appeal —

quiet, instantaneous — but where exactly does one find a guillotine and who would dispose of my head? Or, I could overdose on Valium. Die in my sleep. Never know what hit me. Go gentle into that good night...

But I'm getting way ahead of myself.

⟿

I remember... a crisp autumn evening, close to supper time. The air is alive with the blast of cap pistols, the smell of burning leaves. Buzzy Tannenbaum, Kenny Fishbeck and I are playing Cowboys and Indians in the open prairie of my backyard, although there are no Indians in this game, only cowboys. Nobody wants to be an Indian because it is 1958 and, except for Tonto, Indians are the perennial bad guys. This is the propaganda of the day. Besides, each of us has a black felt cowboy hat, a pair of silver-coated six-guns and a nifty leather holster stitched with shiny white lanyard cord which, like genuine rugged hombres of the Old West, we all got for Chanukah. Fashion dictates. So rather than argue semantics, we are all cowboys, all good guys, all courageous, miniature versions of John Wayne, though we will always refer to the game as Cowboys *and* Indians, absence of Indians notwithstanding.

As soon as we have all been shot dead at least four times, with the requisite torturous death throes (at which I excel), we tire of the game and start aimlessly tossing gravel at my dog, an ancient mass of black fur imaginatively called Blackie, who is sleeping soundly in the back doorway to the garage. A volcanic eruption on West Main Street would not cause this animal to lift an eyebrow, let alone a few poorly aimed pieces of gravel. Soon, we know, one of our mothers will be calling us in for supper, thereby ending the evening's sport, so we are killing time now, waiting to be summoned, trying in vain to get a rise out of the cataleptic mutt. The silence between us has a palpable masculine quality. We are sweaty; we are men.

"Sowadyawandonow?" Kenny asks, hurling a pebble straight up in the air to see how high he can throw. When it descends three seconds later, it bounces smartly off Buzzy's head.

"Dunno," I say.

"You wanna swing off Molson's tree?" Buzzy suggests. He is a pudgy, ruddy-cheeked kid with a greased-up flattop haircut and a face covered with freckles. His expression is one of permanent smugness, a sort of taunting half-smile, though he is not a bully.

I shrug. Kenny Fishbeck shrugs. One day, against all ethnic precedents, Kenny will become the town's Chief of Police, but now he is not sure if swinging on Molson's tree is worth incurring the wrath of Molson, a potbellied, liquor-breathing chain smoker with emphysema and a chronic hatred for nine-year-old boys. A man with a tattoo of a serpent on his arm!

I remove my cowboy hat and wipe the sweat off my forehead with the back of my sleeve, a gesture I have seen Gary Cooper perform to great effect. I spit meaningfully, artfully in the dirt, but as usual half of it lands on my own sneakers.

"You guys are chicken," Buzzy Tannenbaum accuses us, making rooster noises and flapping his elbows like wings. *Bock-bock, bock-bock.* This display is a challenge roughly equivalent to the flinging of the gauntlet in chivalrous times. Honor and credibility are at stake; our fledgling *manhoods* are on the line. Even at nine, we understand this to be true, although we have no idea what it means.

"Oh yeah, like shit," is Kenny's slashing retort. I sigh deeply and take a breath of fresh air, which is not fresh at all but filled with noxious lilac fumes, although there are no lilac bushes to be found in the immediate area. The fumes, I know, originate from our town's principal industry, a chemical plant called Brawer's Frutal Works, which manufactures scents for foods, soaps, fruit juices, candles and anything else that requires artificial redolence. Every morning, the people of Highland Falls wake up to Mr. Brawer's latest concoction spewing forth from the factory's smokestacks. Some days it's lavender, sometimes lilac, occasionally mint, although sometimes Mr. Brawer's adventures with odor go hopelessly awry and the town of Highland Falls is held in an invisible cloud of an indescribably putrescent stench.

I look at Kenny. "Molson doesn't get home till seven," I say. "He has to get drunk first."

"Why?"

"How should I know?"

"You sure he isn't home?"

"Yeah, I'm sure."

"What if he is?"

"Then he'll probably kill us."

"Really?"

"No doubt about it."

"How?"

"Shotgun probably."

"Jeez."

"Or he might breathe deadly emphysema germs on us."

"Oh God."

Buzzy is shaking his head. He socks Kenny in the arm. "You're chicken, Fishface," he taunts.

"It's Fish-*beck*."

"He's not a chicken," I say judiciously. "He's being sensible."

"Takes one to know one, huh Dorfman?"

"Don't call me Dorfman," I say. "I thought we had a solemn pact. You're Pancho, I'm Cisco and Kenny's Buffalo Bob."

"Buffalo Bob's not even a real cowboy," Buzzy says.

"Neither are Pancho and Cisco," Kenny adds. "They're just actors."

This seems to subvert Buzzy's argument. "So what's it gonna be Dorfman? Are you chickenshit like Fishface or what?"

Frankly, yes, but I don't say that. Instead, I sigh for effect. Sighing is a popular part of my social repertoire, the response I use when my mother beseeches me to stand up straight or to pull my hands out of my pockets, two areas in which she is peculiarly obsessive. Rolling my eyes is another faithful standby and occasionally I perform the two together, a sort of mad duet of gestures that never fails to annoy, the art of annoyance being every nine-year-old boy's *raison d'être*. But now I just sigh deeply and amble over to Molson's decrepit split rail fence, leap over it easily and head for the forbidden tree, a dry old maple with a low horizontal branch, ideal for swinging. I notice that I am swaggering and, for a brief moment, I am impressed by my own temerity; we'll see who's poultry in this neighborhood.

I leap the extra foot and grab on with both hands. Swinging my legs, I try for enough counterbalance to hang by the backs of my knees. Then I hear the crack and seconds later I am sitting on my ass, dazed, in Molson's yard, the long horizontal branch at my feet. The world is spinning. As soon as I understand the gravity of what has happened — *I have broken Molson's tree* — I dash for the cover of a concrete wall where I am quickly joined by Buzzy and Kenny. The three of us wait in terror for Molson's screen door to fly open but it does not.

"Holy shit, you're bleeding!" Buzzy observes and now I look at my white T-shirt and I notice that it is indeed splotched with blood. Lots of blood. More blood than I have ever seen in my life! Apparently, the branch had fallen on my head, though I do not remember this clearly. I start to feel dizzy.

"What are we gonna do?" Buzzy cries.

"Make a tourniquet!" Kenny says, yanking at his belt.

"And tie it around what?" says Buzzy, "His *neck*?"

Now I am crying, for the blood won't stop. The side of my face is covered, my T-shirt is ruined. Sobbing, I run for the front door of my house, but before I go in, I look into the driveway to see if my father's tan Buick is there. It is not. I tear open the front door and climb the stairs two at a time. I find my mother in the kitchen. I am hoping for a comforting word, perhaps an embrace, but when my mother turns and sees me, her eyes widen in horror and she says "Oh my God, your father will be home soon!"

Ten minutes later, I am sitting naked in our bathtub and my mother is dabbing the cut on my skull with a damp washcloth. The two inches of water around my naked body are a watery red. I do not cry; it is important that I be the brave little soldier for my mother and not cry. I am not sure *why* this is important, I just know that it is.

"Thank God, it stopped bleeding," my mother says. At 32, she wears her straight auburn hair pulled back severely in a bun, but a stray strand always seems to come loose and fall into her eyes. Now, as she looks at me over her harlequin glasses, she blows the errant strand away.

"Will I need stitches?" I ask.

"I don't think so, Martin."

"Are you sure?"

"Yes."

"How about brain damage?"

"I don't think so."

"Should we get a second opinion?"

"No."

"No offense, but I think I'd like a second opinion."

"Shut up, Martin."

"Okay fine," I say. "But I have a headache."

"And you have only yourself to blame, young man. How many times have I warned you about playing on that tree?"

Even at age 9 I recognize this as a question best left unanswered, so I keep my mouth shut. In the silence, we both hear my father's Buick rumble into the driveway. My mother's face visibly tightens.

"I'll give you some aspirin, but you have to promise me one thing," she says. "Don't say a word about this to your father. Not a word. You know how he is."

⌒

Oh yes, I know only too well *how he is*. This man, my father, is at once not only a practicing physician but a flaming hypochondriac as well. A pessimist. An alarmist! A man fraught with outlandish fears and absurd anxieties. A man utterly incapable of censoring his own lunacy no matter what the impact.

Oh yes, I do indeed know how he is. Every sore throat is mononucleosis! Every stomach ache, colon cancer. Every headache, a brain tumor! And God help you if your bare foot should come in contact with a rusty nail! Even a tetanus shot won't help you. *You want to get lockjaw, young man? You think lockjaw is a picnic? You will never be able to open your mouth to talk or to eat! Imagine that!* Forget for the moment that I have never in my life to this day heard of or read about a single human being who actually *has* lockjaw. I am assured that it exists by my father The Great Felix Dorfman and so I spend half of my youth terrified of rust!

To my father, the human body is utterly incapable of withstanding an invasion of even the most benign bacteria. And bacteria are everywhere, just waiting to get a foothold in the pathetic, defenseless muck of our anatomies. In his book, we have only ourselves to blame if we get sick. You get a chill, you're asking for pneumonia. You drink from a public water fountain, you're asking for a sore throat. You eat shrimp, you're asking for hepatitis. You put an unwashed finger in your mouth and God only knows what dangers await! Botulism, typhoid, myasthenia gravis, polio, malaria, syphilis, diptheria, the list goes on and on. And who are we, the medically uneducated members of his family — my poor mother, 15 years his junior with only a high school diploma — who are we to dispute the word of the Great Physician, Dr. Felix Dorfman, a man with degrees from not one, but *three* prestigious German universities! Is it any wonder I have a duodenal ulcer by the time I reach the ninth grade? Is it any surprise that, two years ago, when my sister breaks her arm after falling off a swing at a friend's house, she offers the kid's mother *hush money* to keep the accident quiet? *We don't have to tell Pop about this do we Mrs. Kipner? Will a sawbuck cover it?* What kind of a family is this when the agonizing pain of a compound fracture does not phase her, a five-year-old child, as much as the prospect of our father finding out about it!

And so, he arrives home that night from a full day of house calls, too tired or preoccupied to notice that I am wearing a cowboy hat at the dinner table. Ordinarily, this breach of etiquette would elicit a stern reproach, but his mind is elsewhere tonight. My mother waits on him as if she were an exceptionally fastidious waitress in a restaurant, taking the old plates away, putting down the new ones, refreshing his coffee, hovering nervously. This keeps her jumping because my father does not eat, he *scarfs*. We all scarf. It is as if we are in a race to see who can finish first. Nobody actually *tastes* anything my mother cooks because the food doesn't stay in the mouth long enough for the taste buds to identify it. I am convinced this is an ethnic quirk that goes back to the days of the pogroms. *Hurry up and eat Moishe, the Cossacks are burning down the shul again!*

Finally, after some feverish scarfing, my father looks up, first at me, then at my sister, Phoebe. My mother anxiously stops in mid-hover. I hold my breath. If the hat goes off, if he notices the dressing on my skull, there will be a big commotion and my mother and I will be blamed for my accident at Molson's tree. We will never hear the end of it. Ten years from now, twenty years from now, he will bring it up. It will become part of the Dorfman family lore. In our family, accidents don't just happen; they are *caused* by negligence, by carelessness, by stupidity. Same goes for diseases. This is a man who would not allow my mother to come near me for the first two years of my life unless she wore a *surgical mask*!

And now, at the dinner table, we all squirm, waiting for my father to mention the cowboy hat that hides my head wound. He is looking right at the offending hat, but it does not register. "You washed your hands before dinner?" he asks my sister and me.

"Yes," we drone.

"Both of you?"

"Yes."

"With soap?"

"Yes, with soap," although the thing called soap in our bathroom is actually a thick liquid surgical cleanser, one drop of which could sterilize all the septic tanks in Christendom.

"You created a nice lather?" he continues. "If there's no lather then you're wasting your time."

We know, we know. Enough already! I roll my eyes. This is a family that uses toilet seat liners in ITS OWN BATHROOM! My father goes back to eating, satisfied that neither of us is ingesting any life-threatening bacteria. I can feel my mother's relief; the cowboy hat has gone unnoticed. When my father is not looking, she gives me a conspiratorial wink. Our secret is safe.

∾

Another amusing little game we play at the dinner table is one called *Make My Sister Hysterical*. My father is the undisputed champion at this one. In fact, if it weren't for him, the game would not exist. He invented it. Here's how it goes: we all sit down to dinner. We cut, we fork, we spoon. We grunt, we scarf. We drink, we slurp. Then my father turns to me and says: "How was school today, Martin?" An innocuous enough question in a normal American household, but a lit fuse in this one. I cringe and, in my usual wordy way, reply "Fine."

"Fine?' he asks. "Is that all you can say?"

"Yeah."

"You can't give me a little more detail?"

I shrug. "Fine seems to cover it."

"Perhaps an adjective or two?"

"Fine *is* an adjective."

"Hah! Some adjective. And you call yourself a writer?"

"No Dad, not yet. I'm only nine."

"And how old do you suppose Mozart was when he composed his first concerto? I'll tell you. He was five."

"Mozart was a prodigy, Dad."

"Maybe you are too."

"Don't you think we'd have noticed it by now?" I ask.

"Not necessarily," he says. "Maybe you're a late-blooming prodigy."

"A late-blooming prodigy? Is that possible?"

"Anything is possible, Martin," he says. "All I'm saying is this: If 'fine' is the best you can do, maybe you should try another line of work."

I roll my eyes and my father goes back to eating. There is silence and I look across at Phoebe, whose face is turning red with mounting anger, a volcano waiting to erupt. You see, she is waiting for my father to ask *her* how school was. He never does. He just eats, oblivious to her anger even though this same scene has played out in exactly the same way a thousand times. My mother clears her throat a few times. Ahem, ahem, AHEM! Wake up, Felix. Yo! You have a daughter, remember, and she goes to school too! But does he respond? No, he just keeps eating.

We all wait about ten seconds for him to catch on, but of course he doesn't. Suddenly my sister throws her napkin down, hurls her chair back and, sobbing melodramatically, storms out of the room.

And what does my father, Mr. Sensitivity, do? He looks up from his plate, perplexity in his eyes, and glances first at my mother, then at me and says, "What in blazes is wrong with *her* now?"

This is where I hone my pre-adolescent skills as a mediator. Don't ask me why, but with the dining room suddenly exploding into an emotional shouting match, with my sister screaming at my father, my mother screaming at my sister, my father wondering why everybody is screaming, and the dog barking insanely at the whole internecine spectacle, it is left to me, a nine-year-old, to arbitrate the dispute. I calmly eat my apple pie while the windows rattle around me from all the commotion and when the noise level has dissipated enough for me to be heard without shouting, I quietly, logically, oh-so coolly explain to each member of my family how and why each one of them is behaving like an imbecile. I am very good at this, articulate, evenhanded, impartial. I smooth things over. At once, I understand everybody's feelings and can put them into words. By the time my mother has poured the last cup of my father's coffee, everyone is on speaking terms again, everything is quiet, everybody is fine again, the dog is sleeping, things are back to normal. I am suddenly, at the age of nine, the only adult in the room.

CHAPTER **2**

The symptoms first hit me about four months after my forti-eth birthday, an occasion I deliberately let pass without fan-fare. Ursula tries to talk me into having an extravagant birth-day bash, a catered affair for forty people or more, but I decline. Why? Because I see no reason to celebrate the fact that I am now one whole year closer to my death. Achieving chronology is, after all, not really much to brag about. If I win the Nobel Prize then bring on the dancing girls, strike up the band! For birthdays I'll be content to have a few stiff drinks and wallow in self-pity. When my father calls, he senses my despair and, in his inimitable way, makes it worse by saying: "Congratulations Martin, you've outlived Mozart by five years."

Like Lewis and Clark (whose motivation was presumably differ-ent from mine), I have by this time managed to put an entire conti-nent between myself and my father. First came a one year stint in New York City in 1974 (75 miles), then Chicago until 1979 (2000 miles), and now finally, I am three thousand glorious miles away, in California. If it were possible to put an entire solar system between us or better yet, several galaxies, I would happily buy a one-way ticket. Not that it makes any difference; one long distance phone call from him and I am instantly reduced to a blubbering twelve-year-old. Even death, I am told, does not succeed in separating you from your par-ents, unless the death in question happens to be your own. And even then, who knows? Hell might just be spending eternity with Dr. Felix Dorfman in a studio apartment with one bathroom.

Anyway, the symptoms first rear up in early April of 1989. A sick, heavy, distinctly *tumor-like* feeling at the lower extremity of my abdomen, as if I have swallowed something that was either meant to be asphalt or Mexican food. This is accompanied by the odd sensation that I am wearing a bad pair of glasses — things seem slightly cock-eyed, as if my eyes are misjudging distances, but ever so slightly, just enough to make me feel queasy, not unlike a mild but persistent case of seasickness. My hearing is suddenly a little weird — voices seem to boom around me, music is irritating. I am suddenly very sensitive to light. Do I attribute my symptoms to a simple case of the flu? To a virus? No. Since I am my father's son, I immediately conclude that I have a brain tumor. Malignant and inoperable, of course.

"Then how do you explain the abdominal pain?" Ursula asks, in her nearly perfect, accentless English, playing devil's advocate. Where Ursula comes from, the standard remedy for everything from multiple sclerosis to indigestion is a shot of schnapps.

"Colon cancer," I say glumly, my head in my hands.

"So you're ruling out colitis and Crohn's Disease?"

"For the time being," I say.

"Colon cancer and a brain tumor at the same time," she says, giving an astounded whistle. "Lucky you. What are the odds of that happening?"

"For someone in *my* family? Hah! Piece of cake! Haven't you heard about the Dorfman Curse? When it comes to long odds, we don't win lotteries, but if a meteorite should fall to earth, guess whose house it will hit?"

"Maybe it was something you ate for dinner?"

"We ate the same thing."

"It's probably just a flu bug then."

"Probably."

"Perhaps a glass of schnapps…?"

It is a fine Spring day and we are driving along the Pacific Coast Highway to Santa Barbara for what Ursula likes to refer to as "a romantic holiday," a chance to relax without being interrupted by an insomniac three-year-old clutching a shredded night-night blankie.

A diehard romantic, Ursula has booked us a room at a bed and breakfast, a romantic hideaway that boasts "charming antique furnishings," a private balcony and a "spectacular view of the Pacific Ocean" (as if we thought maybe we could see the Mediterranean from here). This will be our last opportunity to be alone together, for in two weeks time she is taking the kids to Germany for a month to visit her parents, who live in a small farming town in Bavaria. I dread the separation, in particular that emotional moment at the airport when I will say good-bye to them for *four whole weeks.* As a member of the Dorfman clan, I am of course terrified that the plane will crash and I will never see them again. Good-byes always take on this special paranoid urgency in my family; to us, every farewell is nothing less than a dress rehearsal for the ultimate farewell, death.

Anyway, here we are, off to a weekend of romance, the only problem being that I find it almost impossible to *be* romantic, even under healthy circumstances. Why is it such an effort for me? Why do those three little words get stuck in my throat with the frog and the post nasal drip? Granted, this was not a phrase that saw much traffic in my parents' household, where touching and kissing were considered good ways of transmitting germs but otherwise not of much practical use. Upbringing notwithstanding, I simply cannot get into a convincing romantic mood and maintain a straight face at the same time. For one thing, I just don't see the need for candles when we have the wonder of electricity at our disposal. Soft music just lulls me to sleep. I'm allergic to most flowers. And I am physically unable to coo sweet nothings because I have no idea exactly what the hell a sweet nothing *is.* And how in blazes does one *coo?* Lately, this has become an area of contention between us, my romantic ineptitude, my unwillingness or inability to perform these simple little rituals that she finds so pleasing. And so I ask myself this basic philosophical question: Why do women need us to tell them we love them over and over? Isn't the fact that we take out the garbage without being asked proof enough?

By early evening none of my symptoms have subsided. I am starting to really worry now. The bed and breakfast has turned out to be a disappointment: not only is breakfast *not* included, the "antique furnishings" are actually from someone's garage sale circa 1970, as if anything made of Formica and particle board could be considered antique; the balcony is dilapidated and covered with Astroturf; and to actually *see* the Pacific you'd have to hang from the eaves. I've seen catacombs with more warmth. Ursula is crestfallen and sits weeping on the edge of the bed; another romantic attempt gone sour. Do I console her? Do I offer a word of encouragement? No. I am looking in the mirror at the whites of my eyes to make sure I don't have hepatitis.

The next morning, in a desperate effort to wring something positive out of this disaster, Ursula takes a solo stroll on the beach while I spend the entire day alone in the hotel room, moaning and groaning in bed. None of the old remedies has worked. Even my trusty sidekick Pepto Bismol, the elixir that has saved me from countless bouts of dysentery, fails to relieve any of my symptoms. Ursula is a good sport about it and I manage to get up at dusk and wobble out of the room. We cap off a perfect holiday by eating soggy enchiladas at a badly lit Mexican restaurant that features the musical double whammy of a mariachi band playing *Yellow Bird*.

A week later, after Ursula and I have returned home from our ill-fated Santa Barbara holiday, I am still miserable. I am experiencing a general malaise, a lack of energy and appetite, a listlessness, accompanied by a profound sense of gloom and a vague nausea. I feel unsteady and frail, and I am not sleeping more than four hours a night. The nagging pain in my gut persists and the surface of my skin gives off an odd chill. My tongue is coated white, my weight is down by 5 pounds in less than a week. I look gaunt and ashen. I have no fever but I am clearly not a well man. By now, I have branched out into new pharmaceutical territory, sampling the vast array of antibiotics my father supplies me with, but nothing seems to work. My mystery disease is impervious to both prescription drugs and the usually reliable over-the-counter remedies.

And so I consult my medical library, in particular a book entitled *Symptoms After Forty*, a sort of layman's compendium of diseases one can expect to encounter at middle age. My hands shake as I turn to the chapter on diseases of the intestines; I hold my breath as I read about colon cancer, diverticulitis and Crohn's Disease. My heart is pounding; the hairs on the back of my neck tingle. I slam the book shut but the words reverberate in my head: "Persistent, inexplicable abdominal pain is usually an early warning sign of colon cancer…"

"Omigod," I tell Ursula. "It really *is* colon cancer!"

"Call the doctor."

"I have all the symptoms!"

"Call the doctor."

"Is my will up to date?"

"Call the goddamn doctor."

"Have we discussed cremation?"

Ursula dials the number herself and holds out the receiver, tapping her foot impatiently.

"You're not going to like this, Martin," Dr. Margolis says calmly after I have described my symptoms in the sort of professional-sounding medical mumbo jumbo that would make my father proud. "But it sounds to me like stress."

Stress! Oh *please*! What is this, *Amateur Hour*? Excuse me? Stress? For this you went to medical school for four years? For this you pull in a quarter of a million bucks a year? *Stress*? Come on, give me a break. Stress is the great waste paper basket of diagnoses. Everybody knows that! I'm a doctor's son, you're going to have to do better than that!

"I don't feel any particular stress," I say petulantly.

"Marriage all right?".

"Just fine."

"Career?"

"Good."

"Kids?"

"Healthy."

"Parents?"

"Totally crazy."

"No moves, no vacations coming up?"

"No," I say wearily, "and no deaths in the family."

"Been out of the country lately?"

"Like where?"

"Guatemala, Costa Rica… India?"

"Just to our summer cottage on the Ganges."

"At least you've still got a sense of humor."

"Tell my agent."

"Of course, we can't rule out the flu. There are lots of oddball flus out there."

"It doesn't feel like the flu, Doc," I say. "I've had the flu. Twenty-four hours and it's gone. This feels like something is profoundly wrong. Something *systemic*."

"What are you taking for it?"

"What am I *not* taking for it?"

"Give it a week," he says. "If the symptoms persist we'll run a few tests."

Before I can ask him exactly what tests he has in mind, he has hung up, leaving the answer to my imagination. I mean, are we talking stool sample or colonoscopy? CAT scan or MRI? Upper GI or lower GI? And what if they find something? A polyp? A lesion? An edema? A tumor, a malignancy! Leukemia! Lou Gehrig Disease! Multiple sclerosis! The dreaded myasthenia gravis in which half of your face loses muscle control! Oh my God, what if I need... *surgery?* Transfusions! Tainted blood! General anesthesia! And, horror of horrors, that marvel of modern scientific invention — the dreaded colostomy bag! I'm only forty years old, God; I'm not supposed to go through this for another thirty years!

And suddenly his ridiculous, patronizing diagnosis has become a self-fulfilling prophesy. For what I am now feeling, on top of everything else, is definitely stress.

When I am five, my parents decide to send me away to a day camp called Camp Waywayonda, a name that sounds to me less like an Indian word, as it purports to be, and more like somebody from New Jersey trying to say *way, way yonder*. I do not want to go to Camp Waywayonda; I would rather stay home with my mother and bake cookies or just tag along to the grocery store. I like the routine. I am told that Camp Waywayonda will be fun; we'll make things, we'll take hikes, roast marshmallows over a campfire, sing Indian songs. The fresh air will invigorate me. My mother tells me this in a voice filled with feigned enthusiasm. I'm not buying it; I would rather stay home.

The closer we get, the more I panic. What if I don't know anybody? What if the counselors are mean? What if the food is no good? Finally, I begin to cry. My mother looks at me in the rear view mirror and shakes her head; she is clearly disappointed in me.

"Pull yourself together, Martin," she says. "We're almost there."

"I don't want to go," I say. "Turn around."

"I beg your pardon? Do you have any idea how much it costs to go to camp?"

"How much?"

"Plenty."

"Whatever it is, I'll pay you back."

"Don't be ridiculous."

"You can have all the money in my piggy bank."

"Most children would be grateful to their parents for sending them to a nice summer camp."

"Like who?"

"Don't be smart with me, young man."

"I could work around the house," I say. "Polish Dad's shoes, rake the lawn, reshingle the roof…"

"Don't be silly."

"I'm not being silly. I'm serious."

She looks at me with an expression that appears to my young eyes to be… contempt. She is angry with me, no doubt about it. "My God, you're five years old now, Martin. It's time you acted like it don't you think?"

"I don't want to go," I repeat.

"How do you know you don't want to go?"

"I just don't. Turn around."

"You're going and that's that. There will be no discussion, young man. Now wipe those silly, idiotic tears away."

I do as she says and hold back the tears, although I cannot seem to control the quiver in my lip. She deposits me with a muscle-bound teenager named Rick, gives me a perfunctory kiss good-bye and strides to her car. It is all I can do to muster the courage not to run after her, although Rick is holding my hand so tightly I would have to use my knees to pry myself loose from his grip. So I watch her drive off but I do not cry. Instead, I barf on Rick's sneakers. Half-digested pancakes and bile, a nice combination.

As it turns out, Camp Waywayonda is not so horrible. We make ceramic ashtrays and clay sculptures and lanyards. We swim in a lake and hike through mosquito-infested fields. We are all given Indian names. I forget what mine is, but what it should be is *Craps in His*

Pants, for that is what I do every afternoon at rest period.

And why do I drop a load in my trousers every afternoon at rest period? Because my parents, who are so spectacularly neurotic about cleanliness, so obsessed with toilets, so phobic about germs, have sent me to a place where I am supposed to make doody in a wooden outhouse that gives new dimension to the word filth. I mean, this outhouse, this rickety pile of wood, this rectangular box of unbearable stench is crawling with bacteria that science hasn't even gotten around to naming yet! Not to mention spiders, mosquitoes, huge dragonflies, wriggling white maggots and god-knows-what-else! We are talking about a toilet seat made out of wood here! Not smooth wood, not wood that someone has taken the time to sand. *Splintery* wood! Wood that is hazardous to the naked buttock! Wood with *rusty nails* sticking out of it!

And where does all the accumulated pee-pee and cocky and toilet paper end up? In the sewer? In a tank of disinfectant? No sirree Bob. On the *ground* directly under the outhouse, that's where! That's right, it just sits there, pile after pile of ca-ca, festering in the hot August heat, a veritable Galapagos of evolving life-forms. And you can forget about washing your hands afterward — there's no sink in the area, no soap, not even a lousy towel just a water fountain. People go to the outhouse and then wash their hands in a water fountain! The same water fountain that we're supposed to *drink* from! If my father got an eyeful of this travesty he would have a coronary on the spot.

So I do not venture into the outhouse, not solely because it is nauseatingly filthy beyond all basic civilized standards, but because I am terrified that I will be bitten on the balls by a spider. Some huge tarantula or furry black widow is going to crawl up out of the muck onto that wooden seat and clamp its spidery jaws down on my nuts! They will swell up and probably have to be amputated along with my pecker just to be on the safe side. I will lose my manhood before I even know what it is supposed to be used for! And so, I drop a load every day at nap time. After nap time, I wander off into the forest on some pretense and bury the evidence, my dirty underpants, under leaves and moss and branches. Of course, after awhile my mother begins to wonder why all my underpants are disappearing. When interrogated, I pretend ignorance, but one day I am taken aside by the head counselor and told that I can use the regular bathroom *inside* the camphouse, the one with a real porcelain toilet, a smooth plastic toilet seat and a real sink, if that would make me feel more comfortable. It does. After that, Camp Waywayonda is tolerable.

"All of which is apropos of what?" Nora, my therapist, asks.

It is a warm summer day in 1990 and I am sitting on her couch, a box of Kleenex beside me. She is staring fixedly at me, so I feign interest in the Kleenex; I am utterly *captivated* by the Kleenex. Clearly Nora's previous client made good use of them for I can see a small pile of crumpled up tissues in the trash barrel. They are still damp. From the waiting room, I have heard people bawling in this room, loud horrible sobs of grief, great choking wails of psychic pain. From time to time, I am tempted to cry myself, but I do my best to withstand the impulse come hell or high water and have thusfar been successful. I am proud to say I have not soiled a single Kleenex.

"What do you mean?" I ask.

"I think you know what I mean."

"Spell it out."

"Your experience at this camp," she continues. "What's the relevance?"

"Are Kleenex a deductible expense in your business?" I ask, segueing subtly to another subject. "I'll bet you go through about a thousand boxes of these a year. You could take a nice tax deduction."

"You haven't answered my question."

"I'll bet the Kleenex Company takes out full page ads in all the shrink trade publications. They'd be crazy not to. Visine too. I'll bet most of your patients go through a lot of Visine. By the way, *are* there shrink trade publications?"

"Martin."

"Yes?"

"You think we might get back to the subject at hand?"

"What was the subject at hand?"

"I think you know."

I look away. Nora has penetrating eyes which, when combined with the solemn, Puritan-like expression on her face, could beat anybody in a staring contest and probably melt cast iron. There is a peculiar hardness to this stare, a challenging quality. Of course, my looking away is Mistake Number One. Mistake Number Two is the fact that my arms are folded across my chest. These are all defense mechanisms, physical barriers I erect when I feel threatened. Or so she claims.

"It just popped into my head," I say. "It's apropos of nothing in particular."

"Are you sure?"

"Positive."

"You don't see any connection?"

"No."

"Come on, Martin. You're stalling"

"At ninety bucks an hour I'm stalling?"

"You'll do almost anything to avoid confronting yourself, won't you?"

"That's ridiculous."

"Is it?"

She is still staring at me, boring in like a corkscrew. I slouch back on the couch, another defense mechanism. I look at the clock. Ten minutes left in the session, an eternity. How can I possibly bullshit around for that long?

"Martin, how did you feel when your mother left you at the camp?"

"I don't remember."

"Yes you do."

"Fearful."

"Good. Anything else?"

"Sad."

"Can you recall any physical sensation?"

"Principally nausea."

"Nausea is not how most people experience sadness."

"No?"

"No."

I give this some thought.

"And how did you feel when your wife and kids went to Germany for a month?"

"Fine. I felt fine."

"You think you felt fine."

"Oh please."

"What about your symptoms?"

"They went away."

"When?"

"Two days before they left for Europe. I was fine again."

"But the symptoms came back."

"Okay they came back. So what?"

"You're still not getting this?"

"What are you trying to say, that I got sick because I was sad to see my family go?"

"Is that so hard to believe?"

"Give me a break! I mean, who wouldn't be a little sad? It's a natural reaction. Thousands of people say good-bye to their families, why am I the only schmuck who gets sick?"

"That's right Martin, let it out."

"Huh?"

"All that bottled up emotion and anger, let it out."

"I just did."

"That was the tip of the iceberg."

"That was the *whole* iceberg."

"Come on, have a catharsis," Nora says, gently coaxing. "You'll feel better, I guarantee it."

But I just sit there next to the Kleenex box and sneak a look at my watch.

CHAPTER

It is 1961 and we are the only family in Highland Falls that has a fallout shelter. Down in the basement, just behind the furnace, is a dark, dank room constructed entirely of lead-lined concrete a foot thick. It has the dimensions of an average size bathroom and is stocked with enough canned food to last a month; canned fruit, canned peas, Spam. There are four cots, a number of thermal blankets, a small generator and a transistor radio so that we can listen to the news as the world is being destroyed, assuming there is someone still alive to anchor the news desk. A labyrinthine system of ducts and filters makes it possible for us to breathe clean air, although my father has included in our provisions a box of cigars, two pipes, a tin of tobacco and a month's supply of matches. Under one of the cots is a chest in which my father has stored enough pharmaceuticals to stock the first post-apocalyptic drugstore, everything from Kaopectate to Coppertone sun tan lotion. We all rest easier with the knowledge that, should Armageddon come, we won't have to worry about diarrhea or sunburn while cavorting on some deserted radioactive beach.

Not only are we the only family in Highland Falls with a fallout shelter, we have it *before* the Cuban Missile Crisis! What prescience! What precognition! While everybody else in town is scared to death that Khrushchev will push the button, we are possessed of an equanimity that we have never experienced before as a family. We are *cool*. We are carefree. Let Khrushchev push the button! Let them reduce the world to one huge heap of rubble! Let the Apocalypse come! Who cares? *We'll still be here.*

Of course, it apparently never occurs to my father that being the only survivors in the tri-county area is not such a bargain, either for us or for the rest of the world. Sure we have enough canned food for a month *but then what?* Thirty days after World War Three is over, with Highland Falls transformed into a Nagasaki-like wasteland, we will emerge pale, but fat and sassy from our lead-lined fallout shelter and do what exactly? Go to the A&P and stock up on pot roast? *Radioactive pot roast?* Make a dinner reservation at Howard Johnson's and eat hamburgers that glow in the dark? Everybody else on the planet has a nice quick death while we get to suffer for months with radiation poisoning.

"Fine, Mr. Know-It-All," my father says. "You want to stay above the ground with all the other *schlemiels*, go ahead."

"Okay."

"Don't give me 'okay,' young man. I spent a fortune on this fallout shelter. A fortune! Why? So you and your sister would be able to survive nuclear annihilation."

My father clamps his teeth down on the stem of his unlit pipe. At 48, he is disheveled, a curmudgeon in baggy pants and a misbuttoned vest. A pink patch of eczema colors the area above the bridge of his long nose and flakes of dandruff sprinkle the shoulders of his blue blazer.

"What's the point?" I ask.

"The point is, you will not be staying above ground. You will be staying in the fallout shelter with the rest of us. Somebody has to carry on the family name."

"Why?"

"Why? Because that's what life is all about, Martin. Continuity."

"Fine," I say, trying to head off another lecture on my father's pet theory of life and the universe — his Cosmic Mitosis Theory. We have all heard it at least fifty times. It goes like this: The entire universe and everything in it is motivated by one principle — reproduction. Cells do it, we do it, and the fact that the universe is expanding says to my father that it too is experiencing mitosis; it is reproducing into two universes which will then continue to reproduce for an infinite period of time and so forth... It is Felix Dorfman's Unified Field

Theory.

"Fine," I repeat. "If they drop the Big One, I'll go in your lousy fallout shelter."

"Thank you so much. And in the meantime, do me a favor and don't tell anyone about it."

"Why not?"

My father knocks his forehead with the butt of his palm. "You're such a smart guy," he says. "You tell me."

"I give up," I say after a moment.

"Because comes the H-Bomb, I don't want the whole town lining up to get into *my* fallout shelter, that's why not. Fear can do strange things to people, Martin. Fear can turn people into animals. Better the neighbors don't know. Do you know what the manufacturer suggests?"

"No."

My father beckons me to come closer and he whispers the answer confidentially in my ear. "They suggest that you invest in a firearm."

"Wow! Really?"

"Yes," my father says solemnly. "It is meant as a precaution. In the event you should need to..."

"Shoot the neighbors?"

"Convince them to go away."

This image is so incongruous I have to clench my teeth and look down at my shoes to keep from laughing. Somehow, I cannot picture my father, a man who cannot successfully change a light bulb, drilling the Molsons with a sawed-off shotgun.

"So can I see it?" I ask.

"See what?"

"The gun."

"There is no gun. Do you think I'm crazy? Do you think I would actually purchase a firearm and shoot the neighbors?"

"Then why..."

"I just brought it up to illustrate why we need to keep this little secret to ourselves."

"Oh."

"So do me a favor and keep quiet about it."

"What about the contractors who built it," I say. "What's keeping their mouths shut?"

"I made them promise to keep quiet," my father says. "I took care of them."

Of course, within a month all the neighbors know we have a fallout shelter and think it's one hell of a big joke, especially Mr. Molson who cannot resist the impulse to imitate the whistling sound a falling bomb makes every time he sees one of us. By 1965 the whole town knows about it and we find ourselves giving guided tours of the dark cobwebbed room when the curious come by asking questions. Later, our local paper does a feature article on it (*LOCAL DOC HOPES TO SURVIVE WWIII*). Sometimes I go down there and practice the Flutophone or the violin or the harmonica because the acoustics are so outstanding. My sister and I retreat to this dungeon in the depths of summer because it's the only cool place on the property. And during my high school years, the privacy of the lead-lined concrete walls becomes a popular place to take dates. In fact, I happen to lose my virginity within those cold, drab walls on June 27, 1970. But that's another story.

ᴜꙩᴍ

Two days before Ursula and the kids are scheduled to depart for Frankfurt on a plane that I am certain will crash and burn over the Atlantic, my mysterious symptoms suddenly vanish. Just like that. Gone! I am so relieved that I quickly promise God that I will refrain from anything even remotely sinful for the duration of my life, a solemn oath that will last about a week.

And so we are off to the airport. Ursula puts on her makeup while I drive; the kids bustle with excitement in the back seat. I concentrate on the road. On the way, as we become hopelessly stuck in bumper-to-bumper traffic on the San Diego Freeway, I am reminded of a photograph of my father, my sister and me that was taken in the summer of 1959. In this picture, shot by my mother, we are all standing in front of a lifeboat on the upper deck of an ancient ferryboat called the Nobska just before it is about to disembark from the island of Nantucket for the port of Woods Hole. Summer vacation is over and everyone is going home to the heat and torpor and mad hurly-burly of the mainland. Children will be going back to school, fathers will be returning to the rat race and our Dad will go back to being a physician, a profession he has never been particularly fond of. We have had a terrific summer, for the Island has a special ineffable charm all its own, a dreamlike quality. But now, we are all standing on the deck of this old steamer and three of us are wearing sunglasses, even though the day is gray and overcast, the sun hidden behind a thick layer of altocumulus clouds. For every summer when we leave the island, my father, my sister and I traditionally don shades. Why? Because the three of us tend to become emotional at this farewell and we cannot bear the thought that a stranger will witness the tears that inevitably come to our eyes when the Nobska's whistle blows and the ship begins to creak away from the wharf pilings. God forbid, someone should see that we are human! God forbid that we should demonstrate human frailty to each other! We are despondent about leaving and embarrassed about our feelings, all except for my mother who seems completely immune to sentimentality. She's a tough cookie, my mother. No tears in her eyes. No need for sunglasses. My father, who appears to find the return to real life particularly depressing, is generally the most lachrymose; I have seen him gush with heaving sobs as the old steamer pulls groaning out of its berth. Mortified, he faces the sea, tears streaming down his cheeks. My mother, who seems to find this lugubrious display repulsive, generally retires aft just before the whistle sounds.

And so, as I drive my family to the airport this day in April of 1989, I am wearing the traditional pair of sunglasses. Even though it is overcast.

⌖

Of course, I could have avoided all this emotional tumult simply by going with them to Germany. The choice was mine and I opted for home, so if I am lonely and miserable I have no one to blame but myself. On the other hand, if you have ever spent four weeks on a pig farm in the boondocks of Bavaria, as I did in the summer of 1982, you will understand why I made that choice. After three days, when the quaintness and charm have worn thin, you are confronted with the grim prospect of spending another 25 days swatting flies, eating *kuchen mit schlage* five times a day and discussing the Epicurean qualities of blood sausage, a delicacy that has no practical reason to exist.

Of course, this is not what I tell Ursula. I tell her that I need to stay home and work, which is not entirely bogus. "The script," I say.

"Something might happen."

"That's true."

"It would be just my luck to be out of town when my ship finally comes in."

"My parents have a telephone. Your agent could call you."

"That would be a novelty."

"Well, it's up to you," she says.

"I'd better stay home."

"Suit yourself." She says this a little too quickly, as if she is relieved.

"Admit it. You don't really want me to come, do you?"

"Of course I do," Ursula says. "It's just that…"

"What?"

"Well, it's such a strain on everybody to keep you occupied. For me it's enough to just hang out with my family and schmooze. For you we have to come up with a *schloss* a day just to keep you happy."

"I'm not that demanding."

"Oh yes you are."

"A *schloss* every other day would do."

"You'll be bored."

"Probably."

"It's up to you."

"I'll stay home."

"Are you sure?"

"Yes."

But the fact is I am not sure. It is possible that the script my agent has just sent out to his "A-list of producers" could very well remain unread for the next three weeks, in which case I will be twiddling my thumbs alone at home, bored and undernourished, while my family is having a high old time in Europe, watching pigs wallow in their own excrement.

Fact is, I am experiencing career problems. Work has suddenly dried up. I have hit forty and not one of my scripts has actually been shot; for some reason, that final crucial step eludes me. I am perceived around town as a bad bet. Over the hill. A burnout. So the studios stop calling. And then my agent of ten years, a guy who has lectured me incessantly on the depths of his loyalty when my career is faring well, drops me. Just like that. And makes it sound like an amicable divorce. So I get a new, less powerful agent, a young ambitious 300 pound agent named Gavin, who takes me out for a cup of Cappuccino and a Danish. A big spender. If your career prospects rise or fall proportionately to the amount of money your agent spends when he takes you out on expense account, I'm in big trouble. But Gavin is enthusiastic. He cleans his tortoise shell glasses with his tie and strokes his well-groomed beard and advises me to reinvent my career by writing a script on speculation.

"A nice family comedy," he says. "Something wholesome and sappy with a lot of heart. A nice family comedy I can always sell."

"You mean a kid's movie with *schmaltz.*"

"Exactly. They're very big these days."

"How big?"

"Big."

"But I don't have any ideas."

"You got kids, am I right? What are they interested in?"

"Well, my two-year-old is primarily interested in my wife's nipples. My six-year-old likes Barney."

"Who's Barney?"

"You don't know Barney?"

"Should I?"

"Everybody knows Barney. Barney's a purple dinosaur."

"Okay, so forget your kids. Go out and find a ten-year-old and ask him. Preferably a not very bright ten-year-old."

"You're joking."

"I don't joke, my friend. I leave that to my clients. They're the professionals. Me, I'm just an agent, a mere servant to the geniuses of the writing trade if you will. My advice to you? Go, invent, create."

And, having no other choice, that's what I do.

⌃

From the time I enter the seventh grade, my father no longer refers to me as Martin. No, by this time I have acquired an alias, a sardonic, slightly deprecating nickname. From the age of 12, I am henceforth known to my father as "Dr. Einstein."

This moniker originates as a result of my first day of Hebrew School in October of 1961. I am twelve years old, less than a year away from my Bar Mitzvah. The problem is, Bar Mitzvah or no Bar Mitzvah, I do not want to be in Hebrew School; as a dedicated and longtime atheist, I do not see the point. I would rather be out play-

ing baseball or touch football or riding my new Schwinn. But my
father insists and so, against my will, I find myself sitting restlessly in
a stifling classroom on a perfectly fine autumn morning, listening
inattentively as Rabbi Goldbloom speaks to us about the origins of
Judaism.

Rabbi Goldbloom is a kindly old gentleman of sixty-five who
speaks in a sing-song voice peppered with a slight German accent.
An immigrant from Dresden. He is short, no more than five feet
four, and wears a black fedora over a yarmulke and a double-breasted
suit of pre-War European provenance. He smells vaguely of
naphthaline. A watch chain glimmers from his vest pocket as he begins to tell us about Abraham and the development of monotheism,
the concept, the gimmick that so revolutionized religion. The topic
excites him for I see two little foamy pools of saliva gathering in
either corner of his mouth.

"One God," Rabbi Goldbloom says, thrusting an index finger
upward. "Not many Gods, not a God of Fertility and a God of the
Sun and so on and so forth, but one God, a single God who created
man and the universe. This was the great revelation, children, a great
truth, a great—"

But now he notices me raising my hand and he squints to see
who it is, for I am sitting in the back row. "Yes, Martin," he says. "You
have a question?"

"Why?" I ask.

"Why what?"

"Why was it such a great revelation?"

Rabbi Goldbloom smiles benevolently. "Because it was the truth,
Martin. Because there is only one God."

"I don't mean any disrespect, Rabbi, but how do you know?" I
ask. "I mean, how do we know there aren't fifty Gods out there, a
hundred even? Where's the proof?"

"The proof?"

"Can you prove that there is only one God? I mean, even if you
could, what's the difference? Is praying to one God really any better
than praying to fifty? I just don't see why this one God business is
such a big breakthrough."

Rabbi Goldbloom is momentarily speechless and suggests that,
if I am so interested in the subject, perhaps he can recommend some

supplemental reading. But apparently he calls my parents and relates to them the substance of our debate, because when I get home from Hebrew School that day, my father is waiting for me and he is not happy. "So now after an hour in Hebrew School you're a theological scholar!" he says. "My son, Dr. Einstein!"

"I just asked a simple question, Dad," I say.

"Oh? This is your idea of a simple question?"

"You're the one who's always talking about how I need to have more intellectual curiosity."

"You dispute the word of a man who has studied the Talmud for fifty years? You, a twelve-year-old smart aleck, have the nerve to dispute two thousand years of Jewish knowledge?"

"Why not? It's not two thousand years to me. I just heard about it this afternoon."

"You can't accept the fact that there is one God?"

"Fact?"

"Yes fact. It's a fact, young man."

"Come on, Dad, you're a scientist, sort of. Where's the proof?"

"In the Talmud. In the… writings of wise men. Men who are lot wiser than you."

"Okay, how did they know?"

"Who?"

"These wise men."

"They knew. Okay? God told them."

"God *told* them? Don't you think He'd be a little biased on the subject?"

"Now you're calling God a liar?"

"If the shoe fits…"

"Enough of this! I won't hear another word! There is one and *only one* benevolent God. Period."

"That's another point that bothers me," I say.

"What?"

"This benevolent business."

"Oh? And what bothers you about that, Dr. Einstein?"

"How can you call Him benevolent?" I say. "What about the Holocaust? What was so benevolent about that?"

"God has his reasons," my father stammers.

"His reasons? What are his reasons for creating cancer? Answer me that? Or typhus? Or the polio epidemic? Five-year-old kids walking in braces, what's so benevolent about that? Or myasthenia gravis where you lose muscle control of half of your face? Or—"

"Enough!" my father says. "This discussion is over, young man. Finished! One day you will understand all of this. But for now, I want you to write an apology to Rabbi Goldbloom ."

"Why?"

"Because I say so," my father says firmly.

"But..."

"There will be no further discussion. Now go wash your hands. It's time for lunch. And make a nice lather. If you don't make a nice lather, you're wasting your time."

Two days after Ursula and the kids have safely landed in Germany, my mysterious disease returns. The moment I open my eyes I know it's back. And with a vengeance. It is four A.M. and the house is dark. I have suddenly come awake. My heart is palpitating and I am covered in a cold sweat; my brain feels as if it is racing; my hands are shaking, my legs are weak. As I slowly rise, I feel as if I am on a ship that is pitching in a storm. Suddenly I am nauseous and dizzy. My knees buckle. I sit down on the edge of the bed to get my bearings.

I spend most of the early morning hours chain smoking and walking from one room of the house to another. Hungrily, I suck in the smoke, hoping that the nicotine will produce the usual immediate uplift of spirit, that incomparable keenness of focus, but there is no reaction other than a dry cough. My itinerary requires that I go from the den to the foyer to the living room to the dining room to the kitchen, stopping only to flick an ash in an ashtray or to light the next butt. I have no idea why I am doing this so I try to sit down and watch some early morning TV, but I cannot concentrate.

At about ten A.M. I run out of cigarettes, so I wobble out to the garage and start up the car. I am so dizzy, so disoriented that I wonder if I will be able to drive the three blocks to the HiHo Liquor Store without passing out on the way. Slowly, I back out of the driveway, a Herculean feat given my condition. It feels as if it has taken an hour. Once I am in the street, I carefully put the car in forward. My hands are clammy and holding tight to the steering wheel as I roll at the breakneck speed of about three miles per hour down my street and stop for the traffic light. I feel as if I am going to faint, so I start taking deep breaths and try to focus my attention on the light. When it changes, I veer carefully left. Fortunately there is not much traffic. In a moment I am there. I have made it. I buy a carton of Carltons and when I return home without incident, I collapse from exhaustion on the den sofa.

⟳

"You don't look so hot, Martin."

This keen observation comes from Dr. Margolis, upon whose examination table I am sitting, a thermometer stuck under my tongue. To get here I have had to take a cab because Margolis's office is in Beverly Hills, a good five miles from my house, and I did not think I could drive that far safely. I have not driven anywhere since my perilous trek to the HiHo Liquor Store.

Dr. Margolis is probing the glands in my neck. He is the first doctor I have ever had who is younger than I am. He is short, generally unkempt, and looks like Laurel with Hardy's mustache. The tie he wears crookedly under his lab coat has a ketchup stain hidden in its garish pattern. Or is it blood?

"So what do you think, Doc?" I ask fearfully, after he removes the thermometer. "What does your intuition tell you?"

"You haven't got a fever."

"I could have told you that."

"The fact that you don't have a fever eliminates a number of possibilities."

"Like what? Scurvy? Beriberi? Cholera?"

"Do you have any pain urinating?"

"Why, you think it's a kidney thing? Of course, I should have known, it's kidney failure. My kidneys are shot, I'll need dialysis or a transplant. Oh God."

"Just answer the question, Martin."

"No. No pain urinating."

"Sore throat, headaches?"

"No."

"Any shortness of breath?"

"No."

"Chest pains?"

"No."

"Tingling sensation in the extremities?"

"No."

"Difficulty swallowing?"

"No."

"Good. Lie down."

"Why?"

"So I can feel your abdomen."

"Feel my abdomen for what? Tumors, right?"

"Just lie down, Martin."

I do as he says and he probes my abdomen, gently kneading the skin over my liver and my intestinal tract with his fingers. I can see the hairs in his nose and a little patch of unshaved stubble beneath his chin. I hold my breath, hoping that he doesn't stop at some area, praying that he doesn't find something. He doesn't.

"You can breathe now, Martin."

I exhale and sit up. "What do you think of Crohn's Disease, Doc?"

"Very unpleasant. I wouldn't wish it on anybody."

"That's not what I meant. How about colitis?"

"Not much fun either."

"Are you planning to take this act to Vegas?" I ask. "Or is it just for me?"

"I'm just trying to help you relax, Martin."

"You think this is all psychosomatic, don't you?"

He hands me my shirt and I slip it over my head. The examination is over. Margolis turns his back and washes his hands in the sink. I note that he is using the same industrial strength surgical soap we had as kids, and that he is doing an excellent job of creating a lather.

"No, Martin, I don't think it's psychosomatic," he says, pulling down a paper towel and drying his hands. "I think your symptoms are very real."

"So what do you think it is?"

My heart is beating so loudly I can feel it banging in my ears, as if someone has just turned up the bass on a stereo. Margolis looks at me, sees my anxiety. I have gone pale; my hands tremble…

"Let's just wait for the blood tests to come back," he says. "No point in worrying over nothing."

CHAPTER
4

T he phone rings. It is now five days after my appointment
with Margolis. I have been feeling lousy since my office visit;
disoriented, woozy, nauseous, the same litany of complaints.
My weight is down by eight pounds and I can now completely en-
circle my wrist with my thumb and forefinger. I watch the phone as
it rings three, four, five times. My heart is in my throat and my hand
trembles as I pick up the receiver and croak the word "Hello." But it
is not Margolis. It is Gavin, proving once and for all that he does,
despite all evidence to the contrary, possess my phone number.

"Martin, my friend, how's the world treating you?" he asks.

"Like a baby treats a diaper."

"That's a funny line," he says. "You should use it sometime."

"I have," I say. "Is there any news? About the script, I mean."

"Yes there is," he says and then I hear him shout something to
someone else on his end of the line, possibly his secretary, Clive.
"Can you hold a second, Martin?"

"Sure," I say but he's already clicked the hold button. With the
receiver cradled between my shoulder and chin, I reach across the
room for a cigarette. I look at my watch; it's been thirty seconds. I
begin to fall into a funk.

"So, Martin," he says suddenly, "here's the scuttlebutt. Everybody thought the script was very, very well written…" (In Agentspeak,

this means they hated the story but I spelled everything right).

"Uh huh."

"Several of the producers expressed a genuine interest in meeting with you sometime." (Translation: One of the producer's lowest ranked story editors owes Gavin a favor and will have lunch with me at some unspecified future date, possibly the day after hell freezes over).

"Great," I say unenthusiastically.

"Cheer up, Martin. Who knows, maybe there's a rewrite in it for you." (Translation: Who knows, maybe manna will fall from Heaven).

"Uh huh."

"So we've made some solid progress." (Translation: We're back to square one).

"I suppose," I say, crestfallen. "Is that it?"

"I'm afraid so, my friend. But I'm not giving up, Martin. I am not a quitter. Tenacity is my middle name. I believe in you and I believe in the material. And that's coming straight from the heart." (Translation: He'll send the script out to a few B-List producers and if nothing happens, he'll dump me).

"Thanks Gavin, I appreciate that."

"It's nothing," he says. "You'll be hearing from me very soon, my friend. Stay cool." (Translation: Sayonara sucker).

And then he clicks off.

❧

Two days later, Margolis finally calls with my test results. Everything is distressingly normal. Liver function, kidney function, uric acid, hemoglobin, cholesterol, creatinin. Everything except my white count which is somewhat elevated.

"Aha!" I exclaim, latching on to this one ray of hope. "I knew it. I'm ill. That proves it right?"

"Not really, Martin," he says. "The count is slightly elevated but it's still in what we consider a normal range."

"No anemia?" I ask.

"I'm afraid not."

"Blood sugar?"

"Normal."

"Liver?"

"A marvel."

"You tested for hepatitis?"

"Negative."

"Damn."

"You're disappointed?"

"Of course I'm disappointed!" I say. "I feel like shit and you're telling me I'm in good health!"

"Gee, I'm sorry," Margolis says. "I wish I had some really bad news to cheer you up with."

Suddenly Margolis is guffawing over his own joke, as if he just got it himself. I sigh audibly and consider changing internists.

"The tests you've done," I say tentatively. "They don't rule out cancer or colitis or any of the really horrible diseases right?"

"That's right."

"So what do you think? More tests?"

Margolis sighs. "Martin, do you really want some eager gastroen-terologist sticking a hose with a video camera on it up your colon?"

I gulp at the thought. "They do that?"

"Yes. It's called a colonoscopy. The inside of your colon appears on a TV screen."

"And if it goes into syndication?"

Margolis ignores my feeble attempt at humor. "It's not a pleas-ant procedure, Martin."

"Well if it's necessary…"

"I don't think it is," Margolis says. "Not at this stage anyway. But if it'll make you happy, I suppose we could do a stool culture. Always an enjoyable prospect, particularly for the pathologist. Might be a parasite, who knows? Come by the office for the kit."

"The kit?"

"What did you think, you put it in a plastic freezer bag and drop it off at the front desk?"

CHAPTER

I won't nauseate you with the harrowing details regarding the medieval process of collecting a stool sample. Suffice it to say, if this so-called "kit" is the culmination of five thousand years of medical science, we've got a long way to go. As it turns out, the gruesome exercise is utterly fruitless. Margolis calls two days later to tell me I have tested negative. I am disheartened by the news. A parasite would have been the least of many evils. A parasite is treatable with medication. A parasite would have been a *godsend*.

Frustrated but firm, I tell Margolis that I want to repeat all the initial blood and urine tests just to be one hundred percent sure. Better safe than sorry, I opine. People make mistakes. If nothing turns up we could even try the stool sample again. Won't that be fun? He is neither overjoyed nor encouraging, but I insist.

"It's your money," Margolis says, shaking his head wearily.

And so on a painfully sunny morning in May, I call a taxi and schlep back over the hill for another exhilarating round of tests. As it happens I am twenty minutes early and must wait for Margolis to return from his hospital rounds. It is in his waiting room, my nose buried in an ancient copy of *Variety*, that I first become aware of Delilah Foster.

It would have been impossible not to notice her. She is pacing rapidly in front of an overstuffed wingback chair not five feet from where I sit. Pacing and chewing her fingernails as intently as a beaver nibbling bark from a branch. On top of which, she seems to be muttering something to herself, some sort of whispered reminder or possibly even — could it be? — a prayer. Dressed entirely in black — black skirt, black tights, black ballet shoes, black knit blouse — she is like a dark blur that enters and leaves my peripheral vision. Suddenly I realize I am reading the same sentence over and over and soon I give up, toss the *Variety* back on the coffee table and, with my clip-on sunglasses still on, surreptitiously watch her move back and forth.

She is fascinating, a one-woman bundle of nervous energy. She paces, she chews her nails, she mutters, she sits down, she opens a purse, she rummages, she closes the purse, she gets up, she paces, she chews. And so on. Watching her is making me dizzy, but I cannot take my eyes off her. When she looks away at a clock on the wall, I lift up my clip-on shades and get a quick glimpse of her face. No makeup, a skinny but well-proportioned body and a decidedly sickly pallor contrive somehow to make her attractive in an odd deathbed sort of way. Must be the dark eyes and the well-defined cheekbones, I conclude. And then it suddenly occurs to me that her sickly pallor and gaunt frame might very well mean that she is ill. Very ill. Maybe even terminally ill. After all, this *is* a doctor's office.

Curiosity finally gets the better of me.

"Are you waiting for Dr. Margolis?" I ask pleasantly the next time she passes in front of me.

"No, I'm waiting for a chair lift," she says without breaking stride or even looking at me. "What kind of a question is that?"

"Just trying to make conversation," I say, leaning forward for the *Variety* I had abandoned.

"Godammit," she says. "I hate doctors."

"Welcome to the club."

"I've been waiting an hour. Do you believe that? A whole goddamn hour."

As if suddenly exasperated by her own words, she stalks to the reception desk and starts knocking on the plexiglass window, until a nurse finally slides it open. "The doctor is on his way, Ms. Foster," she says anticipating the complaint. "He just called. He'll be here in a few minutes. Just be patient a little longer."

"You said that forty-five minutes ago. I don't have all day for this you know. I do have a life."

And so, unplaced, she marches back to the wingback chair, falls into it with a weary sigh, crosses one leg, then the other and starts idly rummaging in her purse again.

"What are you in for?" I ask.

"None of your goddamn business."

And so we have our first of many encounters. Not a particularly promising start, but the ice has been cracked.

Our second encounter takes place half an hour later:

Shortly after being bled by Margolis's annoyingly cheerful nurse, a freckled redhead named Dolores, I am in the bathroom trying desperately to urinate in a specimen cup. After consuming several Dixie cupfuls of water, I manage to coax out enough pee pee twenty minutes later to half fill the little plastic cup. This will have to do. With the sample in one hand, I am ready to leave. I try to open the bathroom door but it appears to be stuck. I try again. No luck. Finally, I give it a swift kick, and it flies open. I lose my balance and fall out of the bathroom, spilling the entire contents of my specimen cup on Delilah who happens to be waiting just outside the bathroom with an empty specimen cup in her hand.

"Jesus F. Christ!" she shrieks, recoiling in horror as I pick myself up off the cold linoleum floor. Fortunately, she is wearing one of those paper hospital gowns, the ones that tie in the back.

"I'm sorry!" I tell her. "This is so embarrassing. I'll take care of it." I rush back into the bathroom and pull a wad of toilet paper off the roll and clumsily try to dab the urine spots on her paper gown. She slaps my hand away.

"What's the matter with you?" she asks. "Enough with the toilet paper. You're making it worse. Christ."

"Sorry."

"Just let me in the bathroom," she says impatiently walking past me. "This is really *not* my day."

"I know what you mean," I offer weakly.

"I doubt it."

So much for Encounter Number Two.

Now it is noon. I have completed the last of my tests. Margolis has perfunctorily prodded and kneaded my throat and abdomen, felt my prostate and listened to my heart and lungs. He has searched for tumors, lumps and lesions and come up empty. Disappointed and, curiously, at the same time relieved, I step out of the office, take the elevator to the lobby and exit the building. That awful bright sunlight blinds me instantly and I flip down my clip-ons and duck for shade, hoping to avoid an immediate mega-headache. I light a cigarette and inhale deeply.

"Got a light?" I hear a vaguely familiar voice say. Delilah materializes out of the shadows and leans her chin toward me. I hand her my lighter and she sets her Virginia Slim ablaze. I notice that she is wearing a disposable latex glove on her right hand.

"Sorry if I was rude before," she says. "Doctors make me crazy."

"I know what you mean."

"I'm Delilah Foster."

"Martin Dorfman."

"Nice to meet you."

"Ditto."

She offers a gloved hand and I shake it.

"You can't be too careful," she says.

"Right."

"They don't know," she says.

"Who?"

"The doctors."

"Don't know what?"

"Don't know what I have. You asked me before. What I was in for. Remember?"

"That's interesting," I say. "They don't know what I have either."

"Really?"

"Really."

"How long have you—"

"About two weeks."

"You're lucky. It's been six months for me and they still haven't got a clue."

"Wow," I say. "That's not very encouraging."

"I've had every test known to man. CAT scan, MRI, X-rays, you name it. All of them turned out negative."

"That's good."

"Not really. I'd give anything for a positive result. Not knowing is driving me nuts. You have no idea what I'm going through. I can't work, I can't go out, I can't sleep. Everybody thinks it's psychosomatic, but the symptoms are real, believe me."

"I do. It's exactly the same with me."

"Really?"

"Yes. I wonder if we have the same thing?"

Suddenly my cab appears at the curb. Same guy who took me.

"Your taxi?" she asks.

"How'd you know?"

"I don't feel safe driving either."

"Can I drop you somewhere?" I ask.

"Yeah," she says. "You can drop me off a tall building. Put me out of my misery once and for all."

"Last chance," I say, stamping out my cigarette and heading toward the curb.

"I've got a ride coming. My agent, God bless her."

"Your *agent* is picking you up? That's amazing!"

"Not really. She's not a very good agent."

"Oh," I say. "You're not a writer are you?"

"Actress."

"Well, good luck," I say.

"With the acting or the disease?"

"Both."

"Thanks."

I get in the cab and we drive off.

⌒

It is June of 1972, a full year after I have graduated from college with high hopes and an utterly useless Bachelor's Degree in American Literature, and I am putting my expensive education to good use by working eight hours a day as a professional house painter on Nantucket Island. I am a good house painter, careful and methodical, but it is not exactly what I had in mind for my life's work. I have spent an entire miserable winter trying in vain to break into the publishing business. I will take anything as long as it is connected, no matter how remotely, to writing, but nobody wants me. Not even in the mailroom.

But the real challenge that winter is living in Highland Falls. Being unemployed I have no money, a state of affairs that compels me to take up residence in that lunatic asylum my parents call home. Slowly but surely, whatever self-esteem I managed to accrue for myself over the last four years, evaporates. Suddenly, all my boyhood friends are headed for positions on the Supreme Court or are number one in their classes at Harvard Medical School, the implication being that at the age of 21, I am already a resounding failure. *You remember Ernest Schmeckle, the cross-eyed kid? In one year he finished law school! One year! And now he's with a big firm in New York, making fifty thousand dollars a year!* I am told it is my fault that I cannot seem to get a job. After all, didn't they just put me through college to the tune of three-thousand dollars a year, plus room and board?

That summer, we are all staying in our vacation house on the Island. Every night when I come home splotched with latex enamel and window putty, my father goes into a lengthy warning about the dangers of inhaling house paint. I can expect to get lung cancer and very possibly a brain tumor as well if I continue to work with these highly toxic chemicals. Who knows what they put in that stuff? I should wear a surgical mask and gloves. Then there is also the probability that, in my innate clumsiness, I will fall off a ladder, break my back and become paralyzed for life. *In a wheelchair for the rest of your life! Drooling all over yourself! Making your business in a plastic bag! And for what?* It isn't enough that he tells me this once; I have to hear this five times a day.

But it is my father's anxiety about the dangers of my temporary occupation that eventually motivates him to help me secure a job in the field of publishing.

"I talked to my colleague, Dr. Feldman, this afternoon," he tells me as I stand in the kitchen drinking a beer one evening after work. "I called him long distance. On your behalf."

"On my behalf?"

"That's right. You don't remember? I told you about his brother-in-law, Irving?"

"No."

"Well maybe I didn't tell you, but Dr. Feldman has a brother-in-law who is a big wheel in the New York publishing business."

"Dr. Feldman from Highland Falls?"

"Who else?"

"The one you don't like because he's such a braggart?"

"Never mind that."

I finish the beer and reach for another one, but he grabs it out of my hand, puts it back in the refrigerator and slams the door shut. To my father, two beers means you are an alcoholic.

"When you say the publishing business," I ask skeptically. "What exactly are we talking about?"

"What, you think I don't know what the publishing business is? You think I'm an idiot?"

"Of course not."

"For your information, this Irving happens to be a senior editor at Harpers, a very reputable firm. Maybe you've heard of them?"

"So do they have a job opening?" I ask.

"If he likes you, there's always a job opening," my father says sagely.

"Gee, Dad," I say gratefully. "Thanks."

"Don't mention it," he says with a wave of his hand. "In the publishing business the worst that can happen to you is maybe you accidentally stab your hand with a pencil or drop a typewriter on your foot. It's much safer than painting houses."

As it turns out, my father's colleague Dr. Max Feldman has made a luncheon appointment for me and his brother-in-law, the senior editor, for the next day. I am to take an early morning plane from Nantucket to La Guardia, get a cab into Manhattan and meet Irving Glickstein for lunch at The Saddleback, a steak and prime rib restaurant on Third Avenue.

So I fly to New York and take a cab to the restaurant. I am expecting Irving to be a tweedy type in his fifties, with an unkempt shock of straight white hair, a meerschaum pipe and the upper crust dialect of a Maxwell Perkins. But the man I am lead to in this dark restaurant with old engravings of British racehorses adorning the walls, is something of a disappointment, a bookish, diminutive man with thick glasses and several lonely strands of reddish hair combed strategically over a bald head. He is sitting in a red leather booth and when I shake his hand, I notice that it is clammier than mine.

After exchanging amenities, I order a martini, he orders a glass of milk. We talk about colleges, we talk about New York, we talk about the differences between Nantucket and Martha's Vineyard. The subject of publishing does not come up, but I suspect that this is because he is taking my measure as a man. Character counts. If he is going to recommend me for a position with a company of Harpers stature, he needs to know what kind of a person I am. Am I intelligent, well-spoken, creative? Will I fit in; will I prosper? Do I have the Right Stuff? Over coffee, I learn that he has been with Harpers for twenty years, that it was his first job after he graduated Phi Beta Kappa from Dartmouth, and that he would never even *consider* working for another firm. Throughout the conversation, he keeps looking at his watch. I find this encouraging. He is a busy man. An important man. A man with a full appointment book. And instead of dining with Norman Mailer, he is spending his lunch hour with me, a wet-behind-the-ears kid of 21!

Nevertheless, fearing that the meal will come to a close without the subject of my imminent career prospects arising, I decide to dive in headlong.

"So are there any openings at Harpers, jobwise I mean, Mr. Glickstein, sir?" I stammer. "I'll do just about anything to get my foot in the door. Anything within reason of course, ha ha."

"Harpers is like a big family, Martin," he says. "If we see someone we like, why we take them in and—"

But just then the waiter brings us the check. Much to my distress, Irving does not finish his sentence; he looks over the check, then takes out a few bills and hands both the check and the bills to me. I have no idea why he is doing this. I look blankly at the money for a minute, not exactly sure what it is I am supposed to do with it.

"Mine came to six fifty-two," he says. "That includes the tip and my part of the tax."

I blink. "Right," I say, digging in my breast pocket, hoping I will have enough cash to pay my half of lunch, with enough left over for a cab to the airport. The big publishing hot shot can't even spring for lunch! Why he must make forty, fifty thousand a year! But then I'm not Norman Mailer.

"Come on up to my office," Irving says after we have walked outside into the brutal New York afternoon. "We'll get you to fill out an application. Just a formality of course."

"Of course."

"But we have to hurry," he says. "I'm afraid I have meetings all afternoon."

"Of course."

"As it happens, William Styron is in town."

"Ah."

Ten minutes later I am sitting in an overstuffed chair in Irving's impressively large corner office, gazing out at the spectacular view of Manhattan. Irving is rummaging through his desk, looking for an application. He gives up, looks at his watch.

"Excuse me for a just a moment," he says. "I'll have my secretary get one from Personnel."

"Sure, no problem."

While he is gone scaring up an application, I get up and wander aimlessly around his office. I go over to a bookshelf and look at a row of leather-bound first editions. Impressive. Lodged between them is a nice color photo of Irving and his wife. Nice looking older lady. Good body, nice tan. Only the man in the photo does not really resemble Irving. Strange, I think, to have a photo of some other guy and his wife in your office. But hey, this is New York City, anything goes. Next, I find a plaque, some sort of publishing award, very classy, but the name engraved calligraphically in the polished brass is not that of Irving Glickstein. Suddenly I am beginning to suspect that something is not right. I wander over to the huge desk and casually glance at some of the pink memos lying on the blotter, keeping one eye on the door. Oddly enough, the name on the memos matches the name on the plaque and that name is not Glickstein. Now I am seriously concerned. What's going on here? I grab a recent copy of Harpers from the coffee table and find the masthead. I am scanning past Editor in Chief, Executive Editor, Managing Editor, Senior Editors, Contributing Editors, Associate Editors, Assistant Editors, Researchers but there is no mention of Irving Glickstein to be found. I start reading the bottom lines, the ones *below* the subscription information, the sad dungeon of the masthead, and it is there that I finally find it, his name in minuscule letters, barely readable by the naked eye. I slam the magazine shut. I have been had! My father has been had! We've both been taken in by his braggart colleague, Max Feldman, the lousy son of a bitch! We should have known better!

Glickstein is no big shot. Glickstein is an editorial assistant! A glorified secretary! A goddamn forty-five-year-old *gopher!*

It suddenly occurs to me that Irving is not coming back. He has left me here to be thrown out by security men when the real owner of this office suddenly returns from lunch and finds me rummaging around in his desk. I will be interrogated, frisked and unceremoniously tossed out of the Harpers building on my keester. By then, Glickstein will have conveniently disappeared, gone home most likely.

I peek tentatively through the crack in the door. Fortunately, the lunch hour is still on and, except for a few secretaries eating take-out and a guy from the mailroom wheeling a lopsided mail cart, the office is deserted. On tiptoes, I prance unnoticed through the bullpen and grab a down elevator. Within half a minute, I am safely out of the building and in a taxi back to La Guardia. I have just enough cash left to pay the fare and tip the cabby.

·❦·

"So this experience depressed you?" Nora asks.

"At first, yes."

"And then?"

"And then it didn't. By the time I got back to Nantucket later that day I was in a pretty good mood. Buoyant even."

"Why?"

"I don't know."

"I think you do."

"Oh? What gives you that impression?"

"Because you're a reasonably intelligent man."

"Reasonably?" I say, somewhat hurt. "Is that supposed to be a compliment?"

I sigh. For some reason, I am not in the mood for this today. My mind is too distracted, my thoughts unfocused. The one-liners just aren't coming. I glance at the blinking colon on Nora's digital clock. Forty minutes to go. There's no way even I can bullshit my way through forty minutes. I'm good, but not that good.

"Don't answer a question with a question," Nora scolds. "You'll be in therapy forever."

This prospect is enough to make me say anything. Therapy forever is a nightmare in itself. On the other hand, at ninety bucks an hour, it occurs to me that it is definitely in Nora's best interests for me to be in therapy forever. Drawing out my neuroses would pay big dividends over time. Assuming I live another forty years, at one session a week, that comes to $172,800. And that's only if her rate stays the same for the next forty years. A mere $10 per session raise and we could be looking at a grand total of $200,000. My neuroses are, in essence, buying her a new house.

But then it occurs to me that, in spite of the financial windfall, Nora might *not* be all that thrilled about the prospect of my being in therapy forever. Why should she be? I know I frustrate her. Maybe I bore her as well. Maybe I am her worst patient. Maybe she wants me to get the hell off her roster before I give *her* a nervous breakdown! Who knows how she really feels? Does she discuss me at night in bed with her husband? Do they get a big laugh out of my assorted angsts? Do I have a reputation I don't know about in psychiatric circles?

"Think Martin," Nora scolds. "Why were you feeling buoyant after the Glickstein episode?"

"Did I say buoyant?"

"Yes."

I sigh. She is not going to let up on this one. I take a deep breath. "Okay, because compared to Irving, I wasn't such a big failure. I mean, here was a forty-five-year-old guy doing worse than me; here was a guy who had to carry off a whole charade for a twenty-one-year-old house painter, just to puff himself up! Irving was pathetic, worse than pathetic. My situation might have been pathetic, but it wasn't as pathetic as his. There are degrees of patheticness."

"Good." Nora is nodding. "Very good." It is an ugly winter day in March of 1990 and it hasn't stopped raining in a week. Rivers of foamy water are flowing down the streets. Swimming pools are overflowing. There have been mudslides; people have lost their houses. In the Valley, the streets are filled with lake-sized puddles.

"So you felt uplifted by someone else's misfortune, is that what you're saying?"

"Well, if you put it that way…"

"Yes or no, Martin?"

"What is this, a courtroom trial? Am I on the witness stand?"

"In a way, yes."

"May I consult with my attorney?"

"Cut the crap, Martin."

"Okay, yes," I say angrily. "Occasionally, the misfortune of others makes me feel good. Does that make me a bad person?"

"What do you think?"

"I don't know. My father used to tell me I'd never be a great writer because I was lacking in compassion for my fellow man."

"When did he tell you that?"

"When I was seven."

"And was he right?"

"Maybe. According to most of the evidence, I'm not a great writer."

"Irrelevant. Let's get back to the issue at hand: Do you think you're a bad person because you take great joy in the misfortune of others?"

"Great joy? I never said that I take *great joy*. A slight uplift maybe, a tinge of mirth, an iota of glee, but certainly not great joy."

"Do you feel guilty about it?"

"A little," I say. She is looking at me skeptically, boring in with those baby blues. "No, not at all. There. I said it. You happy now?"

She waves away the remark. "And in your own estimation, does that make you a bad person?"

"It doesn't make me a saint."

"No," Nora says. "It doesn't make you a saint. But if you were a saint you wouldn't be seeing a therapist, now would you?"

It has now been five days since my last appointment with Margolis, two weeks since the symptoms of my mystery disease began. In that period of time, I have felt somewhat normal for perhaps a total of three days. I have taken advantage of these normal days by stocking up on food and doing errands. When I am feeling sick, I stay home for I am terrified that I will collapse or throw up in public, two particular phobias of mine. I have called Ursula and the kids in Germany three times, but as far as they know, I am well. I just cannot bring myself to divulge the truth. I do not want to spoil their vacation. I am my mother's son, a world class martyr.

I do, however, call my sister Phoebe and tell her about my bizarre affliction. We periodically compare symptoms, but the symptoms in question are usually psychological ones. Her inferiority complex, my ragged self-esteem and vice versa.

"That's odd," she says after I have described my symptoms in some detail. "I've been feeling pretty lousy myself for about a week or so."

"Oh?" I ask eagerly, my misery in a desperate search for company. "Lousy in what way?"

"Nausea," she says, "and insomnia. I think there's a bug going around. Some kind of a weird stomach virus."

I feel encouraged by this. Of course, maybe it's just a virus! Aren't there new viruses popping up all the time? Viruses are an evolving species after all. Maybe this is some new strain of flu! Maybe I am at the forefront of some new species of virus which will be named after me! The name Dorfman will be up there with Gehrig and Huntington and old man Crohn! But I soon realize how unlikely it is that I could possibly have the same bug she has, since we live three thousand miles apart.

"Have you told Dad yet?" she asks

"Are you crazy?"

"How about Mom?"

"What would be the point?"

"It might be something serious, Martin."

"Like what?"

"I don't know. You're the expert on diseases. What do you think it is?"

"Colitis maybe. Or worse."

"Cancer?"

The mere sound of that word sends a chill up my spine. "It's possible."

"You should call him."

"Why? What's he going to do?"

"He's a doctor, Martin."

"He's not *my* doctor," I say. "I have a doctor."

"So call him for a second opinion."

"Why would I want a second opinion from a retired, small-town GP who doesn't even play golf, when I have a sophisticated big city doctor who went to Harvard Medical School and shoots three under par?"

"Because it's free?"

"I don't believe you're giving me this advice," I say. "Frankly, I'm appalled. After all the times you vowed never to tell him. Remember that gynecologist he recommended, the one who didn't know you can't go in the sun after taking tetracycline? He recommended that moron!"

"I know, I know," she says. "It's just that… he's our father, so I guess he cares more."

"Maybe not. We can't sue him for malpractice."

"So what's your doctor doing?"

"Doing?"

"About your illness."

"What's he doing about my illness?" I stammer. "You know, he's doing the usual stuff."

"Like what?"

"Okay, he's not doing anything."

"You're kidding."

"No."

"Shouldn't he be doing something?"

"I don't know. I suppose. Yes."

"Call Dad," she said. "That's my advice."

As it turns out I do not need to call my father. He calls *me*. Within twelve hours of our conversation, Phoebe has blabbed the whole gruesome story to him. She has done this, she later claims, because she is truly worried about me and if I die from whatever it is I have, she cannot bear to have me on her conscience along with all of her other problems and guilts. She has done it for her own peace of mind.

"Tell me all about it," my father says seductively. "I'm your father, Martin. I can help you."

"No," I say. "I don't think so. You'll have too much anxiety about it… you'll yell at me, you'll denigrate my doctor, you'll make me think it's all my own fault…"

"Now what makes you say a thing like that?"

Is he kidding? "Nothing," I say, "except forty years of experience."

"I'm a doctor, Martin."

"A retired doctor."

"I still keep up with the journals. I know what's happening. You insult me."

"I'm sorry."

"So tell me."

"Why are you asking me? Didn't Phoebe give you all the gory the details?"

"Yes."

"So?"

"I have always found it preferable to hear them directly from the patient."

Finally, knowing that he will never let me off the hook on this one, I give in with a weary sigh and list my wide variety of discomforts for him. I am growing bored with this tedious lament and consider sending out printed cards or making a video. When I am finished, there is a long interval of silence.

"So what do you think?" I finally ask.

"Are you sure you want my opinion? The opinion of a *retired* physician?"

"I said I was sorry."

"The opinion of a *small-town* GP?"

"All right already."

"And what does golf have to do with it?"

I make a mental note to kill Phoebe the next time I see her. "It was just a joke, okay?"

"With jokes like that it's no wonder you're unemployed."

Ouch.

"Fortunately, I am able to rise above these petty insults," he says. "As for my humble opinion of your symptoms, for what it's worth…"

"Yes?"

"It could be any number of things."

"But?"

"But, I am particularly disturbed by the abdominal pain. If I were you I'd have a colonoscopy. Not a sigmoidoscopy, a colonoscopy. And you might as well have an upper GI too. As soon as possible, don't delay."

"Why? What do you think it is?" I ask, my voice cracking. "Do you think it's serious?"

"Considering the symptoms, I would say there are two good possibilities. At best it's colitis, at worst…."

"Cancer?"

There is another long moment of silence. "We can't rule out the possibility."

"Oh Jesus."

And now I wait for some word of empathy, a little paternal encouragement, but this is a man who diagnosed cancer when I had a stomach ache at the age of six. And so there is no paternal encouragement, no empathy. There is only silence. And so I wonder: Is this how he broke bad news to his patients? *Good morning, Mr. Rapaport. How's the wife? By the way, you have terminal cancer. Two weeks to live. Have a nice day.* I can feel the adrenaline coursing through my veins like a shot of antifreeze. The knot in my abdomen gets tighter.

"Dr. Margolis isn't particularly worried," I say weakly.

"Margolis? You're still seeing that quack?"

"What makes you think he's a quack?"

"I'm surprised he can fit you in between golf dates."

"Very funny."

"So what's his diagnosis?"

I hesitate before answering. "Stress," I say. "He thinks it's stress."

"That's it? Stress?"

"Yes."

"And you pay this man, this so-called doctor?"

"Okay, so it's not the most imaginative diagnosis."

"Imaginative? It's *pathetic*," my father screams. "He should be ashamed of himself for giving a diagnosis like that!"

"Maybe he's right," I say tentatively.

"Fine, you want to believe stress is causing all your symptoms go right ahead. But if you ask me it's a bunch of baloney! Stress! Hah! He's just too damned lazy to sit down and come up with a decent diagnosis. Besides, why should you have stress? You're only a writer. Supposedly."

"What does that mean? *Supposedly?*"

"Now *I* had a stressful job. Doctors are under tremendous stress twenty-four hours a day. You have no idea. But a writer? You forget a comma, you leave out a semicolon, that's stressful?"

"Can we discuss my symptoms please?"

"What's to discuss? You can't say I didn't warn you a million times," he says. "Nobody listens to me."

"You said you wouldn't do this!" I exclaim.

"Didn't I tell you about those power lines? Didn't I send you clippings? You ridiculed me."

"Power lines? What power lines?"

"Behind that house you lived in. The one in the hills, that stilted deathtrap of a house. Five years ago…"

"You said that they could cause high blood pressure, not cancer."

"Who knows what it can cause? And x-rays every time you go to the dentist. It's insane, all that needless radioactivity. I've warned you about that too, time and time again. You think it's a good thing to be exposed to all that radiation?"

"I don't believe you're doing this!"

But my father's on a roll now. "And did you eat oat bran everyday like I told you to? Did you take Metamucil regularly like I suggested countless times?"

"I'm hanging up now, Dad."

"Of course not. You didn't listen to me about the oat bran either. Well, there you are. I'm not surprised. You're sick, it might be something terrible, you have only yourself to blame. A little oat bran and you could have saved your colon!"

And so I slam down the receiver. Suckered again.

CHAPTER

T his is Delilah Foster. We met a few weeks ago at Dr. Margolis's office?"
    I am on a step ladder in the bedroom, fixing an errant blade of a ceiling fan when she calls. "Yes of course I remember," I say, scrambling down from my perch. "How are you?"
    "Lousy, if you really want to know. How are you?"
    "Miserable," I say. "How did you get my number?"
    "You're in the book."
    "Am I?"
    "Listen, the reason I'm calling, I've got your cigarette lighter," Delilah says, "and it's inscribed and everything so I figured you'd want it back."
    "Geez, I was wondering what happened to it."
    "When I asked you for a light that day I guess I pocketed it. Inadvertently of course."
    "Of course."
    "So do you want me to mail it to you or what?"
    "Sure."
    I rattle off my address, but stop halfway into it for I suddenly feel an overwhelming urge to see her. Why? I'm not sure. Certainly I'm not shopping for romance. After all, I am a happily married man with two wonderful children, a reasonable mortgage and an obedi-

ent dog. I certainly don't need to complicate my life with a tawdry extramarital affair. But with Ursula and the kids on the other side of the world, I suppose I'm just in need of a little… empathy. And who better to get it from than someone who might actually have the same disease?

"Listen," I say. "I don't mean to be forward or anything… but instead of mailing it, maybe we could meet for a drink sometime. You know, compare symptoms, cry on each other's shoulder. After all, misery loves company and from the looks of it, we're both pretty miserable."

"A drink?"

"Yeah, you know, like a glass of wine."

There is a long pause. "I can't."

"Right. You're probably married or something. Never mind then, sorry I asked…"

"Sulfates in wine give me a headache."

"Oh. Right. Me too. Then how about a beer?"

"Domestic or foreign?"

"I don't know. Domestic."

"Nitrates."

"Foreign then."

"Water's not distilled."

"No on beer then. A soft drink?"

"Like?"

"Diet Coke."

"Aspartame is carcinogenic."

"Regular Coke?"

"Caffeine doesn't agree with me."

"Is this strictly a beverage problem?" I ask. "Because if it's me you don't like, just say so."

"We could go for soup," she says.

"Soup?"

"Do you have anything against soup?"

"Soup is fine."

"I know a good place for soup. All organic and everything."

"Great."

"It's in Van Nuys."

"City of light, city of magic," I say.

"That's the one."

And so we agree to meet several days later at a little outdoor soup joint in Van Nuys.

⟡

It is a fine spring day in 1959 and my father is conducting the London Philharmonic Orchestra in a breezy, romantic interpretation of Beethoven's Pastoral Symphony, performed before a full house at Carnegie Hall. He is doing this not in Carnegie Hall of course, but in our attic, a large windowless room which been converted into a combination art studio and den. He is using a dry paintbrush as a baton as the music blares from our gigantic Blaupunkt; his conducting style is fitful but energetic, the style of a Toscanini with a bad facial tic; his straight black hair, normally combed back, falls in his face at the temples as he nods with a flourish to the imaginary oboe section. If there was no music it would seem that he is swatting at a swarm of bumble bees. When it is over, he takes a deep bow for the amusement of my sister and me, pushes his hair back and returns to the canvas he is working on, a painting of a man with a gray, skeletal face, a face filled with abject terror. The room is thick with the sweet fragrant smoke of my father's pipe. It is the weekend and he is happy with the painting. Painting is his passion, although each of his many canvasses and charcoal drawings features the same gray, skeletal terror-stricken face. He has had several local exhibitions but has sold nothing; no doubt the town's art lovers do not exactly relish the idea of that depressing ashen face hanging over their living room sofas. Who can blame them?

"Philistines!" my father calls them. "Nothing but a town of Philistines!"

"Maybe you should paint sailboats, Daddy," my sister suggests, hoping to get his attention. "People like sailboats."

But my father fixes her with a withering glance and she slinks away in shame.

As the story goes, my father had been forced against his will into the medical profession by his parents, practical middle-class people who considered their only son's passion for art an amusing hobby, but not something anybody with any sense did for a living. As a result, my father resented being a doctor throughout his professional life and always considered himself a painter first and a physician second. That is not to say that he was not a conscientious doctor; on the contrary, he was so terrified of making a mistake and being summarily sued for malpractice, that he customarily requested more than the usual number of tests and consultations before making even the most elementary decisions. He was miserably insecure and anxiety-ridden for all of the forty years he practiced medicine. Yet for some reason, his patients seemed to adore him, though I doubt that it was because of his bedside manner. Or perhaps he was just cold and clinical with members of his immediate family.

And so, the members of my family, myself included, are able to relate to my father in only two ways — through art and through disease. When we are sick, it is he who administers the antibiotics, the throat cultures, the enemas. There is nothing resembling empathy in his ministrations, but we have his attention at least; he is fussing over us; he *seems* to care. When we are not ill, my mother sculpts, my sister draws with pastels and I create woodcuts. Of the three of us, I appear to be the most proficient; my sister's pastel drawings are colorful, but primitive. On the other hand, my woodcuts are well-balanced and clever; I am equally adept at landscapes, still lifes, portraits. I have a distinct knack for plagiarizing the etchings of Albrecht Durer and, due to my simple preadolescent style, getting away with it. To the chagrin of my sister, who tries so hard to please him and eventually becomes a graphic designer, my father compliments only me, encourages only me to become an artist when I grow up, to fulfill the dream that has somehow eluded him. And for awhile this seems to be my destination. But at age nine, an argument over baseball (more on this later) causes me to forsake my budding artistic career. My father can barely hide his disappointment. *Such a waste! You could be another Picasso!* Practically in tears, he tries to talk me out of it, but I am a stubborn nine-year-old and my mind is made up.

And so, suddenly, I can no longer relate to my father through art. Which leaves only one route — disease.

〜

My first rendezvous with Delilah Foster (I cannot bring myself to use the word "date") is cancelled twice, once when I am feeling too weak to make it unassisted to our meeting place and once when her aching joints have left her virtually immobile. Cancellation for reasons of health eventually becomes the keynote of our peculiar relationship.

It is a hot afternoon in May, the relentless California sun seeringly ablaze. I am sitting at an outdoor table at our meeting place, the Van Nuys soup joint, eating a bowl of bland organic gaspacho when she arrives twenty minutes late. Again she is dressed entirely in black, though this time she sports a pair of small round sunglasses that make her look like she just came from a Communist cell meeting. She seems thinner, if that is possible, but when she pulls off her shades, I see that this time she is wearing eyeliner which has the effect of highlighting those excellent cheekbones and making her eyes deep, dark and (why beat around the bush?)… stunning. The rubber glove is missing this time, but she makes no move to shake my hand.

"Sorry I'm late," she says settling with a sigh into the yellow director's chair across from me. "Traffic."

"No problem."

"Also, I had to stop twice to urinate."

"Thanks for sharing."

"How's the soup?"

"Organic."

"It looks revolting."

"It is."

"You look nauseous."

"I am nauseous."

With a bend of her index finger, she summons me closer. "I actually threw up in this restaurant two weeks ago," she whispers. "I hope they don't recognize me."

"Judging from the soup, they probably get a lot of that here."

"What?"

"Barfing."

She is now fiddling with her brown recycled napkin, tearing it into shreds and carefully arranging the shreds in a line around her fork. Bored with this, she begins turning the shreds into little spitballs. Curiously, I find this neurotic display attractive.

"Aren't you hot, all dressed in black?" I ask.

"I'm in mourning," she says solemnly.

"For whom?"

"Myself."

"But you're alive."

"It's still early in the day."

Jesus, I think, *she's worse than I am.*

By the time the waiter arrives at our table, Delilah has put her sunglasses back on, no doubt because she does not want to be recognized as the woman who regurgitated soup some weeks ago. I can't blame her. But the waiter seems oblivious as Delilah orders a bowl of beef consommé and toast. After two spoonfuls, she pushes the soup away and nibbles on the toast.

"So is nausea one of your more common symptoms?" I ask, getting down to the business that brought us here.

"Yes."

"Same here."

"It's awful," she says. "I can be feeling fine and then, boom, all of a sudden I'm nauseous."

"Exactly."

"I feel so bad I can hardly speak."

"Same here."

"I haven't had sex in six months."

"Wow. It's only been about three weeks for me."

"I carry an airline barf bag on my person at all times," she confides. "Want to see it?"

"Not really."

But she pulls it out of her purse anyway and displays it proudly. "I get my friends to steal them from the airlines. I've looked all over, but nobody seems to sell barf bags."

"How odd."

"Someday somebody's going to make a fortune on these," she says, returning it to her purse. "Mark my words."

After muttering something about how building a better barf bag will have them beating a path to your door, I return to the business at hand. I tell her about all the tests Margolis has performed on me and how they have all turned out negative. She is not surprised. We move on to the subject of alternative medicine. She dismisses acupuncture, biofeedback and aromatherapy as quackery, but holds out some hope for herbal medicine, although it has done nothing to relieve her symptoms.

"I'm at the end of my rope, Martin," she says, her eyes filling with tears. "My boyfriend has left me, my friends have stopped calling..."

"Nobody wants to be around a sick person," I offer.

"Can't really blame them, can we?"

"I guess not."

"I tell you, another six months of this and... well, I don't know what I'm going to do. Something drastic."

"Don't say it," I tell her, putting my hand over hers on the table. "We can't give up, Delilah. We need to stick together, help each other out. Okay?"

She pulls a Handi-Wipes out of her pocket and uses it to dab the area on her hand which I have just touched with mine. She forces a smile. "Can't be too careful."

"Right."

"I don't really know you that well."

"I understand. Really."

Later, as afternoon turns to dusk, we compare symptoms for the third time. As it happens, nausea is not the only symptom we share. She also gets that queer disoriented feeling that terrorizes me so often. She has trouble sleeping as do I. Headaches torment her and her joints ache so badly that at times she can barely move her arms or legs. This achiness, is her primary symptom. I conclude from this that we probably do not have the same disease, although I do not mention this. I am too desperate for a sympathetic ear.

⁓

Two days after my father's cheerless telephone diagnosis, I suddenly take a turn for the worse. I wake up at 3:00 A.M. I am so weak I can barely make it to the bathroom without stopping to lean against the wall for support after every step. I experience shortness of breath and my heart is racing. My tongue is coated with a greenish-white slime; I look sallow and undernourished; there are dark circles under my eyes and I am as pale as an overcast sky; my weight is down to 125 pounds. I feel like I am going to die; I look like I already have.

Five hours later, unshaven, haggard, my whole body vibrating with anxiety, I am in Margolis's examination room once again, having arrived there by taxi. Even the ordinarily sanguine Dr. M. agrees that I look like death warmed over (his description), though he still maintains that I do not have cancer, a word he has forbidden me to utter in his presence. Yet, beneath his placid expression I can detect a distinct trace of apprehension, a soupcon of real concern. He tells me to relax and takes my blood pressure which, to nobody's surprise, is stratospheric. Then he orders an immediate blood test. I am so weak and dizzy, I almost black out as the nurse pokes the needle into my arm. I can almost feel the blood leave my veins and enter the test tube. Margolis returns with the results in ten minutes. My white count is high enough to justify admitting me to the hospital for tests.

"Justify to whom?" I ask Margolis.

"Your insurance company."

"And the tests?"

"MRI, CAT scan, colonoscopy, upper GI… the whole nine yards."

"Oh God."

"If there's something wrong with you, Martin, we'll find it."

Later, I sit alone in Margolis's examination room, waiting for my taxi to Cedars-Sinai and quietly praying. When I get up to leave, I catch a glimpse of my reflection in the mirror that hangs over the sink. The face staring back at me is the gray, skeletal terror-stricken face of my father's many tortured paintings, which I suddenly realize are all self-portraits.

CHAPTER 7

Except for a knock-kneed, bespectacled and overly bookish eighth grader named Leslie Wang, I am practically the smartest kid in all of Rimbaldi Junior High School. I have the highest grade point average in the ninth grade. I am president of my homeroom class, associate editor of the school literary magazine, captain of the debating team. Defying centuries of Jewish precedent I have even managed to obtain a varsity letter (though it is for tennis which is considered a sissy sport). I am respectful to my elders, responsible, well-spoken. A nice boy, a boy adults like to pat on the head. A charmer. Ingratiating but not obsequious. With but a few exceptions, most notably the school's Neanderthal gym instructor, my teachers adore me. They gush with unrestrained superlatives which they scrawl in glorious loops and flowery flourishes on my report cards every trimester. *Martin is such a pleasure to teach! Such a smart young man! So eager to please!* They see great things in my future. *Great things.*

Although the face I present to the world at this time is one of carefree arrogance — after all, I am a fellow who will one day achieve *great things* — underneath it all I am a nervous wreck. I worry and fret over every exam; I tremble at the prospect of every pop quiz; I struggle to comprehend the XYZ Affair. My poor brain is crammed full with facts and dates and the names of all the state capitals. I lie awake at night reciting multiplication tables and square roots. My parents expect no less of me; the letters B through F do not exist in our household; anything lower than A plus is considered a pox on the family name. A catastrophe. A slap in the face of some ancient ethnic imperative. And so I spend most of my time studying. And when I am not studying I am participating in extracurricular activities. Any remaining time is used devising creative ways of getting out of gym class.

By the age of 11, I have temporarily given up the idea of becoming an author, having not succeeded in writing the Great American Novel by the age of ten. For awhile I take up the violin, hoping to outdo Paganini by age nine, but it soon becomes obvious to everyone but my father that I am no musical prodigy and I quickly abandon it. My new plan is to follow in the footsteps of John F. Kennedy, who has suddenly become every young man's idol. I will complete my last two years of high school at a prestigious Connecticut prep school, preferably Choate or Groton; I will go on to Harvard; I will learn to sail; I will write a weighty book in college; and then, after holding a series of lesser political offices culminating in a Senate seat, I will become, at age 35, the youngest President of the United States. How hard could it be? I already have the haircut and I am working on my Boston patrician accent. I know all the musical nuances of "Hail to the Chief," which I whistle in the shower every morning. My campaign speech for student council treasurer in 1962 is a triumph of elocution. *And so my fellow Rimbaldians, ask not what your school can do for you, ask what you can do for your school,* say I, jabbing a finger JFK-style at my adolescent audience, blissfully oblivious to the rude titters and snorts emanating from my nemesis, the gym teacher, Mr. Shoop, a Nixon Republican. But in spite of this rousing act of shameless plagiarism, I lose the election by a landslide to the school's prettiest ninth grader, the stunning but unapproachable Mary Lou Hudsucker. A humiliating defeat. I am crushed. My nascent political career is over. Nipped in the bud. How could they choose beauty over brains? I am thoroughly disillusioned with Mankind, or whatever passes for Mankind at Rimbaldi Junior High. But then one afternoon I see Paul Muni in "The Story of Louis Pasteur," on the Early Show and it makes such a profound impression on me, I decide to forsake politics and devote my life to science, to follow in Pasteur's footsteps. I announce to my family that I will find the cure for cancer before I am twenty. My father chuckles and says *mazel tov*, and I go to the public library and take out Paul DeKruif's "Microbe Hunters," which becomes my bible.

It is between these two brilliant careers that something goes slightly awry with my health. Suddenly, I am waking up each morning with pain, a nagging sourness in the pit of my stomach. It returns before lunch and again before dinner. After a week of this, my mother betrays my trust and blabs my symptoms to my father, who bawls me out for getting ill, and then consults with twenty or thirty of his colleagues and decides, after much wrangling and breast beating, to send me to the local hospital for an upper GI. With my mother holding my hand and my father standing by to make sure I am not exposed unnecessarily to too much radiation, I swallow a cupful of thick barium glop and submit my illuminated digestive tract to the experienced eye of the Pakistani radiologist, Dr. Rajiim K. Gupta. It is discovered that I have a superficial duodenal ulcer. I am put on a bland diet ("No vindaloo for you my boy!" Gupta says, cheerily. "Nosirree Bob!") and instructed to chew a minty chalk-like antacid called Titralac between meals and before bedtime. The doctors inform me that in the seventy-five year history of our local hospital, I am the youngest patient ever to be diagnosed with an ulcer. I ask for a plaque.

And now, thirty years later, here I am again, in the hospital, waiting to have my digestive tract illuminated, probed, photographed and scrutinized.

⌘

For obvious reasons, I do not tell my father about my impending sojourn at Cedars. Who needs the aggravation? If I tell him, he will do his best to make life miserable for both me and my doctors. I do not tell Phoebe because she cannot be trusted not to tell Felix. Nor can my mother.

When I tell Delilah, she is sympathetic but not encouraging. "It'll cost you and your insurance company a fortune," she says. "And they probably won't find a goddamn thing."

"How can you say that?" I say defensively. "Just because they didn't find anything wrong with you doesn't mean they won't find something wrong with me."

"Well good luck then," she says. "I hope they find something."

"Gee, thanks."

"You *want* them to find something don't you?"

"I don't know."

"Yes you do."

"Oh God, what if they *do* find something wrong with me?"

"Then at least you'll have a diagnosis."

"What if it's something really *awful*? Like cancer."

"Cancer of what?"

"How should I know?"

"Margolis would've found cancer if it was cancer."

"Colitis then."

"He would have found that too."

"You think?"

"Definitely."

"You think Margolis is a good doctor?"

"I've never met a good doctor, but that's just me."

"Margolis says my white count was up a little."

"Really?" she says.

"Yes."

"Wow. That's great. I'm green with envy."

"How can you say that?"

"Do you want a diagnosis or don't you?"

"Yes. No. I don't know."

There is a moment of silence on her end. I can hear myself breathing into the receiver. "Look, if they find nothing, you're back where you started. On the other hand, if it's something really horrible either Margolis would've found it in one of his tests or you'd be dead by now."

"You think?" I ask, my voice cracking.

"Absolutely."

"Okay, you're right. I'm being silly. It's probably something minor."

"What tests are they doing?"

"I don't know. CAT scan, upper GI—"

"Colonoscopy?" she asks.

"Yes."

"You'll enjoy that one."

"What could possibly be enjoyable about having a colonoscopy?"

"Demerol."

"Demerol?"

"Demerol. Make sure they give you Demerol."

"Okay."

"And one more thing: keep the plastic cups and pitcher. They cost around three-hundred dollars."

How willing we are to put our lives in the hands of total strangers! I don't know any of these people from Adam, where they were educated, how long they have been on the job, whether or not they are moody or depressed or psychotic. The pimple-faced West Indian orderly who blithely attaches me to an IV could easily make a mistake and pump air bubbles into my circulatory system, thereby killing me instantly, yet I smile and joke amiably about my aversion to the sight of blood. The young gum-chewing nurse who injects me with Demerol two days later could screw up and give me too much and return ten minutes later to find a post-convulsive corpse. A blissfully *happy* post-convulsive corpse, but a corpse nonetheless. Do I make sure she has the dosage right? Do I ask her how long she has been doing this? Do I utter a single contentious word? No! I decide to trust her rather than make a fuss. What if I piss her off? Then she might deliberately give me an overdose! Or worse, an underdose. I have put more effort and care into choosing a mechanic for my battered old car! Into choosing a *barber*! But here, in a life and death situation, I lie back and readily accept the premise that these people have some idea of what they are doing and will not inadvertently murder me. In no other area of life am I this blindly trusting.

So I am stripped, gowned, IV'ed, thermometered, stethoscoped, examined and given a plastic bracelet with my name and number on it. To my chagrin, I am placed in a double room with an elderly bearded man who appears to be in a deep coma. I beg for a single, but am told there are none available.

"Mr. Murphy won't bother you, mon," the West Indian orderly tells me. "He down for the count. Motorcycle accident. Bust his head up good. Poor old bastard."

"At least he's not contagious," I say.

And so I lie there, listening to the monotonous beeping of

Murphy's heartbeat monitor and the raspy sound of his strained breathing amplified by the oxygen mask which feeds him air. I try to read but my concentration is gone. I snap on the TV but the screen is a blur of talk shows and soap operas. After awhile, I am overwhelmed by curiosity. I rise and, pulling my clattering IV stand along behind me, walk over to Murphy's bed. I stand there, watching his chest rise and fall. I notice the twin tubes alongside his bed, carrying his waste from his body to a pair of plastic bags. I notice the inert tattoo of a belly dancer on his forearm. Then, suddenly, I can no longer resist the temptation. I clap my hands. Loudly. No reaction. I wave my palm over his pale blue eyes, but he continues to stare fixedly at the ceiling. I pinch his arm. Cautiously, I tickle his armpits, but he does not respond. I am about to reach under his bedcovers to see if his feet are ticklish when Margolis enters the room.

"We've tried all that already, Martin," he says jovially.

"Tried what?" I ask, my hands flying behind my back, a move that almost topples my IV stand. Margolis deftly catches it before it crashes to the floor and gestures me back to bed. It is then that I notice the other guy standing just behind him, a short fire hydrant of a man with a completely shaved head and a wry smile on his face.

"This is Dr. Herschel," Margolis says. "Your neurologist."

"My neurologist?" I say. "Do I need a neurologist?"

"Let's hope not," Herschel says, giving my hand a hard military squeeze. "Nothing would make me happier than not to be needed by anyone ever again."

"Sort of like the Maytag repairman?" I ask.

They both react by looking at me blankly. "The human brain is somewhat more complicated than the average washing machine, Mr. Dorfman," Herschel says.

"Yes of course," I say. "Bad analogy. Sorry."

"If you don't need a neurologist," Margolis says, "Dr. Herschel is the very best neurologist you could ever possibly hope not to need."

"Excuse me?"

But Margolis's name suddenly booms over the PA system and the smile disappears from his face. "I'll leave you in his very capable hands, Martin," he says, stepping out into the hallway.

When I turn to face Dr. Herschel he is shining a small penlight into my eyes, looking down at me through a pair of bifocals balanced low on his nose. "Just look straight ahead Martin," he says. "That's right. Very good."

He snaps it off and returns it to his jacket pocket. I am seeing dots before my eyes and try to blink them away. "So I understand you've been feeling light-headed, disoriented…"

"Yes."

"All the time?"

"No."

"Any headaches or double vision?"

"No."

"Any loss of hearing?"

"No."

"Numbness in your limbs?"

"No."

"Ringing in your ears?"

"Nope."

"Ever see dots before your eyes?"

"Only after people shine flashlights in my face."

Herschel nods. He is making notes in a small pocket notebook, stopping to lick the tip of his pencil like a racetrack tout. "Dr. Margolis tells me you're a writer," he says, not looking up.

"That's right."

"Did he happen to mention that I'm writing a script?"

"No."

"It's about a neurologist who solves crimes."

I look to see if he is serious. "Interesting idea," I say.

Now he looks over his bifocals at me. "You really think so?"

"Sure," I say feigning enthusiasm. "It's never been done."

"Maybe you would like to read it sometime," he says. "Give me a few professional pointers."

"I'd be glad to."

"I'll have my secretary send it over to you."

"Great."

"In the meantime, I'm going to schedule you for an MRI, just to be on the safe side, although I'm relatively sure this is not a neurological disorder."

"That's a relief."

He folds up his notebook and gives my hand the same curt, military shake, then heads for the door. "Then again, who knows?"

❦

Boredom sets in. After a few one-sided conversations with the comatose Mr. Murphy, I decide to call my answering machine at home. There is only one message and it is from Gavin: "Excellent news, my friend. Call me ASAP. Ciao." Perking up, I immediately ring his office only to hear from Clive that Gavin is at a meeting at Warner Bros. and is not expected to return to the agency until five o'clock, possibly later. Clive asks if I wish to leave a message. I ponder this for a moment and then decide it best not to let Gavin know that I am in the hospital. Bad enough I'm an ancient forty; if he finds out I am dying of some ghastly terminal disease, he'll never be able to get me a meeting anywhere. Death can be a real stigma in Hollywood. I tell Clive that I cannot be reached and that I will try calling Gavin again around five o'clock.

"I know he's simply dying to talk to you, Martin," Clive says. "Try him around six-thirty. I'll give you his home number."

Later that afternoon, I am wheeled slowly down the hospital's long windowless corridors by Lester, my West Indian orderly. My first two tests are to be an MRI and then a CAT scan, two painless, non-invasive procedures that examine my innards by passing harmless rays through my body. In both cases, like an astronaut in a space module, I am mechanically transported into a glass and metal tube and instructed by a technician not to move a muscle which, in both cases, is nearly impossible given the fact that, for some reason, I am experiencing severe abdominal cramps, not to mention profound claustrophobia. But somehow, I manage to cooperate. The CAT scan will reveal whether or not I have an abnormal growth somewhere in my torso, a malignancy on my liver or pancreas; the MRI will ascertain whether or not I have a brain tumor, an aneurysm or multiple sclerosis, all equally terrifying possibilities.

It is early evening by the time Lester wheels me back into my room. My dinner is waiting on a tray: boiled chicken breast, canned green beans, undercooked baked potato, a stale sesame roll and a plastic cup of raspberry Jell-O. You've heard of food that is to die for? This is food that is to die *from*. I am not terribly hungry anyway, so I just eat the Jell-O. Afterwards, though it is forbidden, I light up a cigarette and hope that no one barges into my room and catches me in the act. I am down to my last three butts, so I must ration.

After dinner, I am visited by a tall man with a ponytail who says that he is Dr. Jaffe, my gastroenterologist. He extends his hand and I am reminded of the old maxim "Never shake hands with a proctologist," but I ignore it and return the handshake anyway. I don't know where those fingers have been, but how much worse could I feel?

"Is that cigarette smoke I smell?" Jaffe says, sniffing the air.

I hook a thumb towards the next bed. "It's Murphy," I say. "Smokes like a chimney."

He narrows his eyes skeptically but does not pursue the issue. "So," he says. "I understand we've been having some trouble with our bowels."

"You too huh?" I say.

"No, my bowels happen to be pristine," he says. "You'd be hard pressed to find a set of bowels as untarnished as mine. But enough about me; what seems to be the trouble with yours?"

"Horrendous pain in the lower abdomen," I offer pleasantly.

"I see," he says, reading my chart. "Turn over on your side please."

I do as he says. The next thing I hear is the snap of a rubber glove and within seconds one of his long thin fingers is probing an area of my anatomy which, as the saying goes, receives notoriously little sunlight. Why in God's name, I ask myself squirming slightly, do people go into this godforsaken line of work? What could possibly be so captivating about other peoples' rectums that someone would choose to spend an entire lifetime probing them? Is it a sexual thing? Is proctology school less expensive? What?

"Well," Jaffe says tossing the glove in my bathroom trash bin. "There's no occult blood, which is a good sign."

"Will you be administering the colonoscopy yourself?" I ask.

"Yes. Tomorrow morning at eight. But first we have to make sure our colons are clean as a whistle."

"Oh?" I say apprehensively. "How do we do that?"

Jaffe reaches into his doctor bag and extracts a gigantic plastic bottle and places it beside my dinner tray. It is filled to the top with a clear liquid. "This bottle contains four liters of a very strong laxative," he says. "I want you to drink every last drop of it before eight o'clock tomorrow morning."

I feel my upper lip curl in horror. "What's it taste like?"

"It's not too bad," he says. "You'll get used to it after the first twenty or thirty cupfuls."

"So I guess I won't be getting a lot of sleep tonight," I say.

"Probably not. But you must drink it all, okay? Promise me you'll drink it all."

"Sure."

"If the colon is not completely purged, if there is any… residue, I can't do the test properly," he says.

"Don't worry, Doc," I say. "It'll be so clean you can eat off it."

He smiles. "That's the ticket," he says.

⁓

It tastes like something Brawer's Frutal Works might have come up with on a bad day. Warm Pernod laced with a combination of cheap tequila, Windex and naphthaline is about the best I can do to describe Dr. Jaffe's noxious brew; and it leaves a nice metallic after-taste too. And there's four *liters* of the godawful stuff, twenty or thirty cupfuls! And yes, it is industrial strength; less than five minutes after I struggle to ingest the first cupful, I am urgently dragging my clattering IV stand to the john and ridding my bowels of flotsam and jetsam like there's no tomorrow.

After about the twelfth cupful, I make the big mistake of looking in the toilet. What in God's name could still be coming out? What I see makes my heart stop in mid-beat. For what is in the toilet is *bright red*. Blood! I am passing blood! Lots of blood! Nothing but blood! My intestines are hemorrhaging! My limbs go numb, my heart begins to palpitate, I am suddenly covered in cold sweat and I feel as if I am going to faint. *I am dying. This is it. This is what it's like!* I stumble out of the bathroom and look over at old man Murphy resting obliviously in the next bed, a half smile etched onto his face, a decidedly contented look, and suddenly I *envy* him, a guy in a coma! No more pain, no more anxiety, no more *fear* for old Murphy, the lucky bastard! I crawl back to bed. Feebly, I ring for a nurse.

CHAPTER

The nurse on duty that night is a young, raven-haired, thin-lipped trainee called Connie Snead, or so it says on her name plate. She finds me lying stiffly on my bed staring blankly at the ceiling, a corpse in rehearsal, not unlike my new idol, old man Murphy. It is two in the morning and she seems a little annoyed at being bothered at this wee hour by, of all people, a patient.

"You rang for a nurse, Mr. Dorfman?" she says with a weary sigh and a forced smile.

"I'm dying," I croak, though my mouth is so dry from dehydration I can barely get the words out.

"Oh come now, Mr. Dorfman. According to your chart, you're only in for tests."

"No it's true," I say. "It's all over for me, Nurse. Call a rabbi. I am a dying man."

"Now what makes you say something like that, Mr. Dorfman?"

Without moving from the bed, I point straight-armed, like the Ghost of Christmas Past, to the bathroom.

"I don't understand," she says.

"Go look in the toilet," I whisper. "It's filled with blood. My blood. Gallons of it. I'm hemorrhaging as we speak. My intestines are bleeding like there's no tomorrow. Go ahead. Take a look."

Suddenly a little less impassive, she enters the bathroom and peers into the bowl. I can not bear to watch her reaction, though I do hear a slight gasp, which she attempts to disguise by clearing her throat. In a moment, she is standing by my side.

"See what I mean?" I say.

"When did this bleeding start?" she asks.

"About twenty minutes ago."

"Are you in pain?"

"Yes."

"Terrible pain?"

"No, this is *pleasant* pain," I say. "Of course it's terrible. All pain is terrible."

"Has this happened before?"

"No."

She looks at me for a moment and then, for some reason, at Murphy; she has run out of questions and is trying to decide what to do next. Murphy is no help. "Let me see if I can find a doctor," she says calmly. "I'll be right back. In the meantime, try to relax."

She is gone for about twenty minutes. During that time it is all I can do to hold back the tears. How will Ursula survive without me? What about the kids? They'll be reduced to poverty. They'll have to sell the house, cash in the IRA's and the Keogh, live on Hamburger Helper and Spam. I light a cigarette, possibly my last, and pace, stopping at the large picture window to gaze out wistfully at the bright lights of West Hollywood, wishing I were out there having fun and not in here dying. I pace some more, dragging my IV stand behind me. I stop at the side of Murphy's bed.

"Why me?" I ask him. "Why me? Answer me that, Murphy. Why me and not all those healthy, carefree people out there? I'm a good person... Not perfect, I know that, not a saint, but I mean well... I'm a good father, I give to charity... I try to be honest... Sure, I embellish a little on my tax forms, but who doesn't? I honor my mother and my father, sort of... I don't covet my neighbor's wife... well okay, he's gay but if he wasn't, I wouldn't... The point is, I'm a good person. Is there something I did to deserve this, Murphy? Is there some transgression I'm not aware of? Answer me goddamnit!"

"Mr. *Dorfman!*" Connie says, materializing at the door, and I suddenly realize I am shaking poor old Murphy by the lapels of his jammies. Embarrassed, I let him sink back down onto the bed.

"Where's the doctor?" I ask.

"He's busy in the ER, but he said not to worry. It might just be an irritable bowel thing."

"Oh please."

"Or your uh, whatsit might just be a little bit sore from all the uh, trips to the john."

"My whatsit? You mean my *anus*?"

"Right," she says blushing slightly. "Your uh, anus might just be irritated."

"Give me a break," I say. "It's pouring out of me, the blood. Pouring! Like from a faucet!"

"That's the other thing."

"What?"

"He said to test it."

"Test what?"

"The blood. It might not be blood at all."

"What else could it be? Motor oil?"

But she has moved across the room to the bathroom. "Just try to take a deep breath and relax, Mr. Dorfman," she says. "Look at the bright side. If it is something serious, you couldn't be in a better place."

"Oh yes I could," I say, lying down on my bed, my head bobbing back and forth like one of those plastic hula dancers people put on the dashboards of their cars. "I could be in a morgue."

"You should hear yourself."

"I do hear myself."

"I'm going to test it now," says Connie. "This won't take but a minute."

I watch from behind as she removes a two inch strip of litmus-like paper from her pocket and daintily siphons a few drops of water from the toilet with an eye dropper. She squeezes out a few drops of the red water onto the paper. Then she flushes the toilet. Ten seconds later, when she emerges from the bathroom, she is smiling and shaking a finger at me.

"There. I told you not to worry. According to this it's not blood at all. So there you are."

I sit up. "What?"

"It's not blood," Connie says, holding up the litmus-like paper. "See for yourself."

"Are you sure?"

"If it was blood it would have turned the paper a different color."

"Then what can it be?"

"Beats me," she says, shrugging. "What color is the laxative you're taking?"

"Clear."

"Okay, what did you have for dinner?"

"Nothing," I say. "Just a bowl of..."

And then I suddenly see the light. Instantly, I am a changed man, a man whose death sentence has just been commuted by God. I get up and hug Connie in a tight embrace, the embrace of a man who has just been rescued from a sea full of white sharks. I am Ebenezer Scrooge the morning after. I am giddy. And then I finish my sentence...

"*... raspberry fucking Jell-O!*"

❧

The next morning, as Lester pushes my gurney to Dr. Jaffe's Chamber of Horrors for my colonoscopy, I happen to catch a look at my image in the dark reflective glass of an open door. I do not at first recognize the face. I am unshaven and, having gotten not a wink of sleep all night, there are dark half moons under my eyes. The face is haggard, emaciated, gaunt, a Halloween mask, my skin the color of the moon's surface and just as shadowy. I am appalled, terrified, desolate.

But not for long. The moment Jaffe's nurse shoots me up with Demerol, I turn instantaneously into Bozo the Clown. I am deliriously happy, cracking off-color jokes, making histrionic goo-goo eyes at the nurses, whistling Sousa marches. I am doing a stand-up routine lying down. I am, in short, a complete idiot. I am fully aware that I am acting like a moron, but I can't help myself. My only solace is in the hope that I will probably forget all of this wackiness as soon as I come down from the drug.

Five minutes later, I am wheeled into another room where Dr. Jaffe is waiting for me, like the Roto Rooter man, with his anguine hose, a sobering sight if ever there was one. Somehow, I had imagined the colonoscope to be the size of an ordinary garden hose, green with a little pointed nozzle, but it is no greater in diameter than a small garden snake. Not that this is much comfort. Man's innards were not meant to be explored by small meandering garden snakes, not to mention garden hoses. For some reason, I have run out of shtick. I gulp. Suddenly the epithet "up yours" takes on a whole new clarity of meaning.

"So," Dr. Jaffe says, injecting some new liquid into my IV bag. "Margolis tells me you're a writer. That must be an exciting line of work."

"Not really."

"I've recently finished a writing project of my own," Jaffe says.

"Medical paper?"

"Film script."

"Ah."

"I found the experience very slow, very painstaking, but ultimately very rewarding. It's about a traveling gastroenterologist who helps people solve their problems."

"Right," I say. "Will this hurt?"

"No," Jaffe says. "Not much. You should become drowsy soon. I've put some Valium in your IV."

"That's good. Valium is good. Demerol is better."

"You want more Demerol? More Demerol it is."

Jaffe switches on a video screen. "Have you ever been to the Carlsbad Caverns, Martin?" he asks apropos of what I have no idea.

"No."

"Well, that's what the inside of the colon will look like on the video screen. Carlsbad Caverns."

"Yes, well last night it looked more like Niagara Falls," I say.

My weak attempt at humor falls deservedly flat. "We have to hope that there are no stalagmites or stalactites in the cavern today," he continues.

"Excuse me?"

"Maintaining the cavern image," Jaffe explains, "stalactites and stalagmites would be polyps, metaphorically speaking of course. We don't want to find any of them in your cavern, now do we?"

"No. Definitely not. Or bats either. Or Japanese tour groups, or…"

Jaffe rolls me gently over on my side, moves my legs into a fetal position and picks up the dreaded hose. "Okay, now you might feel a little discomfort…"

I close my eyes and grit my teeth, but miraculously I feel nothing at all. What is he doing? Has he started? I try to look over my shoulder but I cannot. The video screen is still blank.

"Perhaps you'd like to read my script sometime," Jaffe says. "It's only a first draft, but I could certainly use some input from a real writer."

What am I going to say to a guy who is about to do what Jaffe is about to do? I sure as hell am *not* going to piss him off. "Sure," I say. "I'd love to. Send it to me."

"Okay," Jaffe says, and then he snaps on a pair of rubber gloves and pulls down his surgical mask. "Up periscope. Lights, camera, action!"

One second later, I am out cold.

⊙

When I wake up back in my room a few hours later, the Demerol buzz has not yet worn off so I decide to take advantage of this drug-induced state of euphoria and call Gavin.

"Ben Fogelman," Gavin says. "He loves the script."

"You sent it to Ben Fogelman?"

"Sure why not? He's a player."

"Ben Fogelman, the flasher? The guy who exposed himself to old ladies in Griffith Park?"

"Years ago. And he only did it once. People make mistakes. Water under the bridge. He's been rehabilitated."

"They said he'd never work in this town again."

"Who said that?"

"The columnists."

"Ach, they always say that. What do they know? If they had any brains they'd be writing for the movies, not for the trades."

"So he's working, Fogelman I mean?"

"Not only is he working, he's got an exclusive first look deal at a major studio."

"No shit."

"I shit you not, my friend."

"So he liked the script?"

"Liked? Who said liked? He *loved* the script! He's insane for it."

"So he wants to option it?"

"Uh, no."

"Then what?"

"He wants to meet with you. For lunch. When's good?"

"Uh…"

"How's tomorrow?"

"Uh…"

"Okay, Friday."

"Uh."

"Is this a problem?"

"No, of course not. Let me look at my calendar book. Just a second."

I put my hand over the mouthpiece of the receiver. This *is* a problem. What if I make a lunch date with Fogelman and I am too sick to go? What if I am still in the hospital a week from now? What if I am dying? Or dead? Well, then it wouldn't be a problem. I take a deep breath and raise the receiver to my mouth, but just then Lester pops his head into my room, pointing at his watch. Time for my upper GI. Gee, what a busy guy I am, so many appointments. I look at Lester and hold up an index finger.

"Let me get back to you on that, Gavin," I say.

"Okay, but make it soon, my friend. We must strike while the iron is hot."

"Right. We'll be in touch. Gotta go."

I hang up the phone and Lester wheels me out of the room in a wheelchair. He pushes me at a clip, for we are about thirty minutes late for my test, which means I'll only have to wait an hour and a half instead of two. We take an express elevator down to a small basement waiting room that is filled with elderly men of all weights and sizes, some of them pacing nervously, others absently watching a soap opera on television. I am the only person in the room under seventy-five and without significant nose hair. Seventy-five is when you *expect* to be down here, not forty. They look at me quizzically as if I am an interloper in some private restricted club, the lone whippersnapper at the Upper GI Fiftieth Reunion. I try to appear unfazed and pick a magazine up off the coffee table, but they are all back issues of *Modern Maturity*, never one of my favorites. I decide to pace in the hallway. I need the exercise. I need to get out of that room.

About two hours later, my mouth still coated with the revolting barium milkshake they made me swallow in the basement, I am back in my room, waiting for the results of my tests. I drag my IV stand over to the window, twist open the blinds and stare out at the city below. I have been in the hospital for 48 hours, undergone four tests and I do not yet have a diagnosis. For all I know, I have an aneurysm, a brain tumor, pancreatic cancer, colitis, multiple sclerosis, myasthenia gravis, and a gut full of prehistoric ice formations. Margolis has not been in to see me in 36 hours, the lousy bum, and I am a little worried. On top of all that, I am clean out of cigarettes.

Suddenly there is a knock on the door and I turn away from the window, expecting to see Margolis. But to my surprise, it is Ursula who steps into the room. When she sees me she cannot help but raise a hand to her mouth in shock.

"Martin! My God, you look… terrible!"

"Gee thanks."

We both stride for each other, meeting in the center of the room in an embrace. I was not expecting her for another two days, but I am so overjoyed to see her I cannot speak for about half a minute.

"How did you find out?" I ask.

"I've been trying to call you for two days. No answer at home, so I called some of our friends and they didn't know what had happened to you. I was getting scared so I called Margolis's office and they told me you were here. We booked a new flight and…"

"God I'm glad you're here," I say. "It's been hell."

"Why didn't you tell me?"

"I don't know. I didn't want to spoil your vacation."

"That's crazy, Martin. I'm your wife."

"I know, I know."

"When they said you were here, it scared the hell out of me."

"Sorry."

"Do they know what's wrong with you?"

"Not yet," I say. "But I have a feeling we're about to find out."

I nod toward the door. The Three Wise Men, Margolis, Jaffe and Herschel are standing in the doorway, all three of them looking decidedly grim.

☙

I find myself suddenly weak in the knees and I sink to the edge of the bed, awaiting my sentence. Like a jury that has just voted to convict, none of them looks the defendant in the eye. I can feel my heart pulsating in my ears and am conscious of a slight tremor coursing through my body. My gut is tied in knots. Margolis introduces Ursula to his cohorts and after all the handshakes are over, he produces my chart in its metal folder, flips back the cover and clears his throat. Ursula grabs my hand and holds it tightly. Neither of us breathes for the next ten seconds.

"You're not going to like this, Martin," Margolis begins.

"Spit it out, Doc," I say bravely. "Whatever it is, we can handle it, right honey?"

"Right."

"Just give it to me straight."

"Okay," Margolis says, clearing his throat. "You're fine."

"Pardon me?"

"You're fine," he repeats. "Strong as a horse. The picture of health. You should live to be ninety."

I can feel a breeze graze the top of my head as Ursula lets out a heavy sigh of relief. She squeezes my hand so tightly, her fingers are leaving marks. My own feelings are ambiguous. If it is possible to feel elated and crushed at the same time, that describes my response to the news.

"Except for a few minor things," Margolis continues.

"Oh God. I knew it! What minor things?"

Now Dr. Herschel steps forward with his chart. He too clears his throat. "We found a little white area in your brain," he says.

"A little white area? In my brain?"

"Yes."

"How little?"

"Little."

"What does it mean?"

"We don't really know," Herschel continues.

"I don't get it."

"The MRI is a fairly new test and we haven't learned how to read all the results yet."

"Is it a tumor?"

"No."

"A lesion, a polyp..?"

"No."

"An aneurysm…?"

"No."

"A small colony of maggots?"

"Certainly not."

"Then what?"

"A little white area in the brain is the best I can do."

"There's no medical term for this?"

"I'm afraid not, although we neurologists sometimes refer to them as LWAs."

"Okay, answer me this: Can it be the cause of my symptoms, this little white area?"

"No," Herschel says emphatically. "Definitely not."

"How can you be sure if you don't know what it is?"

"Because we've seen these little white areas before in other people and they seem to be feeling fine. Even people with big white areas, or BWAs, are okay."

"I'd feel better if there was a medical term," I say.

"Can't help you there," Herschel says. "Sorry."

Shrugging and a little downcast, as if his inconclusive diagnosis were somehow shameful, Herschel shuffles to the back of the line and now Dr. Jaffe steps forward with his chart and another round of throat-clearing. "The colonoscopy was negative," he says. "Not a single polyp. In fact, Martin you have one of the most attractive colons I have seen in many years."

"I'm deeply flattered," I say.

"Smooth and supple, good width, excellent texture…"

"No shit?"

"None at all. Perfectly clean. Absolutely spotless. Not a speck of debris. You're really an excellent patient, Martin."

"Always one of my big goals," I say.

His smile evaporates as he flips open the chart. "However, we did find something in your upper GI that might be causing your symptoms."

"Oh yes? What?"

"A slight edema in the small intestine."

"How slight?"

"Very slight."

"On a scale of one to ten, ten being worst."

"A one point three."

"Only a one point three?"

"What's an edema?" Ursula asks.

"A swelling," I reply. "An inflammation."

"Correct," Jaffe says. "We can't be sure since it's barely detectable, but I feel intuitively that this edema might be caused by a parasite."

"But my stool culture was negative," I say.

"Some parasites, in particular a hearty little devil called Giardia, can be difficult to detect in a stool culture," Jaffe continues. "If exposed to the oxygen in the air, the little buggers can die leaving no visible trace."

"So you think it's a parasite?" I ask, my excitement mounting. "That's what's causing my symptoms?"

"We can't be a hundred percent sure unless we take a biopsy of the area, but it's a very good possibility."

"Thank God," I say putting my arm around Ursula and giving her a squeeze. "How I've prayed for a parasite!"

They all look at me strangely.

"I'm going to put you on some medication," Jaffe says.

"Metronidazole, more commonly known as Flagyl?" I ask. "Let me guess: Two hundred and fifty milligrams three times a day?"

He looks up. "Yes, how did you know?"

"I keep up with the literature. Kind of a hobby of mine."

"Interesting hobby," Jaffe says, writing up a prescription. "In any case, Flagyl should do the trick. If the little buggers are setting up household in your ileum, they'll be toast by the end of the week. I guarantee it."

"And I'll feel fine again?"

"Hopefully, yes," Jaffe says. "I'd like to have you come into the office next week once you've finished the medication, but I'll be on vacation until the first of the month."

"Carlsbad Caverns?"

"As a matter of fact, yes."

I am elated. I am reborn, resurrected! I bounce to my feet and shake everybody's hand, including Murphy's clammy lifeless one, and thank each of the Three Wise Men profusely. They are brilliant, each one of them, boons to the medical profession, geniuses, humanitarians. I am gushing, ebullient, tearful with joy, deliriously happy, maybe even a little psychotic.

When they are gone, Ursula tosses me my clothes.

"Let's get you home," she says.

Part Two

CHAPTER

Needless to say, I am in a *big* hurry to get started with the Flagyl but, since I am still feeling a bit weak and woozy (partly because Dr. Jaffe's potent laxative concoction has not yet completely worn off), Ursula drives to the nearest pharmacy to fill my prescription. The moment she returns I pop the first pill in my mouth and say "So long suckers" to the insidious little vermin that have pitched their tents in my small intestine. "*Sayonara* fellas, *adios, auf wiedersehen*, good riddance!"

Assuming that I will be cured by the end of the week, the next thing I do is call Gavin's office and make a date to have lunch with Ben Fogelman. "Any place, anytime," I tell my eager agent, who promises to get right back to me with a definite time and place.

Next, knowing that they are probably worried about me, I call my parents. My mother is relieved at the news and tells me so. My father immediately takes full credit for my diagnosis.

"I knew it right from the start," he says. "Didn't I tell you it was parasites?"

"No, Dad."

"Of course I did. You probably picked them up from that housekeeper of yours, the one from Guatemala."

"El Salvador."

"What's the difference? They don't have parasites in El Salvador? She's a walking diarrhea factory. I told you a million times to get rid of that girl."

"She doesn't have parasites," I say.

"How do you know? Diarrhea is a way of life down there. It's part of the culture. They're all carriers. Do you use Lysol?"

"Religiously."

"Good boy. Everyday, Lysol the toilet seats, the sink, the bathroom doorknob, the soap."

"You want me to Lysol the soap?"

"Only if she uses the soap. Does she?"

"Yes."

"How do you know? Do you watch her?"

"Of course not."

"Then Lysol the soap. An ounce of prevention… know what I mean?"

"Not really."

"So," my father says, moving on to a new area of neuroses, "what's that quack Margolis giving you for it?"

"He's not a quack."

"Fine. What's the Great Medicine Man giving you for it?"

"Flagyl."

"Tell me you're joking."

"I'm not."

"Oh God. Not Flagyl!"

"What's wrong with Flagyl?"

"You don't know? They didn't tell you?"

"No."

"Tell me, Martin, you like having a liver?"

"Yeah I suppose. I'm not sure I know much about the alternative."

"Well you can kiss your liver good-bye after a week of Flagyl."

"Excuse me?"

"Don't you read the articles I send you?"

"Of course not."

"Flagyl is toxic to the liver, Martin. Highly toxic. A carcinogen. They gave it to rats and they all died of liver cancer in a week. You'll get rid of the parasites, but you'll lose your liver. Some choice."

I take a deep breath and contemplate hanging up on him. "So

what are you saying, I should live the rest of my life with parasites in my intestines?"

"Better parasites than no liver."

"Come on, Dad. That's ridiculous. Other people take it. I'm sure a week of Flagyl isn't going to kill me."

"Oh I forgot! You know everything better, Dr. Einstein, you went to medical school for four years," he says.

"Can we drop the subject, Dad?"

"Fine. Just don't say I didn't warn you."

"I won't."

"You lose your liver, you have only yourself and your so-called gastroenterologist to blame."

"Right."

"Just answer me this: how do they know it's parasites? I thought your stool culture was negative."

"It was," I say. "They found an edema in my small intestine."

"An edema?"

"Just a little one."

"How little?"

"Tiny."

"And they biopsied it?"

"No."

"Why not?"

"I don't know."

"If they didn't biopsy it, then how may I ask do they know parasites caused it?"

"The gastroenterologist," I say. "He has a hunch."

"A hunch! He has a hunch!"

I see immediately where this is going. "Good-bye, Dad."

"On a hunch, he's going to destroy your liver? On a hunch he's going to prescribe poison?"

"I'll talk to you soon, Dad. So long."

"What kind of medicine do these guys practice?!"

And so once again I hang up on my father.

ᐇ

Delilah was right about one thing. In all, the hospital bill comes to a whopping, unconscionable $15,563.34. Over $2500 for my two unforgettable nights at Chez Cedars, a cool $1000 for the MRI, plus the technician's fee of $456. The CAT scan, upper GI and colonoscopy combined run $4536. The lab gets $2356. The Three Wise Men each receive in the area of $1900 for their forty seconds of backbreaking labor. The Demerol is a bargain at $245; the two Tylenol capsules I receive one night when I have a headache go for $56 each; the red plastic pitcher I use for drinking water costs $232.76; its two companion red plastic cups weigh in at $45 each; the water itself is $4.75 a pint; rubber gloves are $312; the rental on the IV stand is $123.56; the wheelchair lease is $275, which comes to about $700 a mile. And so on and so forth. For the same money, I could have bought a good used car and gone on a two week cruise in the Aegean.

"So did they find anything?" Delilah asks.

"An edema!" I tell her excitedly. "They found an edema!"

"An edema?"

"Yes, an edema. In my small intestine. Isn't that terrific?"

Oddly, Delilah does not sound enthusiastic. There's a grumpy monotone in her voice that I find disturbing.

"Do you know what an edema is?" I ask.

"Do I know what an edema is? Of course I know what an edema is," she says, her voice making a quick transition from dull to annoyed. "An excessive accumulation of serous fluid in the tissues," she sighs. "In your case, an area of minor swelling."

"Yes! That's exactly right," I say. "I'm cured, Delilah. They think it's caused by a parasite."

"Really?"

"Yes. Giardia."

"Uh huh."

"Very common, hard to detect."

"Yes, I'm familiar with the species."

"Delilah, aren't you happy for me?"

"Yes of course…"

"But?"

"I'm just a little under the weather today, Martin. I'm having a bad day, that's all. Congratulations. I *am* happy for you. I assume he's giving you Flagyl for it?"

"Yes."

"That should do the trick."

"Delilah, you really don't sound good," I say. "Do you want me to come over? Can I get you something? Cigarettes? Groceries?"

"That's very sweet of you," she says unconvincingly. "I'll manage. Got plenty of cigarettes and food. Call me next week with an update."

"Delilah, you have no idea how happy I am."

"Oh yes," she says, "I think I do."

September, 1988. It is Amanda's third day of kindergarten and for some reason she is having a severe bout of separation anxiety, a phase we have never experienced before. Ursula takes her to school the first two days, sits with her in the classroom for ten minutes and then, with the aid of the teacher, pries herself loose and walks away, leaving poor Amanda crying her eyes out and screaming at the top of her lungs. Neither of us is quite sure how to deal with this problem, but on the third day Ursula suggests that I take her to school.

"Maybe it's me," Ursula says. "Maybe it's a Mommy thing. Maybe she won't be as sad to see you go."

"Oh thanks a lot," I say.

"You know what I mean."

"And what if she makes a big fuss again?"

"Then we'll know it's not just a Mommy thing."

"But what do I do?"

"Deal with it."

"How?"

"Play it by ear. Be firm."

"Be firm? Me?"

"Fake it."

So the next morning at breakfast, I inform Amanda that I will be taking her to school. I explain to her that Mommy has to go to work early, but that we will both be there to pick her up after school. I promise, cross my heart. I say this in a slow, singsong voice. To my surprise and relief, she seems amazingly unfazed by the news and goes back to eating her Corn Puffs.

"So…" I say, smiling broadly, "is that all right with you, honey?"

"Sure, Daddy."

"You'll be okay today?"

"Uh huh."

"No crying when Daddy leaves?"

"'Course not silly."

"Good girl."

And so she kisses Ursula good-bye without incident and the two of us walk to school hand in hand. It is a warm autumn morning, a beautiful day, Indian summer in California, and I am confident that everything will go well. I can feel it instinctively. Piece of cake. This separation problem is obviously just a phase that she is now over. The tearful farewell scene that I dread will not take place.

I walk her into the area of the playground where she is supposed to line up with her class. Several kids are already there, two boys and a girl, playing catch with a Frisbee. Amanda does not seem to know them. She sits down on a brick pony wall that encircles a large oak tree. I hand her her backpack.

"Well," I say. "Guess I'll be going now, okay sweetheart?"

"Not yet, Daddy," she says. "When the teacher comes."

"Amanda, we discussed this."

"Please."

"Okay," I say, looking at my watch. "But just until the teacher comes, okay? I have lots of work to do, sweetie."

"Okay."

I sit down next to her and watch as the playground slowly fills up with kids. Soon I am the only parent in sight. I have witnessed maybe twenty or thirty children bidding their parents good-bye without a hitch. Not a tear has been shed. And here I am, waiting for the teacher. What I need is a diversion. I spot a familiar face over by the swings and direct Amanda's attention in that direction.

"Isn't that Amy Silverman over there?" I ask. "By the swings?"

"Yes."

"Why don't you go over and play with her?"

"I don't want to," Amanda says.

"Why?"

"I don't know, I just don't."

"I thought you were friends?"

"No. She's too bossy."

"Okay. You don't have to, but she sure looks like she's having lots of fun. How about I push you on the swing?"

But Amanda isn't looking in Amy's direction anymore. She has spotted her teacher approaching. I can see the panic in her eyes, feel her body stiffening. She suddenly takes my hand and holds it so tightly I would need to use my other hand to pry her loose. The teacher, Miss Scott, says good morning and instructs the class to form a line. She is a gangly, soft-spoken woman of twenty-five or so, whose thick glasses make her eyes look large and fishlike. Amanda pulls me to my feet and we both get in line. Miss Scott gives me a sympathetic smile and we all march in single file to the classroom.

"Okay, Amanda," I say as we hesitate by the classroom door. "I really have to go now. Really. Now give me a kiss good-bye."

The other kids file past us, some of them staring at us, a few taunting her. Amanda now has my hand gripped with both of hers and I can feel her little fingernails digging into my flesh. She is doing her best not to cry, but her upper lip is trembling. "Don't go Daddy," she pleads forlornly.

"But I have to work, honey," I say. "I have to work so I can make money to buy you birthday presents. Don't you want birthday presents?"

"Yes."

"Then you'd better let me go so I can work," I say cheerily. "Or I won't have enough money to buy any." But the birthday ruse does not work; we are way beyond blackmail here. Her grip on my hand tightens.

"Please don't go yet, Daddy," she begs me. "Please."

I look down at her and suddenly I am heartbroken. Those big blue eyes of hers filling with tears, that look of utter desperation, dissolve any trace of firmness I may have had five minutes ago. She is clinging to me for dear life. I know this feeling, it is somehow familiar. I feel the tears start to well up in my own eyes and no words will come out of my mouth. Later, Ursula will call me a wimp, a pushover, but what can I do? I can't leave her here like this, turn my back and just walk away. And so I nod and Amanda pulls me into the classroom where I almost break my back trying to sit down in one of those tiny plastic kid chairs.

I stay all day.

CHAPTER

Thanks to my father's paranoia about disease, I am in my mid-twenties before I realize that normal healthy people do not go to the doctor four times a year for a checkup.

"You have a car, you get the oil changed every three months," my father says sagely. "What's good advice for cars is good advice for people."

So every three months, as surely as the seasons and the fiscal quarters change, we are trotted off to our family doctor, an elderly arthritic man we call Doctor Bob, to be probed and kneaded and told to urinate in a cup. We say "ah" to his wooden tongue depresser, we watch our legs kick involuntarily as he taps our knees with the little rubber hammer, we have our fingers pricked. Once every three months, like my father's trusty Buick, we have our oil changed, our tires rotated.

In those days, in the Fifties, I have a healthy respect for medical science. There are miracle drugs and wondrous new technologies for diagnosing diseases and for keeping people alive. Antibiotics! Penicillin! Iron Lungs! Large complex machines, like the one in my father's office, that can suck the phlegm out of your sinuses! Doctors are gods. Titans! They can do no wrong. They are infallible.

I am not sure, but I think this high regard for medical science bites the dust about seven days after I begin to take the Flagyl prescribed by Dr. Jaffe. I am down to my last pill and my symptoms are still with me. I am still waking up nauseous and disoriented; I am morose, dizzy and fatigued. By now the parasites should be long dead. But after fifteen-thousand bucks worth of the latest in medical technology, I am back to square one. All that money and the diagnosis is wrong! Jaffe's hunch is a bust; there are no parasites. On top of which, because of the medication and its adverse effects, I may have irreparably harmed my liver in the bargain. God knows, I hate to say it, but maybe my father is right — maybe Margolis and his cohorts *are* quacks. Not the Three Wise Men, but the Three Stooges. I don't know what to think anymore. I am confused, depressed, discouraged.

Jaffe is out of town, so I call Margolis.

"Gosh, I don't know what to say, Martin," he says, clearly surprised and a little disconcerted after I tell him that the Flagyl hasn't worked. "We thought the parasite diagnosis was a pretty good bet."

"They should be dead by now, right? The parasites? If there really were any?"

"Oh yes, most definitely. Flagyl is a very potent drug. The drug of choice for practically every type of parasite. It kills bugs dead, so to speak."

"Are there any adverse effects?" I ask, testing him.

"To Flagyl? In large prolonged doses it can cause liver damage. But a week of it isn't going to do you any harm."

Thank God, I say to myself. At least he *knows*.

"And give my regards to your father the next time you talk to him."

I ignore this remark and refer to the list I have made, a list of questions. "Look, could this disease of mine be caused by a food allergy of some kind?" I ask.

"Possible, but unlikely. Food allergies are hard to diagnose. There really is no scientific way to tell. Scratch tests are erratic and inconclusive. On the other hand, we can develop new allergies as we age. You might try cutting out eggs and dairy for a week and see if there's any change."

"Thyroid?"

"No, we tested for that."

"Diabetes?"

"Ruled it out."

"Leukemia?"

"No."

"Viral encephalitis?

"No fever, headaches or paralysis."

"How about some kind of new, weird infectious disease?"

"Anything's possible, Martin, but your white count would have stayed elevated. When you left the hospital, it was pretty close to normal."

"So what do you suggest I do now?" I ask, exasperated. "I feel like hell, Doc. It's been like this for over a month now. I can barely function. I have a family, a career…"

"Well," Margolis says. "You can relax about one thing — whatever you've got, we can be reasonably assured it isn't life-threatening. We would have spotted anything really serious on the CAT scan or the colonoscopy."

"But it *is* life-threatening, Doc, especially if I commit suicide, which is an option I will definitely be contemplating if this doesn't go away pretty darn quick. I'm leaning toward the exhaust pipe-garage method, although there are aspects of the Valium overdose that I find appealing."

"You are kidding right?"

I take a deep breath and do not answer. I feel like letting him squirm. Of course I would never really have the guts to commit suicide. Or would I?

"Martin?"

"Yes and no," I say coyly. "Look, just because you didn't find a tumor doesn't mean this isn't serious. It's serious enough to me. I've been feeling sick all day, almost everyday, for a whole month now. I wake up sick in the morning, I go to bed sick at night. My weight is down, I have no appetite. Do you have any idea what that's like?"

"You sound very stressed out, Martin," he says. "Maybe you should see a therapist."

"For what? This isn't psychosomatic, Doc. Trust me."

"I never said it was. But stress has been known to cause physical symptoms."

"Nice theory, but you got it backwards," I say. "In my case, it's the physical symptoms causing the stress."

"Look," he sighs. "Let me talk to Jaffe when he comes back from vacation. Maybe we need to look a little deeper into that edema of yours. Okay?"

"Fine."

"And in the meantime, try to relax. We'll get to the bottom of this thing sooner or later. I'm sure of it."

But sooner or later is not soon enough; in two days I am to meet Ben Fogelman for lunch at Chasen's.

⌒

"To tell you the truth, I'm not surprised," Delilah says after I have told her the disappointing news. "They misdiagnosed me with rheumatoid arthritis. Margolis was *positive* it was the right diagnosis. I was taking meds for no reason for two weeks and nothing happened except I started urinating in the middle of the night."

"I'm very depressed, Delilah. Very, *very* depressed."

"I know, Martin," she says soothingly. "I've been there. Actually, I'm *still* there."

"I might kill myself," I say.

"That's always an option."

"Aren't you going to talk me out of it?"

"Only if I thought you were serious."

"I should have known by the ponytail."

"Excuse me?"

"The gastroenterologist had a ponytail."

"Always a sure sign of an imbecile."

"I should ask Margolis and the other two idiots for my money back."

"Did you save the plastic pitcher at least?"

"Yes. The two plastic cups too."

"Good boy. That's showing them! Bravo."

⌒

After the Irving Glickstein Fiasco, it appears that I will be spending my entire professional life engaged in nothing more challenging than the most routine manual labor. Following Yom Kippur of 1972, once all my friends and family have departed the Island with all the other summer folk, I am still here, painting houses. I am climbing up and down ladders, sanding and scraping, puttying and caulking, breathing in toxic latex fumes. I am living on clam chowder and doughnuts. Soon, the harsh Nantucket winter with its frigid, offshore winds will come, making exterior house painting an unpleasant and largely impossible enterprise. Soon I will not only be lonely and depressed, I will be out of work. Penniless. An unemployed house painter. A bum.

As it happens, I have befriended an old ex-seaman by the name of Captain Chuck, who I meet by chance in an empty dockside piano bar on Steamboat Wharf one stormy night in October. Captain Chuck has a great white beard and a bulbous red nose; he walks with a cane, sports a faded old captain's cap and speaks with a deep gravelly voice, not unlike the actor Robert Newton. A peg leg and a shoulder parrot would not have been out of place on Captain Chuck. Having long ago given up the seafaring life for the lub of the land, Captain Chuck is employed by a local souvenir shop called Pirates Cove as a scrimshaw carver, one of the last practitioners of this dying art. He makes a good living doing this, for the tourists seem to love to spend extravagant amounts of money on the small etchings of schooners and clipper ships that he so painstakingly scratches onto the smooth polished enamel of some dead whale's bicuspid. Captain Chuck has a little booth in a rear corner of the store, where he carves his designs and regales his customers with swashbuckling tales, punctuating his stories with a suck on the old corn cob.

Come winter, when the tourist season is long gone, Captain Chuck goes in search of some poor unemployed fool to polish those whale bicuspids, to make their surfaces smooth enough for him to shaw scrim. I volunteer for the job and he offers me ten bucks a tooth. I grab it, assuming that I can do five or ten teeth a day, thereby earning enough to maintain my spartan lifestyle. At the very least, I figure that one day this will make for an interesting tidbit on the dust jacket of my first novel. *Mr. Dorfman has worked as a merchant seaman, a migrant farmworker, a travelling salesman, a private detective and a whalestooth polisher.*

As it turns out, Captain Chuck has misled me, for my estimate of five or ten teeth a day is way off the mark; I am lucky if I can manage two. If you have ever seen a raw unpolished whale's tooth, it is full of ridges and crevices and fissures, the usual ravages of seagoing tooth decay and plain old wear and tear. Polishing, I soon learn, requires the use of six different grades of sandpaper and a lot of elbow grease. The finished product must be so smooth that if black ink is smeared onto the tooth, none will remain after it has been rubbed off. If I get up at six in the morning and work through until ten at night, with a half hour lunch break, I can just about finish two teeth a day. Twenty bucks for 16 hours of backbreaking labor! If I work seven days a week, I can just pay my rent and get by on chowder and doughnuts.

And that is not the only flimflam Captain Chuck puts over on me. As he later admits one night over fish and chips at Cap'n Toby's, he is not an ex-sea captain at all. Far from it. He has, in fact, never set foot on a ship of any greater dimension than the car ferry to and from Nantucket. And even that short, uneventful journey causes him to blow lunch. Of the seven seas, he has seen only one, the Atlantic, and has no particular longing to see the other six; an anchor, to Captain Chuck, is someone who reads the news on television; he cannot tell a jib from a mainsail, does not know the difference between starboard and port, thinks a poop deck is where the bathrooms are located. For, as he confesses to me one night, Captain Chuck is actually a retired dentist from Passaic, New Jersey. Charles P. Himmelfarb, DDS! A Jewish dentist to boot! A fraud. My faith in humanity is crushed.

In any case, by December of that year, my hands are so calloused from polishing whales' teeth, I can barely brush my *own* teeth at night. On top of which, having to subsist on the paltry $140 a week Captain Chuck pays me, the thief, I am practically broke. In desperation, I dash off a number of letters to the editors of several well-regarded New York magazines, begging for a job, imploring, beseeching, grovelling. I carefully craft these letters, making them humorous in a self-deprecating way, telling my correspondents of my adventures in the whale's tooth polishing racket, noting that I am desperate for work of a slightly less dental nature.

Two months go by before I receive a decent, non-form letter response. One of the editors, apparently tickled by my description of the whale's tooth business, offers me a job as an editorial assistant. I take it without hesitation, despite the low starting salary of $65 a week. It is, after all, a job in the publishing business, a humble, entry-level position, but who's complaining? For once in my life, Lady Luck looks my way, makes eye contact and winks. It is not much, but it is a foot in the proverbial door. I am saved from a life of obscurity! And so I bid Captain Chuck good-bye, return his box of unpolished whale molars and sail for New York.

I arrive in Manhattan eager and raring to go. After looking for three weeks, I find a dreary studio apartment on the Upper West Side, a fifth floor walk-up the size of a padded cell. The job is not particularly stimulating but I take full advantage of the perks: I go to literary luncheons, I meet writers and editors, I make connections, I sleep with one of the assistant editors, I ingratiate myself. Within a year, all this hobnobbing pays off and I manage to parlay myself into a better, higher-paying job at a more prominent magazine in Chicago. It is there, in the Playboy Club of all places, that I meet Ursula, who is putting herself through college working as a Playboy Bunny. I am immediately bewitched by her wavy black hair and dark eyes, by that pale skin, by that exotic accent. With that deep husky voice, she is Garbo in rabbit ears. When, after three martinis, I discover that she is German-born, I leap on top of a chair in the middle of the Playboy Club and recite three verses of poetry in her mother tongue. The Club's patrons, who apparently think I have just recited a romantic sonnet from Schiller or Goethe, burst into applause. But Ursula and I share the secret knowledge that what I have just recited is *Goldilocks and the Three Bears*; it is the only German I know. For some reason, this episode of drunken theatrics wins her over and we immediately begin to date, although in order to do this she must first get permission from her husband. But that's another story.

And then, fortune smiles on me again. During my five years in the Windy City, I write a number of short stories for the magazine, clever little ditties about ordinary people thrust into preposterous situations, fish-out-of-water stories. One of these happens to attract the attention of a legitimate Hollywood producer by the name of Marty Eisenhut, who options it for the movies and offers me 50,000 Big Ones to pen the screenplay. Eureka! Happy to leave the snow-bound doldrums of the Midwest, Ursula and I pull up stakes and move to the Coast. I land a high-powered agent. I take meetings and do lunches. I find a house on stilts in the Hollywood Hills. I put in a spa. I join a health club. I read the trade papers and drive around in a used Mercedes convertible. Life is good.

For awhile.

And then, and then... ten years and six unproduced screenplays later, here I am, an unemployed hack, my Mercedes traded in for a Dodge, my house in the Hills replaced by a common ranch house in North Hollywood, spa full of leaves, my high-powered agent a thing of the past, my calendar book devoid of lunches and meetings, my name stricken from the Rolodexes of the high and the mighty, here I am, hoping that the notorious ex-convict Ben Fogelman will, by some miracle, somehow revive my erstwhile career.

The morning of my fateful luncheon I wake up at four A.M., feeling like death. The house is quiet; the kids are still asleep; even the dog is still snoring on his blanket. I look down at the dog with something resembling envy; he might be a mere canine, he might crap in the grass and urinate on fire hydrants, but at least he's *healthy* and he doesn't have to meet Ben Fogelman for lunch at twelve.

And so I make a pot of coffee and start my compulsive peripatetic journey through the house, stopping every time I hit the kitchen for a sip of java, going outside on the patio once every five revolutions for a cigarette. By the time Ursula and the kids are up, I have finished off the whole pot of strong coffee and smoked about half a pack of Carltons. It is eight o'clock and I have four hours to get my act together.

"Maybe you should cancel," Ursula suggests after I tell her how rotten I feel.

"You don't cancel lunch with Ben Fogelman unless you're dead."

By eleven o'clock I am still feeling nauseous and dizzy, but I am determined to get through this. I figure as long as I don't barf directly *on* Fogelman, everything will be all right. If I do barf on Fogelman, right there in the middle of Chasen's at the peak of the lunch hour, it will probably make the trades (*SCRIBE UPCHUCKS ON PROD! PIX NIXED!*) which is not exactly the sort of notoriety I need at this stage in my career.

And so I dress, shower and shave; I put on a tie, slap on a little aftershave. As usual, I wear the official Writer's Uniform: jeans, running shoes, tweed jacket and tie. Meanwhile, Ursula brings the kids over to our neighbor's house where they will spend the rest of the afternoon. She insists on driving me to Chasen's because she is afraid I won't make it back alive if I drive myself. The way I feel, she might have a point.

"Good luck," she says as we part in front of Chasen's parking lot an hour later. She kisses me good-bye and I watch her pull away in my rattling old Dodge. According to our plan, while I am at lunch, she will go shopping for an hour at the Beverly Center and then park across the street from the restaurant at one o'clock. When Fogelman and I exit the restaurant, I will wait until the valet has brought him his car, say good-bye and, once he has driven off, walk across the street to my waiting Dodge. This will at least spare me the embarrassment of having to get into a car as lowly as my humble old Dodge in front of Ben Fogelman, who probably drives a Rolls or a Bentley.

Chasen's is abustle with waiters and busboys and the bar is thick with patrons waiting for tables or drinking lunch. An extremely attractive blonde *maîtresse d'* leads me through the restaurant to Ben Fogelman's private table. The table is empty; Fogelman will be a few minutes late I am told. She offers her sincere apologies. Still feeling a little rocky, I sit and order a Bloody Mary, not entirely unconscious of the fact that some of the other patrons are squinting my way; after all, this is one of those places where the elite meet to eat, and since I am sitting at Ben Fogelman's table I must therefore be Somebody. But who? I look at my watch and feign preoccupation with the menu.

Fogelman makes his entrance five minutes later. I recognize him from the wanted posters. He is a well-tanned, white haired man of about sixty, very dapper in a yellow blazer and well-creased designer blue jeans. He kisses the *maîtresse d'* as if she were a long lost relative, shakes hands and has a mini-conversation with practically everybody milling around at the bar before he finally heads toward his table. This journey takes him another fifteen minutes, for he has to stop at every table along the way to shake somebody's hand or hug somebody or slap somebody on the back. He is, after all, a mover and a shaker, a big cheese. Of course, the whole time, I am wondering what motivated this nice old gentleman to expose himself to two elderly ladies in Griffith Park.

"Martin!" he roars shaking my hand.

"Mr. Fogelman."

"Ben."

"Ben."

"May I say it is a great pleasure to meet someone as talented as you are?"

"And may I say it is a pleasure to meet someone so perceptive," I respond charmingly. To my surprise, this prehistoric line gets a laugh. He tilts his head back and guffaws.

"I hope you haven't been waiting here too long?"

"No, no," I say. "But President Coolidge sends his regards."

Another laugh. He is either an easy mark or devilishly charming. Or both. Considering how lousy I feel, I am amazed at how well things seem to be going.

"You writers kill me," Fogelman says.

The gorgeous *maîtresse d'* floats by and places a gin and tonic in front of Fogelman. He nods and takes a sip. This is what it means to have power; this is what it means to have a sandwich named after you at Cantors. I stir my Bloody Mary.

"So," Fogelman says. "I assume Gavin has told you that I absolutely love your script?"

"Yes."

"It's funny, it has heart, I love the characters…"

"Thank you."

"I laughed out loud when I read it."

"Music to my ears."

And now he leans forward, a serious expression on his face. "Martin, I just want you to know up front that I have enormous respect for writers," he says. "Without writers where would we be? Nowhere. A lot of producers, they think anybody can write a script, they treat writers very badly. They hire them, they fire them, they take them for granted. I'm sure you have had this experience."

"Oh yes."

"Well you won't have it from me, Martin. You can count on that. I am the exception. I appreciate the contributions writers make."

This speech I instantly recognize as the standard Hollywood disclaimer. I respond with the standard Hollywood reply: "That's good to know."

"I'm hoping that you and I can work together, Martin. I have a few ideas that I think will make the script better."

"If anybody knows how to improve a script, it's you, Ben," I say ingratiatingly.

"I appreciate your trust, Martin. Many writers are not so…"

Obsequious? I am thinking. Sycophantic?

"…agreeable."

"You're a man who gets movies made," I say, laying it on thick. "Who can argue with that kind of experience? Getting movies made is all that really counts. Everything else is just masturbation. So yes, I'd love to hear your ideas."

"Excellent," Fogelman says, practically in tears. "I'm touched by your confidence in me, Martin, I really am. And I am dying to tell you my ideas. But first, shall we order?"

"Why not?"

As if on cue, a waiter suddenly materializes at our table, introduces himself as Joseph and recites the specials. The mere mention of food makes my head swim, but I am hoping the inane smile I have plastered on my face will be enough to cover my nausea.

"I'll have the usual," Fogelman says.

"I'll have what he's having," I say.

"Excellent choice, gentlemen," the waiter says.

"You won't be sorry," Fogelman adds.

The waiter smiles and vanishes. Fogelman gets down to business. He tells me his ideas, some of which are good, some of which are not so good. Nevertheless, I greet each one with enthusiasm, but all the while I am fighting the desperate urge to run to the bathroom. My bowels are in an uproar, but I am not sure that, given the opportunity, I can even make it to the bathroom without help. So I listen and I listen and I nod. Which is fine, since Fogelman seems to love to talk. The good news is that he wants to take the script to the studios and that I will not be required to make any changes until the film has been purchased, until there is an actual deal with actual money.

Finally, the food comes. It appears to be some sort of beef patty covered in gravy and onions. Salisbury steak maybe. Fogelman begins to eat. I cut a small piece of the meat, scoop up a few onions and move them toward my mouth. I am chewing no more than half a second when I feel a strong urge to gag. I immediately realize that the chewy substance in my mouth is not Salisbury steak, but liver. I despise liver. I cannot eat liver. I would rather eat fresh rabbit pellets. Under no circumstances will liver be allowed to make the serpentine trip down my esophagus.

"Good huh?" Fogelman says, relishing the stuff.

"Mmmm," I reply, still chewing the liver into a gray pulp.

"Nothing like a nice piece of liver. A nice piece of liver always hits the spot, don't you agree?"

I nod, conscious that I may be turning purple. Fogelman, carefully arranging some onions on his fork, doesn't seem to notice. The first hunk of liver is still in my mouth. I summon all my strength and close my eyes and swallow it. Somehow, it defies all the laws of gravity and digestion and actually enters my esophagus. I stifle the inevitable gag. I wait for the regurgitation but it does not come. I am home free! I have achieved the impossible! I have succeeded in the Herculean task of swallowing liver!

There is, however, no way in hell I will be able to perform this miracle again and there's still a lot of liver left on my plate. Enough liver to kill me ten times over. What am I going to do? I can't just leave it there and tell Fogelman I don't like it — he'll be deeply offended. And I can't hide it under the onions. Desperate, I resort to subterfuge. While Fogelman isn't looking, I reach behind my neck as if to scratch myself.

"Oh my God!" I say suddenly.

"Something wrong?" Fogelman says.

"There's a hair in my liver."

"A hair?"

"In my liver. Look."

With my fork I lift the hair out of the muck, the hair I have just plucked from the back of my head and surreptitiously deposited on my plate. Fogelman turns pale. He summons the waiter.

"This is an outrage!" he says. "An outrage!"

"I'm so very, very sorry, Mr. Fogelman," Joseph cries. "I don't know how this could have happened! If there's anything I can do…"

"You can get Mr. Dorfman a new plate of liver," Fogelman says. "Pronto!"

"No, NO!" I say. "I, um, seem to have lost my appetite. For liver. It's okay. Really."

"Can I get the gentleman something else?" Joseph asks. "Anything at all, on the house of course."

"Another Bloody Mary would hit the spot," I say.

"Nothing else?" Fogelman asks.

"No thanks."

"You're sure?"

"Positive."

"They make a nice lobster bisque."

"I don't think so."

"Our shrimp diavolo is to die for," Joseph says.

"No thanks."

"Osso Buco?"

"Nope."

Fogelman waves a dismissive hand and Joseph obediently trots off. It has not occurred to me until this moment that for a man like Ben Fogelman, a man so concerned with status and appearances, this sort of gaffe is nothing less than an indication of the very decay of modern society.

"What's the world coming to when you can't even eat a lousy piece of liver at Chasen's?" Fogelman says, pushing his own plate of liver aside disgustedly. "Care for dessert?"

CHAPTER 11

Apparently my luncheon with Ben Fogelman is a triumph because the next day Gavin calls with a rave review.

"Two thumbs up, my friend," he says.

"Meaning?"

"Meaning he loves you. Thinks you're the bee's knees. And this is a man who has worked with the best writers in town, a man who has worked with show business *legends*."

"Did he say anything about the liver?"

"What liver?"

"Never mind."

"You stay on Ben Fogelman's good side," Gavin counsels, "and you've got it made in the shade."

"Did he happen to say when he plans to take the script out?" I ask.

"In two weeks. After he gets back from Cannes. He only just left today."

"Oh."

"Is this a problem?"

"No," I say. "I'm just a little anxious."

"No need to be, my friend. With Ben Fogelman on your team you cannot lose. *Cannot lose*."

Later that day I call Margolis to see if there is any encouraging news regarding my deteriorating health. It has now been exactly six weeks and three days since the onset of my mysterious symptoms and I am no closer to a cure, no closer to even knowing what I have, than I was at the start. I am demoralized by the prospect that I will wake up ill everyday for the rest of my life. My social life is defunct because I cannot plan anything, knowing that I might feel too sick to go when the time comes. I feel a deep, pervasive gloom enveloping me. Besides, Margolis and I have not spoken in a week and I miss the reassuring sound of his voice.

"Nothing much to report," he says gloomily.

"Great."

"I did, however, show your test results to several of my colleagues…"

"And?" I say eagerly.

"Stumped every one of them."

"You're kidding?"

"Afraid not."

"What about the edema?"

"Well, as it turns out, Jaffe might have been wrong about that," he admits. "The other doctors didn't seem to think there was an edema."

"No edema?" I say peevishly.

"No edema."

"How is that possible? One minute I have an edema, the next minute I'm edema-less?"

"Looks that way."

"That goddamn edema cost me over fifteen-thousand dollars! Now you're telling me it was a figment of Jaffe's imagination?"

"I'm sorry."

"This is terrible news," I say. "That edema was at least something to hold onto, a light at the end of the tunnel, a ray of hope. Now I've got nothing. Nothing!"

"I don't know what to tell you, Martin," he says. "Medicine is not an exact science. We do our best, we run the tests, we interpret the results, but there's a lot we still don't know."

"What are you saying?" I ask, suddenly terror-stricken. "You think I have some exotic new disease that science hasn't discovered yet?"

"I don't know. Could be. Anything's possible."

"Oh God. So what do you propose I do now, wait until science catches up to me?"

"I don't know, Martin. I wish I could help you, but I've run out of ideas."

"Surely there must be another test...?"

"Not really."

"Come on, Doc. What if it were you who had these symptoms. What if you felt this sick everyday and you'd had all the tests? What would you do?"

There is a long moment of silence. "Well, I hesitate to say this, Martin, but you might want to investigate some... alternative channels."

"Alternative channels? What do you mean?"

"Acupuncture, homeopathic medicine, biofeedback, that sort of thing."

"You're kidding? I thought you doctors all thought that stuff was a bunch of malarkey?"

"Some of it is, some of it isn't. We don't really know for sure. But if I was really desperate, if I had exhausted all the medical possibilities, I might check it out. Some of my patients have reported good results."

"Okay, assuming you're right, assuming there's some legitimacy to some of this alternative stuff, can you recommend anybody specifically?"

"Not really."

"That's a big help."

"You don't need me for this, Martin. Just ask around. They're all over the place. After all, this is California. They're in the Yellow Pages for God's sake!"

"Under what?" I ask. "W for wackos, C for charlatans?"

And so I bid Modern Medicine adieu and embark on Phase Two of my quest for a cure.

∾

By our third date, Ursula and I find ourselves drifting inexorably toward what in the mid-1970's was commonly known as "a serious relationship." And why not? She is beautiful, warmhearted, intelligent, outspoken, gregarious and amazingly unneurotic. For a German, a race not known for its comedy, she has an excellent sense of humor.

It is on our third date, in the middle of a frigid Chicago winter, that she takes me to her apartment for the first time. She lives in a brownstone walk-up in a funky part of the North Side. I naturally assume we are going there for a night of erotic wrestling since, after two dates, we have not yet consummated the relationship. I am wrong. We are going there to meet her husband.

Consider the context of the times: it is the wild and wacky 1970's, a time when people have all manner of weird marital relationships, open relationships, closed relationships, slightly ajar relationships; a time when the word "commitment" doesn't really mean anything. Yet in spite of all that, in spite of the prevailing cultural mores of the day, I am not crazy about this situation.

"I don't like this," I say in the cab on the way to her place.

"It'll be fine. Trust me."

"How can you be sure?"

"Intuition."

"Does he have a gun?"

"Of course not."

"Knives?"

"Just the kitchen cutlery."

"Is he the jealous type?"

"Insanely."

"Good-bye, I'm out of here. Stop the cab."

"Calm down, Martin. It'll be fine. We have an open relationship. He already knows all about you."

His name is Gary. He is six feet, two inches tall and weighs in at two hundred and thirty pounds. A former college football hero. He is blond, handsome, rugged and well-dressed, a guy who looks like he just walked out of an L.L. Bean catalogue: flannel shirt, khaki pants and suspenders. When Ursula introduces us, Gary is sitting on the living room couch, a Heineken in one hand, watching Monday Night Football. He is friendly, polite, almost ingratiatingly so. In spite of the situation, I like him immediately. Under most circumstances, I would find this meeting awkward and disheartening, but the fact that Gary is sitting on the couch watching Monday Night Football with his arm around another man takes some of the bite out of the event.

"You couldn't have just told me up front he was gay?" I say later in the privacy of Ursula's room. "You had to make me squirm first?"

"I thought you would find it… humorous."

"Well I don't."

"I'm sorry."

"I suffered."

"Forgive me?"

"I'll think about it."

I suddenly realize that I am sounding like a petulant asshole. "So what's the situation exactly, vis a vis Gary?"

"It's a marriage of convenience," Ursula says. "Thanks to Gary, I get a visa and a green card."

"And Gary, what does he get?"

"A free room."

"That's all?"

"That's all."

"You pay the rent?"

"Yes."

I nod. Then I look at her bed. "But you don't…"

"Of course not. He's gay."

"Just wanted to make sure. Sometimes they swing both ways."

"Not Gary. He only swings one way," she says,

A year later, Ursula gets her citizenship papers, divorces Gary and moves in with me.

∽

Everybody I know takes to Ursula immediately. All my friends, the new ones and the old, all my colleagues at the magazine, all my relatives. Everybody except one person. My father.

This does not surprise me. Nobody, has ever been good enough for my father. As long as I can remember, it has always been like that. He never got along with my mother's family; he could never seem to remember the first names of my childhood friends. For no apparent reason, he despises Phoebe's husband Richard Kessler, a very nice guy who happens to be a sculptor. My father regularly makes known his distaste by deliberately referring to Richard Kessler as Robert Kreisler.

"Sculptor!" my father says. "Hah! A tin can with a wire going through it is sculpture? A block of wood with two nails in it is sculpture? Michelangelo was a sculptor. Rodin was a sculptor. Robert Kreisler is nothing but a collector of scrap metal! A fraud!"

The fact that Richard Kessler is a decent, caring man who makes a good living and loves my sister does not seem to matter. To my father, he is nothing less than an interloper who has stolen from him the unconditional love of his only daughter. While most parents try to camouflage this natural hostility, my father, in his inimitable way, revels in it.

On the night before my wedding, after most of the household is asleep, my father takes me aside. It is a balmy night, so we sit outside on the patio. He lights up a cigar and a cloud of fragrant smoke envelopes us both.

"Are you sure you want to marry a German?" he asks, getting right to the point.

"Why not?" I say. "You married one. You *are* one. I thought you'd be pleased."

"Ursula is… a very nice young lady," he says with a complete absence of conviction.

"But?"

"But she's not Jewish."

"Yes, but look at it this way," I say. "I am doing my part for Judaism by marrying Ursula. I am neutralizing a German. If every Jew in Germany had married a German, Hitler would have been out of business."

"This is no laughing matter," my father says.

"Look, she's promised to raise our children Jewish. If we have children. Isn't that enough?"

"*If* you have children?"

"Yes, if. We haven't decided about that yet."

"But you must have children."

"Why?"

"Because that's what life is all about, Martin. Continuity."

"Well, we probably will, okay?"

"Technically they will not really be Jewish. Your children."

"Is that important?"

"Of course."

"Since when are you so religious?"

"That has nothing to do with it."

"Look, I know you don't like her, although I'm not sure why."

"That's not true."

"She happens to be a very warmhearted non-neurotic person and she loves me. Isn't that enough?"

"Where do you get the idea I don't like her."

"Isn't that what you're telling me right now?"

The question goes unanswered. I sigh. I am tired and I want to go to bed. "Is there anything else?" I ask wearily.

"She doesn't even have a Master's Degree."

"Neither do I."

"You couldn't have found somebody with a little more education?"

"What difference does it make? I didn't fall in love with a college degree. I fell in love with Ursula. She's smart enough."

"I just thought you could do... better that's all."

"Better in what way? No matter whom I married, she wouldn't be able to live up to your standards. Nobody ever has. *I* never have."

"That's nonsense."

"Oh really?"

"It's not too late to change your mind."

"Goodnight, Dad," I say. "Thanks for the pep talk."

I start to walk away. "Martin," he says. "One more thing."

"What?"

"Don't forget to wash your hands before you go to bed. And make sure you create a nice lather. You're wasting your time if you don't create a nice lather."

✑

June 21, 1982. It is the night after our wedding, late, around midnight. We are all in the living room of my parents' house, having a nightcap and talking about the day's festivities. It is a family gathering that includes Phoebe and her husband, my one surviving grandmother, my aunt and uncle, and Ursula's parents, who have flown in from Germany for the wedding. The walls of the room are decorated with my father's artwork; every wall has a picture of that gray tortured face silently shrieking into the void. Nevertheless, everybody is in a congenial mood, even my father who, uncharacteristically, has had more than one snifter of brandy and is in a maudlin frame of mind. He is reminiscing tearfully about his romantic student days at Heidelberg to anyone who will listen, in this case Ursula's father, Hermann. Ursula and I are on the floor opening wedding presents and, as a result, there is a large pile of small kitchen appliances and expensive glassware growing in one corner of the room: toaster ovens, tea sets, vases, Cuisinarts, crystal wine glasses. My grandmother, a formidable woman of eighty-five who survived six months in a Nazi concentration camp in the winter of 1944, is sitting on a couch looking through a photo album of Ursula's family. Ursula's mother, a stout woman with a limp, is beside her, explaining who is who.

Suddenly, as I am about to open a box containing a digital alarm clock, there is a scream. I look up. It is my grandmother. She has turned pale and her hand is clasped over her mouth in horror at something she has just seen.

"Der Teufel, Der Teufel!" she shrieks, pointing to a picture in the family album.

"Was ist los?" my father asks, moving swiftly to her side.

"Das ist der Teufel!" my grandmother cries, pointing to a photo of Ursula's paternal grandfather. *"Der Teufel von dem konzentratzion lager!"* With the little bit of German I know, I understand that she is identifying Ursula's grandfather as someone called the Devil from a Nazi concentration camp.

"Sicher?" my father asks.

"Naturlich. Ach Gott, das ist er! Der schreckliche Kerl!"

I am frantic, horrified. No more than eight hours ago I have married into a family of Nazis! The SS uniforms are probably still in the attic! How could I have been so stupid, so gullible? I look at Ursula with absolute horror in my eyes but Ursula herself is mortified and speechless. And then I scream the awful bloodcurdling scream of the gray, tortured man adorning the walls of the living room…

Every time I have this nightmare, I wake up in a cold sweat.

CHAPTER

The Five Elemental Energies. The Six Evils. The Twelve Vital
Organs and Meridians. The Eight Indicators. The Great Prin-
ciples of Yin and Yang.

That's right folks, as the first stop in Phase Two of my quest for a
cure, I choose Chinese herbal medicine. And why not? It is the old-
est continuously practiced form of medicine on earth, five thousand
years old, tried and true. While Western doctors were using leeches
or bleeding their patients to cure anemia, the Chinese were prescrib-
ing herb remedies. One trillion Chinamen can't be wrong. Right?

Question: if I take the herbs and they work, will I be sick again
ten minutes later?

Ahem. Actually, it is less of a deliberate choice and more a simple
matter of convenience. As it happens, one of my friends, an English
entertainment reporter for a London newspaper, has been telling me
about her Chinese herbalist for years. He has cured her, or so she
claims, of debilitating migraines, insomnia and yeast infections which,
according to the Chinese version of human anatomy, are all symptoms of a cold wind in the kidneys, or something like that. Over the
years, she has sung the praises of Dr. Lao Chung and, until now, I
have found this line of conversation infinitely dull. Now, however, I
am all ears.

"Why the sudden interest, Luv?" she asks suspiciously.

"Let's just say modern medicine has failed me."

"Modern medicine has its head up its arse."

"It has a lot more than that up its arse," I say. "Hoses, index fingers and such like, but that's another story."

"The problem with modern medicine is that it treats the symptoms. The Chinese treat the root causes of the symptoms."

"Uh huh."

"It's all about imbalances and the internal energies that effect the whole body."

"Uh huh."

"Yin and yang pertain to the body too. For example, the yin heart is linked to the yang small intestine."

"Fascinating."

"If the wind is too hot, the herbs cool it. If it's too cold, they warm it."

"You've sold me," I say. "How do I get in touch with this great healer?"

"You don't, Luv."

"I don't?"

"It's first come first serve."

"I don't call for an appointment?"

"No need. You just stand in line like everybody else."

"Take a number? Like at the bakery?"

"Something like that."

"He doesn't make house calls?"

"Afraid not, Luv."

And so I write down his address, a street in Chinatown. One weekday afternoon, when I feel up to it, I drive down there. With Dr. Chung's street address clutched in my sweaty hand, I walk up and down Spring Street searching in vain for his building. For some reason, I simply cannot locate Number 543. There is Number 541 and Number 545, both office buildings, but between those two buildings is a one-story Chinese grocery store with no numerical address displayed on its door or its window or anywhere else. I walk back up the street and back down. Still no luck. Finally, I decide to go into the grocery store and ask for directions, hoping that the Asian lady behind the counter speaks English.

"You at right place. This number 543," she says.

"Excuse me?"

"Doctor Chung in back by tofu. You stand in line."

"But this is a grocery store."

"You stand in line. Dr. Chung here. Go."

I stand there indecisively for a second while the counter lady exchanges a giggle, no doubt at my expense, with her attractive teenage daughter. I mumble a thank you and move cautiously to the back of the store where I find a small crowd of Asian men and women, both young and old, standing in line.

Seated at a card table directly in front of a large wooden cabinet with numerous small file drawers is Dr. Chung. He sports a small skullcap and a Ming the Merciless mustache. His hair is wispy and gray, his expression calm and beatific, reflecting, I am quick to assume, the wisdom of the ages. He wears a black Chinese collarless silk blouse, sleeve garters, shorts and tennis shoes. I decide to stay.

In twenty minutes, after inspecting the fifty or more variations of tofu on the shelves, I am at the head of the line. Dr. Chung tilts his head slightly in a half-bow and takes my hand. He places it palm side up on a silk pillow.

"I've been having all kinds of problems, Doc," I say.

"No talk," Dr. Chung says.

"Right. No talk. Sorry."

I shut my yap and watch silently as he places his index finger at various locations on my upturned wrist. "Liver bad," he mumbles. "Kidneys tired, too much heat. Other hand please."

I extend it, he places it gently on the pillow and starts inspecting its pulse points. "Heart good. Lungs bad. Too much wind in intestine."

"You got that right."

"No talk."

"Sorry."

Now he gives me back my hand and takes out a notepad and a short stubby pencil. Evidently the examination is over. He licks the tip of the pencil and writes out my prescription in Chinese symbols. This he then hands to another man, the herbal pharmacist, who places three pieces of thick brown paper side by side on the table. He then opens several drawers to the wooden filing cabinet and takes out a series of dried herbs. These he places on scales, carefully measures each group, then sprinkles them into three piles on the brown paper squares until he has fulfilled the instructions. Each pile has the same mixture of different herbs. He then pours each of the mixtures into five individual plastic Ziploc bags.

"Twenty dollar," the pharmacist says.

I hand him the bills and he gives me my herbs. They smell woodsy, like old dried moss. "What are these exactly?" I ask. "Just curious."

"Dried cicada bodies, ginseng root, wolfberry, asparagus, lotus seeds. Use earthen teapot only, no metal. Take whole pack, mix with five cup water, boil. Stir with wooden spoon only, no metal. Drink two time each day. Okay?"

"Okay," I say. "And how long will it take before I start to feel better?"

"Maybe one week only."

"Great. Thanks."

"And then what?"

"You come back for more medicine."

Later that night, I can hardly wait to start. I have purchased the required earthen teapot from Chung for an extra ten bucks; he throws in a wooden spoon for free. Methodically, I set out my utensils and the packet of herbs. I boil the water as instructed and pour in the mixture. Almost immediately, the kitchen begins to smell like a lumberjacks' locker room in a damp, moss-infested part of the Pacific Northwest. I have never smelled the odor of death, but it couldn't be much worse than this. Ursula and the kids hightail it to the den, all three of them holding their noses as I proceed to stink up the entire house. Even the dog ducks for cover under a coffee table.

"Bubble, bubble, toil and trouble," I say, stirring the thickening broth and bending over it to breathe in its pungent healing aroma.

"What exactly is causing that horrendous stink?" Ursula asks nasally.

"Must be the dried cicada bodies," I say.

"Cicadas are…"

"Insects."

"Oh God. You're not going to actually drink that?"

"Watch me."

As soon as it has boiled down completely, I strain it and pour the contents into a ceramic mug. With something vaguely resembling gusto, I hold my breath and take a tentative sip. Not so bad really.

Tastes like liquefied mud. Okay, liquefied mud that someone has peed in. Maybe even wallowed in. Maybe even shat in. Sipping is clearly the wrong approach here. So I hold my breath and swallow the remainder of the stuff in one nauseating gulp. There. Done. Finito!

"I'm on the road to recovery folks," I tell my family. "Won't be long now."

Five days later, Ben Fogelman returns from Cannes with a bad chest cold and some moderately good news. He calls me from an airport pay phone with his limo driver standing by. For some reason, the connection is spotty.

"How was Cannes?" I ask.

"Terrific," he says. "The women, the parties, the food. The French, they don't know shit about making movies and their toilet paper is from the Spanish Inquisition, but they really know how to live."

"So I've heard."

"I put on six pounds, can you believe it?"

"No kidding?"

"And a nasty case of hemorrhoids on top of that."

"Really?"

"From playing polo. I can't help it, I'm a nut for horses. You like horses, Martin?"

"Horses? To me, horses are what the Cossacks rode on to chase my ancestors through Eastern Europe."

"Same here, but I don't hold a grudge."

Suddenly the line fills with loud static and I cannot hear his voice. When the static clears, I catch him in mid-sentence. "...but it wasn't all fun and games, Martin. I want you to know that I used every opportunity to hype your script."

"You *typed* my script?"

"Is this a bad connection?"

"So so."

"I said I *hyped* your script."

"Oh."

"Everybody loves the concept. *Loves* it. I had to fight them off with a sharp stick."

"Everybody?"

But before he can answer, he falls into a fit of coughing that lasts about thirty seconds. A deep, phlegmy seizure that sounds like it's coming from somebody with terminal tuberculosis.

"Goddamn airlines," he says, wheezing and struggling to keep from coughing again. "They don't circulate the air properly. Every time some asshole sneezes, the whole plane gets the germs right in the face. Where were we?"

"Everybody loves the concept."

"Right. I hyped it to people from Warners, Columbia and Paramount for starters. They're all dying to get their hands on it."

"What about Fox, Disney, MGM and Universal?"

"I'm deliberately not hyping it to them."

"Why?"

"Why? You don't know much about salesmanship, do you Martin?"

"No."

"I didn't hype it to them because I want them to feel left out. That way they'll want it even more than the other guys."

"I see. Good strategy."

"'Good strategy,' he says! It's basic Machiavelli. You're a laugh riot, Martin."

"Thanks."

As if to prove his point, Fogelman starts laughing, but the laughter soon degenerates into another long coughing fit. I hold the phone a foot away from my ear and count slowly to five. Even at this distance I can hear him hacking convulsively. Wouldn't it be just my luck if Ben Fogelman dies right there in the airport before he can even send my script out to one lousy studio? The moment I have this grim thought, I am deeply ashamed of myself.

"You better take care of that cough, Ben," I say. "Maybe some Chinese herbs might help. Get rid of that heat in your lungs or the wind in your spleen."

"No way," Fogelman says. "I heard a rumor from a very reliable source that the so-called herbs those Chinese guys use are actually dried up cow turds."

"What!?"

"Cow turds. Is this a bad connection?"

"No."

"So look, here's the plan," he says, getting back to business. "I'm sending the script out on Friday. We'll get a weekend read and be in business, hopefully, by the beginning of next week."

"*Cow turds?*"

"What?"

"Nothing."

"Did you hear me, Martin? I said I'm planning to send the script out on Friday for the weekend read. By Monday you'll be a rich man."

"I wish you hadn't told me that."

"Told you what? About the cow turds or about the weekend read?"

"The weekend read."

"Why not?"

"Because now I'll be on pins and needles all weekend. I'll be miserable. Come Monday morning, if the phone doesn't ring, I'll be anxious and depressed."

"You writers kill me!" he exclaims. "You guys crack me up, you really do."

"It's just that I hate that kind of pressure," I say. "It's better if you don't tell me anything."

"Okay, I won't tell you anything."

"About what?"

"About the script."

"What about the script?"

"You said not to tell you."

"Tell me."

Fogelman sighs. I have exasperated him. "Not to worry, *bubela.* This is a sure thing. A sure thing!"

"There you go again!" I say. "I wish you hadn't told me that either."

"Why not?"

"Because now it won't be a sure thing. If you say it will, then it won't. It's the Dorfman Curse. It's always better to say it won't because then it will."

"Says who?"

"The Cosmos. The Evil God of Script Rejection. It's a karma thing."

"Karma schmarma. Have a little optimism, Martin."

"I've tried optimism. You can't fake out the Dorfman Curse. It doesn't work."

"So try pessimism"

"Doesn't work either," I say. "Look, you can't trick these subtle forces of nature, Ben. The Cosmos has a mind of its own, an agenda of its own. It's all part of a bigger Master Plan that governs the Universe." Only after these words have left my mouth do I realize how completely idiotic they sound.

"Trust me, Martin, I know this town. This script will sell. You have a good solid story, sympathetic characters and a lot of very funny stuff. Forget karma and all that superstitious baloney. I can feel it intuitively in the marrow of my bones. And my bones never lie. You've got nothing to worry about."

13

CHAPTER

After ten days of Dr. Chung's pungent herbal libation, I am feeling no better. In fact, I am feeling worse. For one thing, I now wake up with a tremor in my hands. It's so bad, I have to wait an hour to shave. Then there's Super Belch. Shortly after ingesting the dubious beverage, I get a bubble in my stomach that expands past my diaphragm, up my throat and, to the delight of my children, explodes in a belch that can best be described as volcanic in force and timbre. No doubt this is the passing of the notorious wind in the lungs. I also seem to be suddenly experiencing reflux at night when I go to bed. I lie down, fluff the pillows, switch out the light, kiss Ursula goodnight and five minutes later, I get to experience dinner again. Half-digested dinner. Dinner that, for some reason, refuses to progress to the next stage of my digestive tract. At this point, I need more symptoms like a moose needs a hat rack, and the possibility that I may be ingesting dried cow dung is hardly encouraging. And so, I bid a fond farewell to the last of Dr. Chung's inscrutable packets, flushing them down the old WC.

Onward and upward. By my count, more than seven weeks have passed since I first came down with this mysterious bug and for most of that period, a mixture of ennui and general malaise has caused me to become something of a hermit. Most days, I do not feel strong enough to go anywhere; I sit for hours immobilized at my desk, concentrating on my symptoms, gazing out the window at the world outside, watching spring turn to summer and wallowing in self-pity. Why me? I ask myself. Why not the gardener or the meter reader or the mailman? Why do they get to live healthy, happy lives while I am consumed by nausea and gloom day in and day out? Ursula tries to get me out of the house but I simply do not feel well enough to mingle successfully with other members of my species. Captivating conversation has always been something of a strain even under the best of circumstances; my illness has killed off whatever minuscule vestige of charm I might have once possessed.

⁓

Of course, I could have saved myself the trouble had I consulted Delilah on the Chinese herbal business before visiting Dr. Chung. It seems that she has already been down every path; she has climbed every mountain, forded every stream. When I mention the herbal business on our second meeting, she tilts her head back and breaks into a hearty guffaw, one of those deep, gravelly laughs that comes from years of lung pollution. This gives way to a serious coughing fit and, after about thirty seconds of this, I find myself on her side of the table smacking her on the back and pulling her arms heavenward until it subsides.

"I gotta quit smoking," she says, struggling to light another cigarette with trembling fingers.

On her insistence, we are at the same outdoor table at the same Van Nuys soup joint. The same waiter is hovering in the same supercilious way as we halfheartedly peruse the same menu. I am in an adventurous mood and, throwing caution to the wind, order the vichysoisse; Delilah opts for the beef consommé.

"So how are you feeling?" I ask.

"Crummy. You?"

"Awful."

"Everyday?"

"More or less."

"Same symptoms?"

"Same symptoms."

We both breathe inaudible sighs of relief. If one of us starts to feel better, the other will be left high and dry. This prospect throws me into a fright.

"I don't know if I can stand it much longer," I say.

"Same here," she concurs. "I mean what's the point of living?"

"There is none."

"Exactly."

"We can't go through life like this."

"No way."

"Margolis wants me to see a therapist," I tell her.

"Waste of time."

"That's what I told him."

"And?"

"He can be stubborn."

"They're all going to try to convince you it's psychosomatic, Martin," she says sagely. "The shrinks, your wife, your doctor. You can't let yourself give in to that. You have to be strong."

"Maybe it *is* psychosomatic."

"Don't even say it, Martin. I don't want to hear it. I'm not listening. That word is taboo."

"Well if it's not psychosomatic, then why does it come and go? Wouldn't I feel sick all the time?"

"How should I know? Am I a doctor? Maybe it's some weird new virus. Maybe it likes to take a day off now and then."

"A virus that takes vacations?"

"Or sick days."

"I see."

Just then, the waiter comes by and, with an ambivalent snort, deposits our soups before us. I gaze hesitantly down at mine. It looks like tepid bath water.

"Maybe I need to see a specialist," I say. "An infectious disease man or an endocrinologist."

"Come on, Martin. You had all the tests. As far as the doctors are concerned you're healthy as a horse. You really want to blow another $15,000?"

"It's only money."

"That's one way of looking at it."

"I've met my deductible."

"Congratulations."

Frustrated, I push my soup away. "So what the hell am I supposed to do?" I ask. "My career is fizzling. My family is about to fall apart. My sex life is over. I'm losing my mind. What the hell am I supposed to do?"

Delilah looks up from her soup and, seeing the look of plaintive terror in my eyes, places her hand over mine. "The only thing you can do," she says gently. "Just hang in there."

⸱⊙⸱

It is May of 1956 and Mr. Brawer's chemists have either come up with *eau de corpse* or accidentally set their laboratory on fire. The whole town reeks of burnt chocolate chip cookies and onions, a sweet caustic smell that permeates every acre of Highland Falls and makes the eyes water. It starts in the morning when I wake up, and by the time I come out of school that afternoon at three o'clock, the noxious fumes are still with us; I can feel my nostrils burn when I breathe. Except for the kids walking home from school, the city's streets are empty of pedestrians; the stench is so bad, the few motorists on the street drive with their car windows closed even though the temperature is in the mid-seventies. The place looks like a ghost town, as if someone has just called an air raid drill. Buzzy Tannenbaum, Kenny Fishbeck and I join up at the Rimbaldi basketball courts and trot home together, all of us coughing and holding wet tissues over our noses and mouths the whole distance.

"Jesus," Buzzy keeps saying, "it smells like God farted."

My father, I know, will be livid. He has, on a number of occasions, written angry, illegible letters to the town's newspaper, condemning Brawer (whom he calls Dr. Frankenstein) and his chemists for recklessly sending toxic fumes into the air we breathe. These fumes, he has speculated in his unreadable script, will poison the air we breathe, the food we eat, the water we drink. Our children will get lung cancer or leukemia. In this, my father is way ahead of his time. But Brawer's Frutal Works employs five hundred of the town's citizenry and so my father's complaints generally fall on deaf ears, although in retaliation, Mr. Brawer suggests that those of his employees who are treated by my father find themselves another internist. Which infuriates my father even more. And so I wince at the thought of coming home to find him pacing angrily in the kitchen, ranting to my mother over this latest explosion of toxic stench.

But he is not home that afternoon and neither is my mother, for their cars are not in the driveway. Oddly, a car which appears to be my grandparents' old gray Mercedes sits on the street in front of my house. They live seventy miles away in Queens and I am not expecting them. It is not Yom Kippur, Thanksgiving or anyone's birthday, so why are they here? When I lope up the stairs to the porch and try to open the front door, it is locked. This has never happened before. My stomach leaps into my throat; I am gripped by fear. Frantically, I pound the doorbell and eventually, to my relief, I hear the sound of footsteps from inside.

Phoebe comes barreling down the stairs and opens the door.

"What's going on?" I ask. "Why is the door locked?"

"Mommy and Daddy are in the hospital!" she screams.

"What?"

And now I see my grandmother standing on the landing. "Come Martin," she says. "Come upstairs, *bitte kommen, schnell.*"

I take the stairs two at a time and we all go into the kitchen where my grandfather is calmly sipping black coffee at the breakfast table.

"Ach, Martin," he says. "How you've grown! Come here my boy."

My grandfather is a stout man with a bulbous nose, a bottle-brush mustache and a few wisps of hair combed horizontally across the top of his head. He smells of cigars and moth balls when I hug him. He is the patriarch of our family and he takes this role seriously. He is also a great source of capital, always giving us kids money for no reason, squeezing ten dollar bills in our little hands or letting us beat him at gin rummy for nickels and dimes. Phoebe and I are crazy about him.

"So," he says. "You had a nice day at school, Martin?"

"Yeah sure. It was fine."

"Good. Sit down and Oma will pour you a nice cold glass of milk."

"Are Mom and Dad sick?" I ask. "Phoebe said they were in the hospital."

My grandfather doesn't say anything. He points to the glass of milk my grandmother has just poured. I swallow it in one gulp. An oatmeal cookie materializes in front of me and I gobble that down too. When I look up and wipe the milk mustache off my upper lip with a napkin, I notice my sister's pink Minnie Mouse suitcase and my yellow Lone Ranger suitcase standing side by side next to the refrigerator.

"Are we going somewhere?" I ask nervously.

"Yes. You are going to spend a few weeks with us in New York," my grandfather says. "Both of you. How do you like that?"

"What about school?"

"There won't be any school for you for awhile."

"How come?"

My grandfather reaches into his breast pocket and pulls out a long metal cylinder. He turns it upright, removes a fat green cigar from its metal housing, and carefully snips off the end with a small silver tool. I watch as he lights it, turning it in his thick fingers until the flame surges. My grandfather is a meticulous man.

"Your Mommy and Daddy are sick, Martin," he says finally. "They both have…" and now he looks at my grandmother for help, but she only shrugs.

"A disease of the liver," he continues. "Also known as jaundice. You have heard of it?"

"Hepatitis," I say. "There's been an epidemic in town. Lots of people have it. Mr. Fishman from across the street has it."

"That's right. And now your mother and father have it too. Most likely your father got it at the hospital, from a patient. Your mother, who knows? Maybe she got it from your father. But they will be all right, Martin. I promise you that."

"Are they in the hospital?"

"Yes."

"Can I see them?"

"No. It is very contagious, this hepatitis, and we don't want you or your sister to get it, do we?"

"But I saw them this morning," I say. "I've already been exposed."

"Me too," Phoebe says.

"It makes no difference," my grandfather says, waving his cigar.

"How long will they be in the hospital?"

"Nobody knows for sure."

"*Villeicht drei wochen,*" my grandmother shrugs.

"Maybe three weeks, maybe longer," says my grandfather. "So now you know, Martin. I hope you will be a big boy and not cry or act up. I hope you will be a man, Martin."

"Sure," I say. "I'll be fine. Don't worry about me."

And so, we drive to New York City in my grandparents' Mercedes. That night, warm and secure beneath the fluffy eider down quilt on my grandparents' daybed in Queens, I am lulled to sleep by Phoebe's gentle sobbing. But I am all right. I am fine.

‿☙‿

"Like hell you were."

Nora's office is being repainted and recarpeted, so we are sitting at her breakfast nook, the sun glinting through the slats of her Venetian blinds, the rays picking up dust motes. Workmen are hammering and drilling nearby. A radio is on, tuned to a Latino station and as a result, my therapy session's musical accompaniment is *Guantanamera*, never one of my favorites. Before me is a cup of lukewarm Cappuccino and a piece of bundt cake. I feel like we are a couple of *yentas* having coffee and gossiping about the neighbors at the kitchen table. It is a warm summer day in July of 1991 and I long to be through with this session.

"No really," I say. "I was okay with it."

"You weren't worried?"

"About what?"

"Come on, Martin," she says. "About your parents?"

"Not that I can recall."

"Angry at them maybe?"

"Why should I be angry? They were sick."

"They could have called you at school to let you know instead of having you find out this way."

"They had hepatitis," I say. "It's no picnic, hepatitis."

"You're making excuses."

"I'm being honest."

"Are you sure?"

"Reasonably."

"Don't commit to anything, God forbid."

At close range and in bright sunlight, Nora's eyes are even harder to avoid. The office was better; it was dark and we were farther away from each other. I yearn for the relative safety of the office. I shift in my seat; I play with my bundt cake.

"Do you use a bundt cake mold for this?" I ask.

"Is that important to you?"

"Not particularly."

"Then let's not change the subject," she says. "You were how old when this hepatitis thing happened?"

"Seven."

"You're seven and your grandfather gives you the same song and dance about repressing your emotions as your mother."

"Of course," I say. "He's her father. Where do you think *she* got it from? This has probably been going on for generations. How come I'm the first one to get sick?"

"Maybe you're not," she says. "But that's beside the point. Assuming you really were okay with it, what happened next?"

"We stayed in New York for three weeks."

"And after that?"

"We went home."

"Both of you?"

"Yes."

"And your parents were fully recovered?"

"I guess so."

"You guess so?"

I stop to think about it. I cannot seem to remember what happened next. No images come to mind. It is a blank spot. And then...

"My father grew a beard," I say. "I remember the beard. It was a goatee. He looked ridiculous, like a Jewish Thelonious Monk."

"Is that all?"

"I don't know," I say. "I suppose we went back to our normal life."

"If you call what you led a normal life."

"You know what I mean."

"But you don't really remember."

"No. Not vividly."

"Don't you find that a little odd?"

"Not particularly. There's lots I don't remember about my youth. Most of it actually."

"I wonder why."

She takes a small clean bite of her bundt cake, but does not take her eyes from mine. A second later, as she sips her coffee, she looks over the rim of her cup at me. She is like the famous Greek sculpture whose eyes follow you around the room, everywhere you go. Her strategy is to wear me down. Or she is suspicious I am pocketing the silverware. One day those eyes will give me nightmares.

"So what are you saying?" I ask facetiously. "That there's some deep, dark, terrible secret here that I have stricken from my memory?"

"Maybe."

"That's ridiculous."

"Is it?"

"Absolutely."

"Three weeks isn't really enough time to recuperate from hepatitis, Martin. Not if it's bad enough to put you in the hospital. I've had hepatitis. Six weeks minimum."

"So maybe it was more than three weeks. It was a long time ago."

"Have you talked to your sister about this?"

"No."

"Maybe she'll remember something."

"Maybe."

"Or, we could try hypnosis."

"Really? You can do that? Hypnotize people?"

"Some people."

"No extra charge?"

"No extra charge."

"Gee, I don't know."

"What are you afraid of?"

"Nothing. Why should I be afraid? It's like taking a nap with your eyes open. You take off your clothes and flap your arms like a chicken for half an hour and then you wake up and don't remember anything. Right?"

"Fine. We'll set it up for your next session."

I look at the clock. Time's up, thank God. I drain the last dregs of my coffee and polish off the last bite of bundt cake. God I love bundt cake.

❧

"Who is Delilah Foster?"

Ursula is standing in the doorway of my office, fanning her face with a bunch of pink message slips. I have just returned from a particularly pointless meeting with an endocrinologist in Beverly Hills.

"Delilah Foster?" I say vaguely, feigning ignorance.

"She called several times."

"Oh Delilah *Foster*," I say. "She's one of Gavin's new assistants."

"She seemed… a little strange."

"Oh? How so?"

"I don't know. She whispered."

"Yeah, well, she's a little neurotic," I say. "Wet behind the ears. Comes from Nebraska or something. Doesn't know the ropes yet. Give her a week."

I immediately feel guilty about lying. *Why am I doing this?* I ask myself. Nothing's going on here. Do I *want* something to be going on here? I don't think so. Can Ursula, who is fairly intuitive, see through my phony little song and dance? I lower my eyes. A second passes quietly. Ursula hands me the pink slips, sighs and leaves the room.

As it happens, Delilah has been calling me all afternoon from Twain's Diner in Sherman Oaks, not far from my house. She has been nursing the same Coke for three hours waiting for me to return her call. She sounds bad — frantic, depressed, disoriented. Her voice croaks, a fragile whisper and I can barely understand her. She had an audition at Warner Bros., she tells me. She started to feel nauseous in the middle of it. She thought she was going to collapse. A sympathetic secretary called her a taxi and deposited her in it. She was suddenly very thirsty and had the cab driver drop her at Twain's for a Coke. Now she hasn't got the energy or strength to look in the phone book and call another taxi. And her hands are trembling so badly she hasn't been able to lift the Coke glass to her lips. She asks me to come pick her up. She pleads. She beseeches. She begs.

"The lady on the phone, wife or girlfriend?" she asks me as I help her wobble out of the diner and into my car. I have managed to slip away for ten minutes on the pretense of going to Kinko's to fax some script changes to Gavin. When I tell her this, Ursula is in the kitchen chopping onions and does not even look up. Two points. Another successful lie. I'm on a roll.

"Wife," I say.

"You never told me your were married."

"It never came up," I say.

"I assumed you were unattached."

"You assumed wrong."

"Where's your wedding ring?"

"Can't wear it. It turns my skin green. I must be allergic."

This causes the conversation to screech to a stop. No words pass between us for twenty seconds. Then I begin to hear her sobbing.

"God, Martin, I thought I was going to die," Delilah says, turning to me, tears in her eyes. "I thought I was going to die right there in a booth at Twain's. Can you imagine anything more pathetic?"

"You're not going to die," I say reassuringly, but I can hardly look at her. Her forehead is covered in sweat. Her complexion is somewhere between hospital pale and morgue gray. Her hands still tremble; even her hair is somehow lifeless, like an old mop.

"I'm telling you, I just can't take it anymore," she says as I get on the Hollywood Freeway. "Does this car have a passenger-side airbag?"

"No."

"That's good," she says.

"Why is that good?"

"A nice head-on collision with a Mack truck would be great," she says. "No seat belt, I'll go right through the windshield. DOA."

"Stop talking like that," I say. "Nobody's going to crash. I happen to be a very good driver. Not a single citation in 15 years. And put on your seat belt, for God's sake. You want me to get a ticket?"

"If I could just get over this phobia I have about the sight of blood, I'd slash my wrists. But it would me too messy, wouldn't it? They'd have to hire a cleaning lady. I'd feel too guilty about that, the poor woman. Blood stains are hard to get out."

"I'm not listening to this."

"I hear sleeping pills is a pretty painless way to go."

"Stop it, Delilah."

"But Margolis discontinued my prescription."

I get off the freeway at Griffith Park and head for Los Feliz where Delilah lives. I pull up at an old pink stuccoed apartment house with black wrought iron balconies and tall lit palms in the front yard. A very nice place. Supposedly, Rudolph Valentino once lived here.

"I could always hang myself."

"Enough, Delilah. I mean it."

"A bullet in the old cranium would probably do it."

"Too messy. Think of the poor cleaning lady. Blood on the walls, blood on the floor, on the—"

"May I kiss you?"

I look at her. A real conversation stopper. This has caught me by surprise. "You must be feeling better," I say.

"May I?"

"Why?"

"I have an urge. You look very cute in the moonlight."

"But not in the sunlight?"

"In sunlight too. In any light."

"Fluorescent?"

"Nobody looks good in fluorescent."

"Do you think kissing is wise?" I ask. "I mean, how do we know one of us isn't contagious?"

"Jesus, you're right!" she says suddenly moving back towards the window. "I hadn't thought of that. What's come over me?"

"Besides, I'm happily married."

This seems to put her in a funk.

"Give me a rain check," I say. "You can kiss me when we're both feeling better."

"What about your wife?"

"You can kiss her too if you want."

Delilah opens the door and steps out. Amazingly, she is no longer wobbling. I even detect a bit of color in her cheeks.

"And promise me, Delilah. Don't do anything foolish. No suicide attempts. We have to stick together. Promise me."

"Fine."

"Promise me."

"Okay, I promise."

"I'm not kidding."

"Neither am I. You're the only friend I have, Martin."

"I'm going to call you tomorrow," I say. "And you damn well better be alive."

⁂

Gavin calls on Friday, the day Fogelman sends the script out to the studios. This is the fifth time in one month *he* has called *me*.

"Ben did a super job of hyping the script," Gavin says. "I'm getting calls from everybody in town."

"Everybody?"

"They're begging me, Martin. *Begging* me to send them a copy. I love it when they grovel. I love having *leverage*."

"Like who?"

"Studio people, independents. You're very hot right now, Martin. Very hot. Scalding even. I could fry an egg on you, you're so hot."

Why, I ask myself, do I have the feeling that if this script doesn't sell, Gavin will be going back to selling hot tubs, used cars or aluminum siding?

"I just hope he didn't overdo it," I say cautiously. "The script might not live up to its lofty reputation."

"Get outa town! It's a great script, Martin. You shouldn't have any doubts. Besides, you got Ben Fogelman telling everybody it's great. Even if it sucked big time, with Ben saying it's good, it's good. He has credibility."

"He also has a parole officer."

"Water under the bridge, my friend," he assures me. "Look, I gotta run. Do me one favor?"

"What?"

"Monday morning, stay close to a phone. Okay?"

"Okay."

"If there's a bidding war, timing will be critical."

"Right."

"And picture in your mind lots of zeroes."

"How many?"

"You have to ask? At least six."

"Right. Six is good."

After I hang up, I tell myself over and over not to get my hopes up, much as I like the sound of the phrase "bidding war." Who wouldn't? God knows, I have fallen into this trap too many times in the past, and I should have learned my lesson by now. In this town, hope and disappointment are Hollywood's yin and yang. Every screenwriter knows the axiom: talk is cheap and everything is meaningless until actual money has changed hands. Period. Unfortunately, I do not have the luxury of being as blithely apathetic about the fate of this script as I would like to be. If it does not sell, if Gavin's groveling minions reject me, our financial picture will become, in a word, desperate. The bank will foreclose on my house. The repo men will take my car. My children will starve. Then what?

And so I spend this crucial, nerve-wracking weekend pacing and biting my nails; I avoid broken mirrors, black cats and ladders. A rabbit's foot dangles from a chain around my neck. I wear my lucky underpants. Occasionally, I catch myself staring longingly at the phone. It does not ring. For the most part, it is a miserable weekend except for one thing: Oddly enough, although my stress level that weekend is at an all time high, my symptoms *disappear*. I wake up Saturday morning feeling normal for the first time in weeks. Same thing happens on Sunday. No symptoms. The one time I *should* be feeling awful (according to Margolis), I feel fine.

What does this mean?

CHAPTER

14

onday, June 5, 1989, 8:00 o'clock A.M. Against my better
judgment, I station myself at my desk and wait for the
phone to ring. I have a thermos full of coffee, a pack of
cigarettes and a brand new copy of the *American Medical Association's
Family Medical Guide* in front of me for light reading. I know that,
like the proverbial watched pot, the phone will probably *never* ring if
I spend all day staring at it, but I cannot help myself. I am fidgety,
taut, a chain-smoking, nail-biting bundle of exposed synapses. My
ego is doing the mambo blindfolded at the end of a shaky limb.

To pass the time, I close my eyes and try to conjure an image of
the generic studio executive who is possibly, at this very moment,
reading my script. I visualize him as young, glib, well-tanned, sitting
by a black-bottomed pool in jeans and a silk shirt, sipping a *café au
lait*, laughing, sobbing, then madly turning the pages to see what
will happen next; he is really into it now, caught up in the suspense,
unable to put it down; he is thinking *it's funny, it has heart, it's a
movie*, for he is clearly a *brilliant* studio executive, a veritable Irving
Thalberg in Guccis and jeans. Finally, he comes to the last page and
as soon as he is finished, he calls two other studio executives and, in
a three-way conference call, they decide to make an offer; a few minutes later, one of them calls Gavin and makes a low bid which, in an
inspired moment of negotiating brilliance, Gavin turns into an as-

tronomical bid (this part requires some serious imagination). The deal is finalized. My life is saved. The bank won't foreclose. My children will get orthodontia if they need it. My dog will get orthodontia if he needs it. Excitedly, Gavin dials my number and now… and now… my phone should be ringing…

But it does not ring. It is dead, dormant, lifeless, a dull hunk of inert white plastic. I pick up the receiver to listen for a dial tone. Yes, the line is working. And so, I run the whole upbeat scenario through my mind again, this time with a generic *female* studio executive (ballsy, hard-nosed, attractive, small-breasted but athletic etc.) and when I come to the part where the phone is supposed to ring, I sneak a cursory glance at the receiver and once again ABSOLUTELY NOTHING HAPPENS.

"Ring you lousy piece of shit," I say out loud, but it does not obey. So much for telephonic telepathy. It is only 8:05 and I am conversing with inanimate objects. This promises to be a very long day.

So I turn to the Big Red Book in front of me. Seven hundred and fifty-six pages of lavishly illustrated diseases, maladies and syndromes, lesions, polyps, pustules and malignancies, their symptoms and cures spelled out in alphabetical detail for the layman, a hypochondriac's Gutenberg. Later this week, I have an appointment to see a chiropractor who treats chemical allergies, a woman who comes very highly recommended, but now I am hedging my bets, giving medical science another chance on the sly. In spite of Margolis's protestations, I am still not entirely convinced that my mysterious illness is not some exotic syndrome that has, by its sheer rarity, slipped by all the pathologists. I am determined to read every one of these 756 pages to see if my symptoms match up to something in the book. I mean business.

～

Monday, June 5. 9:05 A.M. Anal fistula, anorectal abscess, amebic dysentery, acetylcholine disease and achalasia do not fit my symptoms, but make for fascinating reading nonetheless. So many lovely diseases! So many different forms of pain! So many equally torturous cures! I move onward to acid reflux, acrocyanosis and acromegaly when the phone finally rings. I sit there and watch it jingle with a mixture of excitement and terror and finally pick up on the third ring. It is Gavin.

"So how's that ulcer coming along?" he asks.

"Fine. How's yours?"

"Me, I'm not the nervous type," he says. "It rolls off me like water off a duck. I used to bite my nails but no more. Now I am always calm, a cool customer. Life is too short. Of course the Valium helps."

"Not if you're waiting for the phone to ring," I say impatiently. "Can we maybe cut to the chase now?"

"You're wondering if there is any news, am I right?"

"Good guess."

"You're wondering if any of the studios have called."

"Right."

"You want to know if you've sold the script."

"Don't do this to me, Gavin. It's not funny."

"You're wondering if—"

"IS THERE ANY NEWS YET GODAMMIT?" I shout into the receiver. A second of silence passes during which I imagine Gavin is either poking an index finger into his ear or banging the side of his head with the butt of his palm to see if he can still hear.

"Nothing yet," he says finally.

My heart sinks into my stomach. "They hate it. It's finished, dead, I knew it," I say dispiritedly. "They would've called by now."

"Martin, it's 9:05 in the morning, my friend. Relax. Nobody even gets to work until ten in this town. And then they're in meetings half the morning and when the meetings are over they go to lunch for two hours. Have a little confidence in yourself. Have a little more self-esteem."

"So now you're my shrink?"

"Interestingly enough, psychiatry was my second career choice. But unfortunately I'm not a very good listener."

"A tragic loss for the world's neurotics."

"That's what my mother says."

"You'll call me as soon as you hear anything?"

"You got it, pal."

I hang up and turn back to my book.

⟳

Monday, June 5, 3:00 o'clock P.M. After lunch, I call Delilah to make sure she is still alive. She is. Barely. We keep the conversation short because I don't want to tie up the line. She understands and wishes me luck. Later, I doze off at my desk somewhere between acute granuloctyc leukemia and Addison's Disease. I wake up with a start at 4:00 o'clock and the first thing I look at is my message machine. Of course, if the phone had rung, the noise would have certainly awakened me, but I look anyway. No messages. The work day is almost over; the executives are probably back from their two-hour power lunches by now. I'm dead.

Out of sheer boredom, I turn back to Addison's Disease which, on the surface, appears to have some real potential. The symptoms — loss of appetite and nausea — fit me like a glove. I read on. It is a disease of the adrenal glands, I learn, curable by taking small doses of steroids. This part does not appeal to me, for I have witnessed the side effects of steroids. My Aunt Marga from Passaic was on them for medical reasons in the Seventies and they made her cheeks puff up so much she looked like Alvin the Chipmunk. Also, you should have seen the biceps on her. But I mark the page anyway and make a mental note to consult Margolis about it. Just then, the phone rings. I don't watch it ring this time, I grab for it madly, so madly that I knock the whole apparatus to the floor. I fumble clumsily under my desk for the receiver.

"Okay, we got an offer," Gavin says calmly.

"We did? Hot damn! That's great! From who?"

"Paramount," Gavin says, but there is something in his voice that bothers me, something uncharacteristically subdued. "That's the good news anyway," he says.

"There's bad news?"

"Yes."

"Well?"

"It's a low ball offer. Seventy-five against two hundred."

"That's not that low," I say.

"It's an insult," Gavin continues. "A slap in the face. It's practically Guild minimum. The seventy-five includes a two year option and your rewriting services. Two drafts and a polish. Everything but the kitchen sink."

"What did you tell them?"

"I said I'd talk it over with you and with Ben. I said I didn't think either of you would go for it. Ben is absolutely livid, he screamed at me on the phone, like it was my fault. How do you feel about it?"

"I don't know."

"Wrong answer, my friend."

"Okay, okay. Question: If we turn it down now, can we come back to them later if nothing else pans out?"

"Sure, but they'll know why and probably lower the offer. You'll practically be paying *them* for the script at that point."

"Have we heard from anyone else?"

"Not yet. Which leads me to believe we'd be fools to take this offer. What if another studio comes in with a much higher bid?"

"What if nobody comes in with anything?"

"I would find that hard to believe, but anything's possible in this crazy town."

"Seventy-five would solve a lot of my problems."

"Not as many as two hundred would solve."

"I'm not a gambler," I say.

"Then you're in the wrong business, my friend."

"If you were me, what would you do?"

"Find a new tailor."

"Funny."

"I'd throw it back in their faces," Gavin says with casual bravado. "Only a wuss would accept an offer like that. Are you a wuss, Martin?"

"Definitely."

"So take the offer. Work your butt off for chump change. It's your career, my friend. You take seventy-five now, you'll have a hard time getting more than that next time."

"How soon do you need a decision?"

"Half an hour ago."

"Jesus, can't you stall them?"

"I don't think so."

I suddenly realize that I am still kneeling under my desk. I pick up the phone and crawl into my chair, banging my head as I go. I feel like there is probably more oxygen up there. I can hear Gavin breathing impatiently on the line. Only an agent can breathe impatiently. The clock is ticking. Suddenly all this wuss business has changed the issue. There is more at stake than just money. My manhood is on the line, what there is left of it anyway. A gauntlet of sorts has been dropped. Besides, if one studio is willing to spend $75,000, surely another studio will be willing to spend more. It is on this dubious logic that I finally make my decision.

"Turn it down," I say.

ᥱ

Monday, June 5, 6:30 P.M. My lonely vigil continues. *The Family Medical Guide* is laying open on my desk. I have read through the A's and just started on B12 deficiency anemia and bacillary dysentery, neither of which works for me. The phone has not chimed since my last conversation with Gavin, the one in which I blithely instructed him to turn down seventy-five thousand dollars. I am having second thoughts about the wisdom of that move. Call it "seller's remorse." How could I have let him talk me into this? How could I have been so impulsive? What could I have been thinking? Am I out of my mind? Has my mystery disease affected my brain? I said *no to seventy-five thousand dollars?* SEVENTY-FIVE THOUSAND DOLLARS? And now, the work day is almost over and nobody else has offered one brass farthing. I am not going to get a penny for the goddamn thing! I'm ruined! When Ursula pulls into the driveway at 6:35 that evening, I do not have the nerve or the heart to tell her what I have done. She will kill me. So much for my manhood.

"Any offers?" she asks, standing in the doorway.

"Not yet," I lie.

"Is that bad?"

"It ain't good."

Seeing the hangdog look on my face, she enters the room and kisses the top of my head. "Don't be depressed," she says. "You're very good at what you do."

"That's what every wife tells her husband. That's probably what Himmler's wife told Himmler."

"Well in this case it happens to be true."

"Thanks," I say, forcing a feeble smile.

She looks at the bright red tome laying open on my desk. "You haven't been sitting here all day, waiting for the phone to ring?"

"Of course not," I say, laughing deprecatingly at such a preposterous accusation. "I'm not that crazy."

"Somebody will make an offer," she says. "I just know they will."

"And if they don't?"

"Then we'll muddle through somehow. It's not the end of the world, Martin. Try to have a little perspective on things."

As soon as she has left the room to start making dinner, I frantically dial Gavin's office number. It is 6:45 and he is probably still there, waiting for a late offer to come in. I am wrong. Nobody is there. The office is closed. An answering machine picks up. What kind of a literary agency shuts down at 6:45? A literary agency that would have *me* as a client, that's who. I slam down the receiver. Now what? I do not have Gavin's home number and he is not listed in the book. Nobody is listed in the goddamn book. But somehow, I must talk to him. I must tell him to call Paramount back and get them to remake that offer before they change their minds completely. Beg even, grovel if necessary. I'll take seventy, sixty-five, even sixty! There must be some way to undue this mess.

And then I remember. When I was in the hospital, Clive gave me Gavin's home number. Did I keep it or toss it? I can't remember. I try to think back. I wrote it down on a slip of hospital stationary and put it in my wallet. Yes, that's it! I take out my wallet and dump out the contents on my desk. I give them a thorough going over, but nothing turns up either between the plastic or among the random receipts and miscellaneous paper in the billfold section. I repeat the process. Nothing. Could I have put it in a pocket?

Suddenly, I am in the kitchen. Ursula is at the stove stirring pasta. The kids are eating uncooked strands of spaghetti. I try to appear less agitated than I feel.

"Remember back in May," I say casually, "when I was in the hospital?"

"Who could ever forget?"

"You don't happen to remember what I was wearing?"

"A hospital robe with your butt hanging out."

"After that. When we went home?"

Ursula stops stirring and stares off into the middle distance. She is very good at visualizing the details of the past. "Your green flannel shirt... running shoes... the patched blue jeans and... the brown tweed jacket with the elbow patches."

"Thanks!" I say and I am off to the closet.

The tweed jacket is my best bet since it is the only item that has not been washed since my hospital stay. I rifle the pockets. Nothing. My last hope is one of those little secret pockets inside the side pockets. I practically rip them out of the fabric. But I find nothing. I'm dead.

Tuesday, June 6, 3:30 A.M. Clad only in a pair of boxer shorts and a Harvard T-shirt, I am pacing barefoot on the back patio, cursing the sun for taking so goddamn long to rise. I have smoked through an entire pack of cigarettes for I have been out here pacing since midnight. My mouth is raw, my nerves are shot and I am dead tired. The moon is full and I feel like howling. Five more hours to go.

Dawn finds me at my desk, drinking strong coffee and strumming through my Big Red Book. Sometime around 5:30 A.M. my symptoms suddenly return. One minute I am fine, the next minute I am not. First comes that peculiar disoriented feeling, followed by the inevitable queasiness. When I return to my *Family Medical Guide*, it is with renewed purpose. Why am I suddenly feeling sick again? What *is* this insidious disease? I look to the C's for answers: Cancer takes up fifty pages. I speed read them and move on to canker sores. I know I do not have cancer. If I did, I would already be dead.

Tuesday, June 6, 8:30 A.M. After putting me on hold twice, Clive tries to give me the runaround, but I am adamant. I must speak to Gavin immediately. If he is in a meeting, pull him out; if he is on the toilet, yank him off it; if he is still at home, give me his home number. Whatever it takes. At this point, I am temporarily insane, possibly even borderline psychotic, and I suppose this must come through to Clive because he finally gives in and connects me to Gavin.

"Yes Martin?" Gavin says, sighing audibly.

"Don't give me 'yes Martin,'" I say. "What the hell's going on?"

"How do you mean?"

"How do I mean? HOW DO I MEAN? Did you have brain surgery last night?" I ask. "You know goddamn well what I mean!"

"This is no reason to get testy."

"This is a *perfect* reason to get testy!"

Another sigh. "Hold on a second," Gavin says. I hear him giving instructions to Clive about something, another client with another deal pending. I am pacing now, frothing at the mouth, my heart in my mouth. Every second that I am on hold takes a year off my life. "Where were we?" Gavin asks finally.

"We were discussing the great bidding war that never took place," I say. "Have we heard from everybody?"

"The studios all passed," he says.

"All of them?"

"I'm sorry."

"You're *sorry*? You talked me into turning down seventy-five thousand dollars!"

"I didn't talk you into anything. I simply gave you the pros and the cons. You made the decision. You're a big boy."

"Says who?"

"Hey, we gambled, we lost. It happens."

"Go back to Paramount. Tell them we reconsidered."

"I did that already," Gavin says. "Unfortunately, they withdrew the offer."

This crushing news takes all the remaining wind out of my sails. I collapse into my chair, my face in my hands. I feel like banging my head on the desk but I resist the impulse. My mouth suddenly feels like it is filled with gauze. "Oh great," I say. "So that's it? End of story?"

"More or less."

"More or less?"

"We haven't heard from Octagon yet."

"Who's Octagon?"

"Mini-studio. Lots of Japanese capital. Distribute through Universal. Mostly low-budget stuff. You really should read the trades more, Martin."

"Is it a good sign?" I ask, grabbing for a life preserver.

"Is what a good sign?"

"That they haven't responded yet?"

"Might be. Then again, it might not be."

"Thanks for clearing that up," I say. "How's Fogelman taking it?"

"Fogelman? He's got deals all over town. One falls through, there are six others pending. He's like that fish that never stops swimming. Eventually one gets made."

"In other words he doesn't really give a shit."

"That's not what I said."

"Right."

"Is there anything else, Martin?" he asks impatiently. "I've got a meeting I'm late for."

"So you'll call me if Octagon responds?"

"Sure."

"Either way?"

"Either way."

I'm not sure why, but when I hang up the phone I have the distinct feeling I will never hear from him again.

15
CHAPTER

At the age of seventy, my father finally retires from the medical profession. Most of his patients are either dead of natural causes or in nursing homes and he is not making enough of an income to justify paying the astronomical malpractice insurance premiums required by the State of New York. He has never actually been sued for malpractice, but the threat of ruination via lawsuit hangs over his head at all times and causes him considerable anxiety, anxiety that he takes out primarily on us. Besides, retirement means he can devote all of his days to painting, something he has been wanting to do his whole life.

He is still energetic at seventy. Ironically, while my mother is constantly in and out of hospitals for one ailment or another, my father, who has lead a sedentary life rich in pastries and tobacco smoke, is remarkably healthy for a man of 70. Every morning he rises at seven A.M. sharp, makes himself a pot of coffee and trudges upstairs to his studio to work. He is locked in there all day long, according to my mother, and only comes down for lunch at noontime. For some reason, he has taken to locking up the place every night after he finishes, which is usually around five o'clock. Around that time, he comes downstairs to watch the Evening News and eat dinner on a tray in the den with my mother. Later, he sits in a corner smoking his pipe. When my sister and I call, he seems excited about the work he is doing in his studio.

"I am creating quite a significant body of work," he says modestly. "Once I am dead and buried these canvasses will be worth a lot of money. The name Dorfman will be up there with Cezanne, Monet, Picasso. Mark my words."

"When can we see them?" my sister asks.

"Soon."

That was in 1983 and neither my sister nor I have seen anything yet. Nobody has, for it has since become clear that my father has not created a single canvas in ten years, though he will not admit to this. He has the artist's equivalent of writer's block. He stands there everyday with his brushes and palette and stares at a blank canvas for several hours. Then he retires to an old easy chair in the corner and smokes his pipe and reads the paper to the accompaniment of a classical record playing on the old Blaupunkt. He reads every word of the paper, classified ads included. He can tell you how much a 1978 Volvo with 50,000 miles on the odometer and automatic transmission is selling for. He knows real estate prices and the going rates for used upright pianos. Sometimes, he writes an angry letter to the editor of the local newspaper, protesting something that has gotten his goat. After that, he takes a little nap and then, around four o'clock, tries painting again. I can picture him there in his old light brown corduroy trousers and apron, hunched over his paints, the pipe between his teeth, flecks of dandruff on his wide-frame glasses. My mother asks us to spare his feelings by pretending to believe him when he talks about the work he is doing in his studio. We agree to go along with the ruse. When we talk to him on the phone, we always ask how the work is going and he usually says "fine, fine," and we move on to other areas, most notably the respective states of our health. This has been going on for years.

In between creating nonexistent works of art, my father keeps his hand in the medical racket by treating my mother's various physical ailments. He becomes her personal physician and, like a good patient, she manages to provide him with a constant array of new symptoms. Three times a day, he monitors her blood pressure which, as a direct result of his ministrations, rises steadily. To prevent her from getting a heart attack, he advises her to take aspirin regularly which causes her to develop a stomach ulcer within three months. This he also treats with a steady dose of bland food and prescription

drugs, the latter eventually causing my mother to develop bowel problems, which my father then treats with something else that causes
her to develop new symptoms. Whenever she is symptom-free for
any length of time, she makes up for it by conveniently breaking a
wrist or twisting an ankle or getting a bad case of the flu. Then out
comes the old black medical bag. It is a vicious cycle, but it keeps
them going.

"He's going to kill her," Phoebe tells me. "She looks terrible."

"Be glad he has a hobby."

"Martin, this is serious. I'm concerned."

"So am I," I say, "but what can we do? They're adults, chrono-
logically speaking anyway."

"Why does she let him do this to her?"

"I don't know," I say. "It must be a symbiotic thing. According to
my therapist it takes two to tango. If Mom didn't need whatever it is
she gets out of this weird relationship, she wouldn't put up with it.
And Dad's totally dependent on her."

"Right. That makes sense, I guess."

"She needs the attention, he needs to feel needed, something
like that."

"Uh huh."

A moment of silence passes and then, completely out of the blue,
Phoebe asks me: "Do you think I'm stupid, Martin?"

"No, why?"

"I don't know what the word 'symbiotic' means. I'm stupid, aren't
I? Be honest."

"You're not stupid."

"I feel stupid. Richard and I go to parties or out to dinner with
friends, and I'm afraid to open my mouth for fear that I'll say something really moronic."

"Everybody says things that are moronic," I say. "The art is being
able to say something truly moronic with great strength of conviction."

"Like what you just said for instance?"

"Exactly."

And so we maintain the ruse about my father's nonexistent body
of artwork and keep our mouths shut as my mother's health steadily
deteriorates under my father's vigilant care.

"Are you sleeping with her?"

"Of course not."

"You can tell me the truth, Martin."

"I am."

"Honestly?"

"What would be the point?" I sigh. "We're both nauseous all the time."

For some stupid reason I have confessed to Nora the details of my platonic relationship with Delilah. Ever the conscientious patient, I am running out of things to talk to her about, so bringing up Delilah seems like a good idea at the time; a subject that we haven't dissected, bisected and trisected yet. Fresh material. New Meat.

Immediately, I regret it.

"I see. Have you *attempted* to have intercourse?"

"She carries around a *barf bag*, for Christ's sake."

"If you were both feeling well would you be having intercourse?" Nora asks.

"I don't know."

"Of course you do."

"Yes, no. What's the difference? Look, we're both miserable so we cry on each other's shoulder. That's the long and the short of it. Really."

"Do you find her attractive?"

"Can we drop it?"

"Do you?"

"When she's not talking about vomit, yes."

"I see."

"You see what?"

"How are things going with Ursula?"

"What things?"

"Clearly you're feeling the need to go outside your marital relationship for empathy. Why is that?"

"Gee, let me see. Could it be that I'm not getting enough empathy at home? Just a wild guess, mind you…"

"There's no need to get sarcastic."

"Sorry."

"But you're headed in the right direction."

"Fine. So I need to go outside the relationship for empathy. So what?"

"Don't you see?"

"Don't I see what?"

Nora shakes her head. "Oh no you don't. You'll have to figure that out for yourself."

But my mind is going numb. I suppress a yawn. "While we're on the subject," I say, filling up the silence. "I'm not getting a lot of empathy lately from you either."

"Is that what you want from me, empathy?"

"It couldn't hurt. I mean, at ninety bucks an hour, couldn't I earmark say ten bucks for five minutes of empathy?"

"Stop and think, Martin."

"About what exactly?"

Nora rolls her eyes; again I have disappointed her. "Where is this train going?" she says. "Think, dammit."

I hold my breath and do as she says, but nothing comes to mind. I must have gotten off the train at the last depot. I'm marooned, stranded, high and dry.

Finally, she comes to the rescue. "Think of what we've been talking about in the context of your youth."

"Empathy?"

"Yes."

"In the context of my youth...?"

"In other words," she says softly. "Where did you go for empathy as a boy?"

I blink. "I don't know."

"Did you get empathy from your father?"

"No."

"Your mother?"

"No."

"So where did you go to get empathy?"

"The dog was always eager to—"

"*Where, Martin?*"

"Nowhere, I guess."

"Exactly! You internalized it, Martin. Your mother was terrified of your father and your father gave you his anger when all you needed was a little empathy from someone. What a sad little boy you must've been. I don't know how you survived, I really don't."

When I look up at her, I am astonished to see that *her* eyes have welled up with tears. This has never happened before. I'm fine, she's crying.

Finally, some empathy.

☙

Following the Great Bidding War Fiasco of 1989, my symptoms disappear again, this time for an entire week. After the fifth day of good health, I am convinced that I am cured. I am so chipper, so buoyant, I don't even care about the pathetic failure of my script. My appetite returns along with my spirit and, to celebrate my rebirth and maybe put on a few lost pounds, I take Ursula and the kids out to dinner at a popular seafood restaurant where we all gobble down copious quantities of fried shrimp, Australian lobster tails and succulent Alaskan King Crab. I am myself again. It is good to be back. Life suddenly has possibilities again. I cancel my appointment with the chiropractic allergist.

Which turns out to be a mistake, because the very next day when I wake up, it is back. I can tell as soon as I open my eyes in the morning that things are not right. I am dizzy, disoriented and there is that awful brick-like feeling in my gut. I feel weak and devoid of energy and an overpowering gloom envelopes me. Since it is Sunday, I see no reason to get up so I lie in bed half the day. Finally around noon, the kids convince me to arise by mercilessly jumping on my stomach, always a persuasive gambit. I force myself to take them for a bike ride but there is no joy in it for me. I pedal slowly and sulkily around the block twice and spend the rest of the day on the living room couch staring silently at the ceiling. Ursula calls the chiropractor's answering service and reschedules my appointment for Monday afternoon, claiming that I am an emergency. Ursula is still sympathetic, but I suspect her patience is wavering. So is mine. This is not a life. I must get to the bottom of this, although I confess a certain lack of faith in the very notion of a chiropractic allergist. But I am quickly running out of choices.

And so the next day, I find myself sitting awkwardly once again on yet another doctor's examination table, skeptically reading the framed diplomas that cover the wall. I have never heard of even one of the institutions calligraphically scrawled on the diplomas. My potential savior's name is Dr. Nancy L. Guff and she is about 40, tall as a basketball player and possessed of a beatific smile that I find irritating from the start. I run through the tired old *spiel* about my symptoms in record time and she says nothing at first but just looks me over from head to foot as if she were about to fit me for a tuxedo.

"So can you help me?" I ask. "I'm desperate."

"Yes, I can feel that," she says, taking a step back but never removing her eyes from me.

"You can *feel* it?"

"Oh yes," she says. "It's in your aura. Heavy nervous tension. The colors are very bright."

"And that's bad?"

"Yes, but not incurable."

"I'm in your hands," I say hopefully, although in truth I remain highly skeptical.

And Dr. Guff's subsequent explanation of her so-called allergy test does not do much to assuage my doubt. In fact, I have trouble containing an overpowering urge to guffaw as she reveals it to me in detail.

She calls it her Muscle Resistance Exam and its goal is to "scientifically" determine what specific elements my body is allergic to, and to then purge these elements from my diet. To perform the test, I will be told to lie down flat on my back on the examination table and extend my left arm as if I were saluting someone of higher rank in the Gestapo. I am to try my best to keep the arm as stiff and straight as I can at all times, while she pushes against it with her right hand. No matter what, I am to resist. As she pushes against my arm, she will wave a series of small vials over my stomach and lower abdomen. Each vial contains a mineral or a food such as iron, nitrogen, wheat, sugar, barley or oats. If she succeeds in bending my arm, if my resistance fails, that means I am allergic to whatever is in the vial that "causes" the arm to bend.

Ordinarily, I would have dismissed this as pure horseshit, but lately, what with the dismal failure of medical science in solving my health problem, I do not know what to think.

"I sense that you are skeptical," she says before we start.

"My aura again?"

"Your face. The smirk is a dead giveaway."

"I don't mean to be rude," I say, "but I just don't see how this allergy test can possibly work."

"Neither did I at first," she tells me. "Frankly, it sounded preposterous, but I have had excellent results with a number of patients over the years."

"Really?"

"I can show you testimonials if you like?"

"No, that's okay."

"Let me put it into context for you, Martin," she says sitting down next to me on the examination table. "You see, from the time we are children we fill our bodies with all kinds of poisons. We eat refined sugar in candy, we eat yeast in bread, we drink caffeine, our teeth are filled with silver and mercury, we breathe in an assortment of household chemicals and industrial pollution. Some of us can go through life without having any problems. But most of us develop some sort of illness as a result of our exposure to all this junk. It might be cancer, it might be arthritis, or it might be what you have."

"Uh huh. Makes sense," I say feigning enthusiasm. "Let's try it. What have I got to lose?"

"I like your spirit, Martin," she says. "Okay, lie down and raise your arm."

And so I lie on my back and raise my arm and we go through this cockamamie ritual. Sometimes my arm stays rigid, sometimes it bends. I cannot tell if it is the vials or if it is the way in which she is applying pressure, although I would guess the latter. At six foot two she's not exactly petite and I have the distinct feeling that, beneath that beatific exterior lies one tough lady who works out a lot. The whole idiotic procedure takes about half an hour. When we are finished, she asks me to sit up and open my mouth. She counts the number of fillings in my teeth, consults a book and then writes something down on a clipboard.

"Okay," she says. "It's not as bad as I thought."

"Really?"

"You'll have to quit smoking for starters. Immediately. Can you do that, Martin?"

"Piece of cake," I say.

"And I'm going to put you on a strict diet. There will be a lot of things you will not be allowed to eat. You might feel a lot worse before you feel any better because your body will crave the foods you are denying it."

"Worse before better," I repeat. "No sweat."

"Also, I am going to recommend that you have all your fillings replaced."

"What! Why?"

"The mercury in the fillings might be leaking into your system, causing your symptoms. I'll refer you to a chiropractic dentist."

"Does he use Novocain?"

"Of course. This isn't the Middle Ages, Martin."

"Right. So Novocain doesn't poison the body?"

"Actually it does, but there are some poisons we are forced to endure and Novocain is one of them."

"Anything else?"

"Yes. I want you to have your house inspected for chemicals, radon, toxins and so forth by another one of my colleagues."

"A chiropractic house inspector?"

"In a manner of speaking."

"Sounds good."

"I'm going to give you several bottles of vitamins and supplementary nutrients. These will help your body cope better in these tough days ahead."

"Uh huh."

"If you stick with this plan, I know you'll be feeling much better in about a month or so, Martin. Think you can do it?"

"I love a challenge."

"Excellent."

Ten minutes later, I find myself at her cashier's desk, writing a check for $350, which covers the cost of the exam and the four huge bottles of vitamins and nutrients she sells me for about $30 a bottle. While the cashier writes down my insurance information, I steal a glance at the diet Dr. Guff has created for me. It has a familiar ring: The recurring word "no" as in no candy, no pastry, no coffee, no decaf, no meat, no fruit, no vegetable juices, no bread, no alcohol, no dairy and so on and so forth. I am, it seems, allergic to practically everything on God's earth, which makes one wonder why He put them there in the first place. On top of that, I have to see some other charlatan who is probably going to charge me another $250 or more to replace all my fillings. Then there's the environmental guy; no telling what that will cost. I might even have to move out of my house.

The question boils down to this: do I believe in Dr. Guff and her dubious version of science enough to put myself and my family through all this aggravation? The Diet from Hell, a mouth full of new fillings and possibly a new address? Not to mention a bill which could eventually come to several thousand dollars? More importantly, am I desperate enough?

As always, Ursula provides the sensible answer. "Try it for two weeks," she says. "What can you lose?"

⌒

My sister and I come up with a name for it when we are in our twenties. We call it Medical Terrorism. That is what my father practices. He is a medical terrorist.

Once a day, beginning when I am ten, he starts taking everybody's blood pressure. My sister's, my mother's and mine. Every morning before school, just after breakfast, we stand in line in the kitchen, waiting for him to strap up our arms and pump the little rubber bulb. Nobody says a word as he listens intently with his stethoscope. If we are even one point too high, a fraction of a point, he goes bananas with worry and starts to take readings *three* times a day. As a result of the anxiety this causes, all three of us eventually develop hypertension.

Once all of us have high blood pressure, the medical terrorism moves into the area of food. My father becomes the Salt Police. We cannot eat salt because salt can contribute to hypertension. Every time we are about to put anything in our mouths, he wants to examine its salt content. That means no potato chips, no popcorn, no ketchup. The problem is, practically everything that tastes good has salt in it, so the three of us are forced to eat only the blandest of foods while my father, whose blood pressure is disgustingly normal, stuffs his face with pastries and pretzels. He is a real pleasure in restaurants, where he tells us what we can order and then sends all the food back at least three times until it is completely salt free. We can eat spaghetti without marinara sauce, coq minus the vin, veal but no marsala. All beef must be cooked until it is a disgusting, unappetizing gray. Fish can come from the cool waters of Washington, but not the warm, garbage-infested waters of Mexico. Shrimp must be boiled until you need a screwdriver to extract them from their shells. In Nantucket, he requires precise details about the provenance of every seafood dish on the menu. Oysters and cherrystones are out of course. He keeps a list of all the mercury-infested rivers in the continental United States. When waiters see us coming, they dash for cover.

And of course it does not end with salt or mercury or garbage. No sir! Life, to my father, is a dark treacherous path through a jungle of land mines and booby traps. Salt is merely the tip of the iceberg in a peril-filled world that features radon, high tension wires, PCB's, strontium 90, mercury-consuming salmon, e coli, toxic waste, chloroflorocarbons, good and bad cholesterol, pesticides and God knows what else. And to document all of this, my father keeps a file cabinet full of clippings from every newspaper, magazine and medical journal he can get his hands on.

In the fall of 1967, the day before I am to go away to college for the first time, my father gives me a large manila envelope that has been sealed securely with tape and staples. He orders me not to open it until I have arrived at the campus. I am dying with curiosity, but I keep my promise. I am assuming it is either some money or a sentimental letter wishing me good luck on my new life as a college student. Perhaps a few philosophical pointers. My father is big on philosophical pointers.

But there are no philosophical pointers, no sentimental ruminations and no cash to be found in this envelope. How could I have been so naive? What the envelope contains is five pages of color photographs, torn from an issue of a medical journal, with the attending article highlighted in yellow magic marker; five pages of photographs depicting the ravages of syphilis and gonorrhea in their final gruesome stages. Pictures of purple penises, pictures of penises with horrible brown purulent growths, graphic photographs of penises with ghastly gangrenous malignancies, with open sores and chancres, penises that have been amputated and placed in jars of formaldehyde.

This is my father's unique way of warning me about the dangers of promiscuity. This, he is saying, is what will happen to me if I engage in premarital sex, if I engage in any sex at all, if I utilize my penis for anything more compelling than urination. A man-to-man talk will not suffice; no, he has to *terrify* me into abstention.

⁊

Dr. Guff is right about one thing. It is definitely worse before it gets better. Much worse. Close to horrible. Three days of the Diet from Hell and I am not only sicker in every respect, I am climbing the walls. I am a bundle of fits: nicotine fits, caffeine fits, sugar fits, fructose fits, doughnut fits. My digestive system is in open rebellion. My mind is staring straight down into the abyss. My legs are weak. Even my kidneys ache. I sit at home in my pajamas, unshaven, my hands trembling uncontrollably, my mind both racing and numb at the same time. I cannot concentrate on anything. I am in a dark pit. The future looks unaccountably bleak in every respect. I want to die.

Somehow, with the help and encouragement of Ursula, I get through the first week. By Day Eight there is still no light at the end of the tunnel. I am gripped by nausea for twenty-four hours a day, unable to sleep, unable to even close my eyes, unable to talk. Sunlight makes me dizzy; food turns to chalk in my mouth; there are deep pangs of pain in every part of my body.

I can barely swallow the huge vitamin pills and nutrient supplements Guff has prescribed. My lips feel swollen and my tongue is furry. My head is pounding.

On Day Nine I am close to losing my mind. I sit there, in the den, staring at the television, unable to understand what the news anchor is saying. Nothing makes sense. Is he even speaking English? Is he even a news anchor? I close my eyes and open them again and now the newsman is Captain Kangaroo. I do it again and Captain Kangaroo is Adolf Eichmann. Have I changed channels or am I hallucinating? My head is splitting. I have a cold compress on my brow for my brain feels as if it will explode any minute. Suddenly, I cannot bear it anymore.

I go outside and totter toward the garage. I cannot even tell what time of day it is. I look at my watch but nothing registers. Is it 5:15 or

3:25? Is it twilight or sunrise? I have no idea, but the light is blinding and everything is a blur. Something sharp and metallic is jingling in my pocket. Somehow, I manage to make it to my car. I open the door and sit down in the cool leather of the driver's seat. I find the car key and put it into the ignition. Where am I going? My hands are white and shaking madly, but I manage to turn the car on. I open the car windows and then reach up to the visor and push the button. I hear a click and then a rumble as the garage door begins to descend. It hits the concrete floor with a thud and now, except for the purr of the engine, there is silence. Suddenly it is dark. I lie back in the seat and wait for the fumes to reach my nostrils. Finally, five days of sleep-lessness catch up to me and I begin to doze off…

And then… and then suddenly there is a loud noise, a rolling noise and another thud and I am enveloped by bright light. Have I died? Is this it? Is this the bright light they talk about? I blink my eyes and look around. I am still in the car, still in the garage, but something is different. Yes, now I see… the garage door has mysteriously opened.

"Daddy, there's a telephone call for you," an angelic but familiar voice says. I turn to see Amanda knocking on the car window.

"Hi honey," I say squinting at the sun. "Who is it?"

"It's Mr. Gabby," she says.

"Who?"

"Mr. Gabby," she repeats, a little annoyed. "Daddy, are you all right?"

"I'm fine, honey."

"What were you doing in the garage?"

"Nothing," I say, and I pick her up and go inside the house.

As it turns out, Mr. Gabby is Gavin. Octagon has made an offer for the script. Sixty thousand against one-hundred and eighty.

CHAPTER

When I am miserable, when I feel myself slowly sinking into the warm protoplasmic goop of self-pity, I am reminded of a newscast I saw some years ago in Chicago. An elderly black man is being interviewed by an impossibly coiffed female news reporter, a handsome woman with a multi-ethnic name. A disaster has occurred. The elderly man's house has caught fire and burned down. In the blaze, two generations of his family have succumbed — his wife, his three grown children and his two toddler grandchildren. On top of this, he has lost all of his belongings, his car, his two dogs, his life savings which he kept under a floorboard, his scrapbooks, his TV, the photos on the mantle. Everything of any value to this wrinkled, seventy-two-year-old man has gone up in flames.

The blond news reporter, professionally blasé over the magnitude of this man's tragedy, shoves a microphone into his face. "You've lost everything, Mr. Jones," she says as if, with the smoldering ruins of his life caught dramatically in the background, he needs to be reminded. "You've lost your family, all of your money, your pets. How does that make you feel?"

The man scratches his stubbled chin, looks at the black chimney that is all that remains of his house, looks at the reporter, and shrugs.

"Well, Brenda," he says in an oddly chipper tone. "This is the

kinda thing that happens to somebody every day. And today it happened to me."

And today it happened to me. I love that! What morale! What
courage! What total madness! How incredibly comfortable that degree of fatalism must be! His number was up, that's all. Forget the
fact that he fell asleep with a cigarette dangling in his mouth. Not
his fault. No sir. God pulled his ticket out of the Great Celestial
Lottery and that was it for the Jones family. Poof. Up in smoke. Toast.
And today it happened to me! Hah!

I decide not to tell anybody about my nutty little escapade in the
garage, not Delilah or Nora, at least not right away. There is no reason to upset Ursula and the kids, and I would have to be a certified
lunatic to let my parents in on it. *There aren't enough ways to die? You
have to breathe in carbon monoxide? Don't you know it's dangerous?*
So for several years it remains my dirty little secret. Of course, under
duress, I do eventually disclose it to Nora, but that is two whole years
after the fact, long enough for the episode to have faded somewhat
into the nostalgic haze, although Nora takes three whole miserable
sessions to dissect it in its entirety. Did I really want to commit suicide that day in 1989? I don't know. I do know that the prospect of
feeling that sick everyday for the next forty years of my life was truly
a fate worse than death. So in a way, I suppose I did. Would I have
gone through with it? Probably not. Why? Because at the end of the
day I am, as the pugnacious Buzzy Tannenbaum once so aptly pointed
out, chickenshit.

In any case, the garage episode is enough to convince me to abandon Dr. Guff and her improbable allergy diet. After all, is health really worth dying for? And so, directly following my conversation with
Mr. Gabby on that fateful day in 1989, I make myself a strong cup of
coffee, smoke two cigarettes at a time and eat twelve stale miniature
Snickers bars left over from Halloween. This self-indulgent rampage
immediately brings me back to the land of the living, or at least close
enough to keep me away from exhaust pipes, shotguns and nooses. I
am still definitely feeling lousy, but on a scale of one to ten, ten
being death, I drop a few notches from a desperate seven down to a
tolerable four.

Not surprisingly, the unexpected career boost from Octagon Productions causes Gavin to undergo an immediate attitude change. That annoying aloofness of a few days ago has vanished and we are suddenly back to the old intimacy, if you can call it that. Once again, he is my biggest fan, obsequiously laughing at my jokes, offering to buy me lunch at expensive restaurants, claiming that he never lost faith in me, blah blah blah. And suddenly he is calling me again. Often. I get my revenge by putting *him* on hold. And by calling him Mr. Gabby.

Since the details of the pending deal with Octagon will take a few weeks to hammer out, Gavin tells me to relax and take it easy and leave the rigors of negotiation to him and Ben Fogelman. He offers to keep me posted on a daily basis. As I understand it, fifteen thousand of the sixty will go toward a one year option; the remaining forty-five thousand will cover one rewrite to be performed by me at a later date. In other words, within two or three weeks, the script will be in development and I will be required to take regular meetings with Octagon's story editors. I will be called upon to have ideas and to express them intelligently, although not too intelligently lest I frighten them off. I find this prospect worrisome. What if I am still feeling ill three weeks from now? What if the nausea and the dizziness do not abate? What if I start feeling worse? Suddenly, I am terrified. And so I decide to utilize this down time by reading the last few chapters ("Warts" through "Yellow Fever") of The Big Red Book in hopes of finding a cure before the meetings begin.

I zip through it in record time and call Margolis with my findings.

"How's the world treating you, Martin?" he asks.

"Like a cat treats a catbox."

"That's a funny line. You should use it sometime."

"I have."

And so we leap through the amenities in this clever fashion and I start laying diseases on him. I begin with the dreaded Addison's Disease. "The symptoms fit me like a glove," I say.

"You don't say?"

"That's right," I continue. "It's all here in my book, *The American Medical Associations' Family Medical Guide.*"

"Funny, I didn't notice the darkened complexion the last time you were in."

"The darkened complexion?"

"One of the most obvious symptoms of Addison's Disease is a darkened complexion."

"Okay, scratch that," I say, disappointed. "What about thyroid?"

"We tested you for that. Negative. Try again."

"Chronic Fatigue Syndrome."

"Are you fatigued?"

"How fatigued?"

"Extremely fatigued. Do you sleep half the day? Does the slightest undertaking exhaust you?"

"No."

"Sorry. Next."

"Epstein Barre Syndrome."

"Doesn't exist."

"What?"

"Since that book came out, research has disproved its existence."

"Oh."

"You got anymore? This is kind of fun," Margolis says.

"I'm glad you're enjoying it," I say. "Maybe I could come down there and play Disease Charades with you one day. You know, act out the symptoms. Barf… sounds like scarf."

"Sorry. Continue."

"How about labyrinthitis?"

"Does it come and go?"

"Yes."

"Labyrinthitis doesn't come and go. It stays and gets worse. Got any more?"

"Celiac disease?"

"A gluten allergy? Not unless you've been having the symptoms since childhood. Next?"

"Pancreatitis?"

"Are you running a fever?"

"No."

"Scratch that one then. Anymore?"

"Just one. Spangler's Gastritis."

There is a long pause. "Never heard of it," Margolis admits.
"Aha!"

"What are the symptoms?"

"You're the doctor."

"Can I get back to you on that one?" Margolis asks, suddenly diffident. "I'll have to, uh look that one up."

"Tsk tsk," I say condescendingly. "Fine. Go, look it up. Call me when you know."

"Spangler's Gastritis, huh?"

"That's right."

"Okay," he says, sounding more than a little embarrassed. "Talk to you later."

And he hangs up. I slam shut my Big Red Book and imagine Margolis frantically pulling thick medical tomes off his shelf and strumming madly through their indexes in search of Spangler's Gastritis, an utterly futile undertaking since there is no such thing as Spangler's Gastritis. I made it up.

⸎

At about this time — early July of 1989 — Delilah suddenly disappears.

We had agreed to rendezvous at our usual spot in Van Nuys, but she does not show up. I wait around for a good hour, polish off two absolutely putrid bowls of low-sodium, clamless clam chowder, and finally call her apartment from a pay phone at the restaurant. Her message machine picks up after the second ring, and I leave a short, slightly annoyed message. I have been feeling miserable for days and am in urgent need of some serious commiseration. Of course, the logical reason for her absence is ill health — perhaps she is simply not feeling well enough to make it. I have been there myself. But why hasn't she called?

And so I totter on home and wait for her to respond, but she does not return my call that day or the next or the next. After leaving about six messages, all to no avail, I begin to worry. Could her ailment have taken a turn for the worse? Is she hooked up to a myriad of life support machines in some intensive care unit, sucking oxygen out of a tube, unable to move or to speak? Is she in a coma? Or — and I cringe at the thought — has she committed suicide, hanged herself from a rafter in her apartment and kicked away the chair, or taken an overdose of Valium, or jumped off a building?

Two more days pass with no sign of her and so I decide to snap into action. First I call every hospital in the greater Los Angeles area and ask if she has been admitted. This proves fruitless. Next, I phone the police and ask if she has been reported missing. No one by that name, I am told. I contemplate reporting her missing myself, but decide to wait until I have checked out her apartment.

Delilah lives on the third floor. From a narrow vestibule, I locate her name on the roster and buzz her apartment. Predictably, there is no response and so I buzz the super.

From the foyer I can see him, still in robe and slippers, peer out from his ground floor apartment. I wave tentatively and he shuffles towards me. He is unshaven and clearly annoyed. We speak through the glass door which he does not open for fear, I assume, that I might be a criminal of some sort.

"One of your tenants, Delilah Foster, Apartment 7," I say. "I'm worried that she might be sick."

"Haven't seen her," the super says gruffly.

"I know. That's the whole point. She might be, well… dead."

The super scratches his unshaven chin.

"She was supposed to meet me somewhere a week ago," I say. "I haven't heard from her."

"Are you a cop?" he asks.

"No, just a friend."

"So what is it you want?"

A rocket scientist, this one. "I want you to let me into her apartment so I can make sure she's not sick or, uh, dead or something."

The super yawns and puts a hand through his hair which causes a tuft or two to stand on end.

"Wait here," he says finally and I watch him head back to his apartment for the master keys.

Five minutes later I am following him up the stairs to the third landing. He leads me down the carpeted hallway and we stop in front of Apartment 7. He knocks several times and once he's reasonably certain nobody's home, unlocks the door.

With more than a little trepidation, I enter Delilah's apartment.

For some reason, I had expected it to be dark and forbidding, a gloomy, claustrophobic cell, but I am wrong. On the contrary, it is bright and airy, a spacious, minimally furnished one-bedroom apartment with high ceilings, ornate moldings along the tops of the walls and French doors which lead to a balcony enclosed by twisted wrought iron fencing. No rafters.

"Yo, anybody home?" the super yells. He is poking his head into the rooms. I am in the empty bathroom, having just swept back the shower curtain to reveal… nothing.

"Guess not," I say, following him into the bedroom. "Boy, that's a relief."

"Can we go now?" he mutters looking at his watch. "I'm missing Oprah."

"Sure," I say. "Sorry to trouble you."

And so I drive home, relieved but more than a little perturbed, the mystery of Delilah's whereabouts still preying on my mind.

17

CHAPTER

In the Spring of 1986, three years after his retirement begins, my father becomes inexplicably obsessive-compulsive about, of all things, electricity. Lights are to be kept off unless absolutely necessary. Appliances are to be used only sparingly. The electric toothbrush is traded in for a manual one, as is his electric razor. The TV set is clicked off during commercials. Nobody seems to understand where this compulsion comes from or what it means. Apparently, it has been going on for close to a year by the time I hear about it. My mother never mentions it of course. It is Phoebe who fills me in.

"It's the strangest thing," she says. "He follows us from room to room and turns off the lights."

"Why?"

"I have no idea."

"Did you ask him?"

"Sure. He says we have no consideration."

"No consideration?"

"Right."

"What does that mean?"

"I was hoping you would know."

"Why would I know?"

"You're smarter than me."

"No I'm not."

"Yes you are."

"Can we get back to the subject at hand please?"

"Okay," Phoebe sighs heavily. "So what do you think?"

"I haven't the slightest idea. No consideration. It must have something to do with the bill."

"I don't think so. Richard got so ticked off the last time we were visiting, he wrote Dad a check for fifty dollars to cover the electric bill."

"Good move. Did it work?"

"No. Dad tore it up."

"Then what happened?"

"Richard said we're leaving and we left."

"Good strategy."

"It didn't help. He begged us to stay, pleaded with us and we said okay but he had to promise to stop this electricity thing."

"And did he?"

"For about an hour. Then he started following Richard around again, switching off all the lights, muttering 'no consideration' over and over under his breath. Finally, I went out to the car and got a flashlight and we kept that on all night."

"And that made him happy?"

"Yes."

"What did Mom say about all this?"

"Not much. The usual. She told us to humor him."

"That figures."

Why does my father do these things? I ask myself. Why electricity and not gas? And where in God's name does this insane behavior come from? His youth? His parents? Six thousand years of accumulated genetic neuroses? Who's to blame here?

He was an only child, my father, born a few years before the start of World War One, raised in northern Germany primarily by his mother and a number of doting aunts while his father was off sitting in a trench at the Somme. I've seen photographs of him in his youth. Little Felix, dressed in skirts and kneesocks, his hair cut in a ridiculous pageboy style, was spoiled, his every need attended to, his every utterance heeded as if he were some Grand Child Potentate. Little Lord Fauntleroy, the German version. At some stage in his early life, my father must have discovered that the rest of the world wasn't going to react to him in quite the same way as his mother and his doting aunts, and I suppose he's never fully recovered from the disappointment.

"What are we going to do Martin?" Phoebe asks.

How should I know? I want to say. He's a lunatic! A crazy old coot! A parsimonious nutcake! But this would not be in keeping with my role in the family. As usual, it falls to me to make sense out of this irrational behavior, to bring the warring parties together, to interpret, to arbitrate. And so I consider the problem carefully, as any self-respecting professional oracle would.

"The next time you visit," I say. "Bring candles."

∽

Two weeks after my fruitless search of her apartment, Delilah finally calls.

"Where have you been?" I ask testily. "I've been worried sick."

"You didn't get my postcard?"

"No."

"I've been back east. New York. Visiting my parents."

"Oh," I say, trying not to sound too plaintive. "You could've told me."

"It was a last minute decision."

"I was so worried I actually—"

"Martin I'm *cured!*" she says.

"What?"

"I'm cured. I'm healthy again!"

At first, I don't know what to say. This is a bombshell I am not prepared for. On the one hand, I am sincerely happy for her; on the other, my heart sinks, for I suddenly feel marooned, Robinson Crusoe deserted by Friday.

"That's wonderful," I croak.

"You'll never guess what I had."

"I can't imagine."

"Fucking Lyme Disease," she says.

"Lyme Disease?"

"Do you believe it?"

"So you're taking antibiotics?" I ask, having spent a few minutes on the Lyme Disease chapter in The Big Red Book.

"Yes. Margolis, the schmuck, didn't have a clue of course. My parents' doctor figured it out. I guess they get more Lyme Disease cases back east."

"Are you sure you're cured?" I ask. "I mean, how long have you been feeling okay?"

"Ten days and each day gets better."

"But you've gone a week without symptoms before," I point out. "Maybe this is a false alarm."

"I don't think so," she says. "I think this is really it."

"I certainly hope so."

"You don't sound all that happy about it, Martin," she says.

"I'm happy for you," I say in an unconvincing monotone. "Really I am. I'm just not feeling that well myself today."

"Can I help?" she asks. "Groceries, pep talk, cigarettes…?"

"No, but thanks anyway."

"Listen, can you meet me tomorrow at the usual place? To celebrate. Soup's on me."

"Tomorrow's no good," I say.

"Next week sometime?"

"Sure," I say. "I'll call you Monday."

"Great. Take care, Martin."

"You too."

Of course I do not call her next Monday or the Monday thereafter. I just cannot bring myself to call her. I am just too depressed and, suddenly, lonely.

∾

Spurred on by Delilah's success, I try homeopathy, acupuncture, biofeedback and aromatherapy, all to no avail. Nor has The Big Red Book provided any insight whatsoever, and I find myself running out of options. Plus, my three Lyme Disease tests all come back negative. It is Ursula who finally convinces me to see a therapist in the fall of 1989. Ursula's patience is wearing thin. She is tired of looking at my haggard face, tired of making excuses to our friends about why we have to cancel dinner, tired of doing things alone rather than as a couple. And so, without telling me, she enumerates my various symptoms to her gynecologist during one of her biannual checkups. Dr. Leslie Feingold, a female ob-gyn with a medical degree from UCLA, a woman I have never met, a woman, I am quick to point out, who spends her days looking not at brains but at *vaginas*, explains to Ursula that, in her opinion, my symptoms point unquestionably to anxiety-depression disease. Ursula, who has not been as skeptical as I regarding Margolis's original (and, in my estimation, pitiful) stress diagnosis, does not ask me to see a therapist. She *tells* me to see a therapist. Period. End of discussion. It is, in the purist Teutonic sense, an order. I mutter a peevish *sieg heil* and toddle obediently off to Nora's office.

Choosing Nora was also not up to me. Had it been up to me, I would have dithered endlessly over the choice, weighing the pros and cons, looking into references, reading up on gestalt, procrastinating until Kingdom Come. Something about the idea of seeing a therapist frightens me. Getting in touch with one's emotions requires that one have emotions to get in touch with. I was not sure I had any, and less sure that I wanted to get in touch with them.

Nora is recommended to us by Ursula's aerobics instructor, Heidi, a single woman of 45 who, by her own admission, has been plagued by problems making emotional connections with members of the opposite sex. Six months with Nora have apparently cured her of this flaw and she is now engaged to be married to a man she met in Nora's waiting room. Nora is to give the bride away. Heidi's review of Nora's abilities as a therapist is a glowing four stars.

And so, having no real choice in the matter, I have my first session with Nora. During the first four weeks, she asks me questions about my childhood, my parents, my sister, my adolescence and the current emotional status of my life. I muddle through as best I can, careful not to reveal too much, tentative, resistant, emotionally inscrutable. Whenever I can be vague, I am vague; whenever I can meet one of her questions with a one-liner, out it comes. I can detect early on that Nora regards me as a challenge, but that she soon grows impatient with me, frustrated by my unwillingness to open up, to reveal myself. After four weeks, she claims that she does not know me any better than she did the first moment I walked into her office. I am a cipher to her, a talking head that knows how to turn a phrase and make a sarcastic comment, but who the hell am I? And so I repeat my name, rank and serial number and we continue downhill from there.

Gradually, over a period of about six months, Nora wears me down. Slowly but surely, she peels away the layers of protective armor I have donned throughout my life to deflect the spears and arrows of... what? Of intimacy, of emotional truth, of trust and passion and the expression of affection. In the end, she finds a man with a little boy struggling to get out, a little boy who was never really allowed to be a little boy when that was all he was supposed to be.

And so, many months later, I find myself sitting on her couch with my eyes closed and my limbs inert, waiting for a hypnotic trance to descend upon me like a soft dark cloak. She is counting backwards from twenty, slowly, lethargically, soporifically, in a languid monotone. I yawn. I relax my muscles. I feel my eyelids flutter, but I cannot seem to erase from my mind the comical expression I am wearing, a sort of bemused blandness. In the end, it does not work; I will not allow myself to give in to it. I will not relinquish control. Frustrated, Nora gives up.

"Okay," she says. "Open your eyes."

"Am I hypnotized?" I ask dumbly.

"Of course not. If you were hypnotized you wouldn't have to ask."

"Sorry," I say. "I'm new at this."

"It doesn't work on everybody," Nora says sympathetically. "Especially diehard skeptics like you. I should have known better."

"So what now?" I ask.

She points to the phone on her desk. "Pick up the phone and call her."

"Call who?"

"Your sister, who else?"

"Right now?"

"Right now."

"But the phone bill..."

"Don't worry about it. I'll tack the bill onto your next session. Go ahead. Dial."

Hoping, praying that I get her answering machine and not her or Richard, I slowly dial the number. No such luck. Phoebe picks up on the second ring. She had to be home.

"It's Martin," I say quietly.

"Is something wrong, Martin? You sound… weird."

"No, nothing's wrong. It's just that I'm calling from my therapist's office."

"Really? She lets you use her phone?"

"Yeah. Why?"

"I don't know. My therapist doesn't."

"Have you ever asked your therapist?"

"Well, no."

I look over at Nora who makes a hurry-up sign by shaking her hand at me.

"Look, Phoebe, I need to ask you a question and the meter is running," I say.

"Right, of course, go ahead."

I clear my throat. "Do you remember when Mom and Dad had hepatitis?" I ask.

"Sure. How could I forget? We got to spend five blissfully *normal* weeks in New York with Opa and Oma. We even got to eat *salt!*"

"Right. I remember that part too. More or less anyway. But what happened after Mom and Dad got better? I'm drawing blanks on that."

"You're kidding?"

"No."

"How could you forget?"

"I don't know. I just forgot. Can you tell me?"

There is a long pause on her side of the line. And then a deep, anguished sigh. And then she fills in the blanks.

Part Three

CHAPTER 18

It is July of 1989, just after the long Independence Day weekend and I am to show up at the offices of Octagon Films in Beverly Hills on Tuesday afternoon for my first official meeting with the story editors. This is not my first safari into the dark wilderness of Development Hell, so I know what perils await me. I know where all the land mines and booby traps and trip wires will be hidden; I know how to tread carefully, to be agreeable but not to roll over and play dead, for that will only encourage them. Most of all, I must always keep in mind our opposing purposes: Their job is to make sure I destroy the script so that it will never be made into a movie. My job is to make it appear as if I respect their input without actually using any of it. A delicate balance must be struck if I am to survive. And survive I must, for if this script does not get transformed into celluloid, if it ends up on the shelf of some story editor's office for all of eternity, then I might just as well take down my shingle and find another line of work.

Of course, I am still not feeling very well. On the morning of my first meeting, I wake up with the usual nonalcohol-induced hangover. I feel as if the world is at a slight angle, that I am oddly detached from the people and objects around me, that my voice sounds hollow and faint and unnatural. My eyes do not seem quite able to focus. And then there is that awful sinking feeling in my gut and the weird cold flush that passes through my limbs and causes my hairs to stand on end. All of which is accompanied by the inevitable nausea and sense of dread, not to mention the almost paralyzing depression that comes from so many consecutive weeks of illness.

Nevertheless, I am determined to go through with the first meeting. After three months of this, I am growing more apathetic to the crippling aspects of this disease, and I have learned that if I force myself, if I take things one step at a time, I can get through these difficult situations without barfing or fainting or otherwise making a disgusting spectacle of myself. Mine has become a life only barely worth living, but a man's got to do what a man's got to do, and so I brace myself, pop the script into my briefcase, climb into my car and slowly negotiate my way over the Hollywood Hills and into Beverly Hills on that arid, windless day in July of 1989.

It is a modern, sterile office, tastefully decorated with sleek black leather sofas, light gray industrial carpeting and a lacquered gray coffee table. Bare pipes crisscross the ceiling and halogen track lighting illuminates the waiting room. I am greeted by a receptionist tastefully clothed in black leather and instructed to wait while she notifies Ted, the guy I am supposed to see. I settle into an armchair, pick up a copy of the trades and try to take my mind off the fact that I feel like I am about to vomit.

Within five minutes, a secretary comes out, offers me a soft drink and accompanies me to a large corner office where Ted is sitting behind a round desk, talking animatedly on the phone. I wave hello and he motions for me to sit. I strategically choose the highest chair, the power chair. I estimate Ted to be about 29, glib, prematurely jaded, an up-and-coming mover and shaker in pleated slacks, a blousy white shirt and red suspenders. Behind him is an enormous bookshelf completely covered with scripts stacked one atop the other, their titles magic-markered in black along the spines, a veritable screenplay graveyard, no doubt a testament to Ted's talent at successfully sabotaging all movie projects that have had the misfortune to float across his desk. His phone conversation drones on; he is doing all the talking, making plain his knowledge of writers, directors, producers, dropping names like an ingenue at a premiere party, and I begin to wonder if there is really anybody on the other end of the line or if this is a one-sided conversation solely intended to impress me. On the other hand, why would he feel compelled to impress *me*, a writer, the lowliest of all Hollywood species.

Finally he hangs up and strides over to me, his hand extended.

"It's wonderful to meet you at last," Ted gushes. "You are so incredibly talented. We all absolutely adore the script."

"Music to my ears," I say unoriginally.

"Can I get you a soft drink or a muffin or something?"

"No thanks," I reply. "But if there's any Lobster Newburg around, I'd love some."

Ted points a finger pistol-style at me and pulls the trigger. "Funny man," he says dully. "Funny man."

After some more hilarious small talk we are joined by Ted's secretary, who is there solely to take notes, and another woman named Jen, who is Ben Fogelman's assistant vice-president of development. My power chair is suddenly surrounded by three predatory development people and I shift nervously about like a deer caught in the headlights, trying to find the right angle, the right sitting posture, hoping that my sickly pallor is not too obvious under the bright halogen lighting. Jen appears to be in her early twenties; she is attractive in a business-like way, although she seems physically unable to smile. She is wearing a tasteful brown business suit, a conservative bow tie and a pair of thick glitter stockings, which make such an abrasive noise every time she crosses her legs, I am afraid her lap will burst into flames.

"So," Ted says, clapping his hands together. "Shall we get down to business?"

And so these people who profess to adore my work, begin methodically hacking it to pieces until whatever it was they adored in the first place is nowhere to be found. They have each made copious notes which, more than a few times, appear blatantly contradictory. They love the characters but want to change them; they adore the story but want to modify it, and I am left to wonder what it is they liked about the script in the first place. There must have been *something*; after all, they're shelling out sixty-thousand American Dollars for 120 pages of words on paper. It is an arduous, grueling process that leaves me in a despondent trance.

Four hours later, I leave the meeting haggard, humbled and laden with a pile of notes thick enough to roll into a Yule log and worthy of the same fate. I have done my best to keep the structure of the script intact, to keep the "integrity" of the project alive (as Ted is fond of saying), while somehow managing to assuage their respective egos in the process. This I accomplish by prefacing every one of my responses with "Yes Ted, I agree wholeheartedly but..." or assuring them that "nothing is written in stone." After all, I am a professional at this game and, health notwithstanding, I know my way around the Development Inferno. By the end of the second hour, however, I am too exhausted to reply strategically and readily agree to almost everything they say simply because I am tired of listening to them and want to go home and curl up into a fetal position in the corner of my bedroom.

Unfortunately, I have no time to waste. I have my marching orders. I am to alter the script to their specifications and I am to hand it in to them with said changes within the next four weeks. The script, I am told, is on the fast track.

⤳

The fact that Octagon is only paying me for one rewrite has ominous implications: it means that Ted and his gang of saboteurs fully expect to be hiring another writer to rewrite my rewrite shortly after my rewrite is finished. Most likely, they are planning to bring in a high-priced ringer, a professional script doctor to whom they will pay several hundred thousand dollars for three lousy weeks of work. For all I know, they are already sending the script around to the agents of a long list of prospective hacks before I have even *started* my rewrite. If he is smart, the script doctor they eventually hire will gratuitously alter as much of my work as he can and thereby end up with a screen credit on the completed film, should it defy all the odds and actually make it to principal photography. According to my contract, if I have to share credit with another writer, I will only receive half of the back end money. If I lose credit entirely I end up with *bupkis*. Worse, I will be quietly and politely kicked off the project and my participation will summarily end. In other words, the bastards will make the film without me. My baby will be torn from its biological father's arms and put in a foster home. I will be cut off, their filthy lucre my only consolation.

I am determined to prevent this from happening by doing a superlative job on my one meager rewrite. I'll show them! I will take their notes and turn the script into a masterpiece! They'll be so impressed with the finished product they will practically beg me to stay on and do the polish.

And so I spend the next four weeks locked in my home office, reworking the script, fleshing out the characters, honing the plot line, livening up the dialogue. It is therapeutic work for it takes my mind off the dismal state of my health. The month of July flies by and before I know it, the first week of August has passed. When I hand them the finished product exactly thirty days after our meeting, I am confident that Ted and Jen will be delighted. After all, they are professionals like me; they know a good script when they see one. They're not fools. But when I do not hear from them a week later, my confidence slowly begins to crumble. When the week turns into ten days, I am forlorn. After two miserable weeks of silence, I call Gavin. I spend the first half of the conversation ranting and raving about common courtesy and writer's egos and the exasperating guile of development people. Then I get down to business.

"Have you talked to them?" I ask bluntly.

"Me?"

"Yeah you. You're my agent, remember. Did they at least tell *you* what they think?"

"Actually, now that you mention it, Ted did call last week…" Gavin stammers.

"Last week! LAST WEEK? And you didn't call me?"

"I forgot."

"Baloney. What did he say?"

"Well, they really liked you," Gavin begins. "They liked working with you. They thought you were very professional, very agreeable, very patient…"

"But?"

"But they feel you're a little too close to the material."

"Oh boy, I know where this is going," I say. "I'm off the project right?"

"I don't know if I would phrase it exactly that way."

"How would you phrase it?"

"Look, they just feel you're too close to the material, so they've hired somebody else to give it a little… oomph."

"Oomph?"

"Oomph."

"It already has oomph. I gave it lots of oomph. It practically reeks of oomph!"

"They wanted some… fresh oomph."

"Fresh oomph?"

"Fresh oomph."

"I see. So when does the oomph guy start?" I ask.

"Actually, he's been working on it for about… oh ten days now."

"Ten days! TEN DAYS? When did they hire this guy, while I was still working on it? While I was in the meeting?"

"Of course not. I wouldn't have allowed that."

"So I'm off the project."

"I don't know if I would phrase it exactly that way," Gavin says.

"Oh? How would you phrase it?"

"Uh…"

"Never mind. Tell me this: Is it still on the fast track?"

"Yes. Absolutely. They're all still very excited about the project. In fact, they're already looking for a director. An A director."

This is some consolation. "Tell me the truth, Gavin. Is it a page one rewrite the oomph guy is doing?"

"No, no. Just a dialogue polish. No biggie."

"Are you telling me the truth?"

"Have I ever lied to you?"

What agent in his right mind would ask a question like that?

"I don't know if I would phrase it exactly that way," I say and then I mutter a good-bye and hang up.

⟨✧⟩

One month later, I receive a messengered copy of the rewritten script from Ben Fogelman's office. Just as I suspected, the script doctor (whose name is Larry Bud Pushkin) has done a lot more than add fresh oomph. He has gratuitously changed every single word of the original script. The protagonist, who I called Noah, is now Sam; his romantic interest, once named Sally, is now Megan. Where I had a character saying "Hello," he has the newly-named character saying "Hi." And vice versa. Where the characters were once interesting, they are now one-dimensional. Where the plot once twisted, it now meanders; where the story was once unpredictable, it is now formulaic. A pointless car chase now takes up eight pages in the middle of the picture. But the worst part of the whole pathetic mess is the title page which now reads: "Screenplay by Larry Bud Pushkin and Martin A. Dorfman." I take my only solace in the fact that they spelled my name correctly.

Over the next year, I am given regular bulletins on the erratic course of the script by both Gavin and Ben Fogelman. It is first sent to Octagon's A-list of directors; it is roundly rejected by all of them. In the spring of 1990, one B-list director expresses interest, but he is booked through 1993. Several months later, another B-list director becomes interested but will not commit until an acceptable leading man is signed. Then it is sent out to actors. Several express interest in the leading role, but none is willing to commit until an acceptable director is signed. Finally, Octagon gives up on the project and puts the script into turnaround; another minor production company called Icarus Films finally picks it up for a song and the script's circuitous journey begins anew.

By 1991 even I lose interest in the script. Who but a masochist would still dare to get excited after all these ups and downs? Besides, on the strength of my deal with Octagon, I have gotten several rewrite jobs myself and am scraping out a decent living doing to other writers what Larry Bud Pushkin did to me.

19
CHAPTER

After five weeks of bivouacking at our grandparents' apartment in Flushing, five glorious neurosis-free weeks in which we are not required to wash our hands thirty times a day, not expected to create a nice lather, not even instructed to use toilet seat liners, Phoebe and I are summoned home to Highland Falls. The hepatitis epidemic is finally over and our parents have recovered. Or so we are lead to believe.

It is, according to Phoebe's recollection, a humid day in late June of 1956 and although we have had plenty of fun with Opa and Oma, although each of us is about thirty-five dollars richer after repeatedly clobbering both of them at gin rummy every night, we are glad to be home again. We have missed our parents and our school friends and our toys, although not necessarily in that order. We have even missed the narcoleptic mutt we call a pet. But when my grandfather's Mercedes pulls up into our driveway, only my father steps out of the house to welcome us home. My father and a tall, stout woman with long blonde braids, a Swede whose name, we are told, is Helga.

"Where's Mommy?" Phoebe asks.

My father bends to one knee and takes our hands. He is wearing a surgical mask and rubber gloves, presumably to protect us from any lingering hepatitis germs he may still harbor. Oddly, there appear to be tears in his eyes. "Mommy's not all better yet, kids," he says.

"Where is she?"

"In the hospital."

"Can we see her?"

"Of course not. She's still contagious."

"When will she come home?"

My father glances at my grandfather. "Opa and Oma will be taking Mommy to New York for awhile," he says. "To recuperate."

"Why can't she recuperate here?"

"Because she can't."

"We'll be good."

"That's not the point."

"But when will she come home?" I ask again.

"I'm not sure. Soon, very soon. Daddy has to work, so Helga will be taking care of you until Mommy feels good enough to come home. Now say hello to Helga."

We mutter an unenthusiastic greeting to the giant Valkyrie who stands before us, arms akimbo, legs planted firmly, mouth a humorless straight line across her face, expression severe and impatient, a woman who exudes less warmth than most inanimate objects. She is Swedish and she speaks with a strong Scandinavian accent. Every consonant is hard, every vowel has an umlaut. To us, she sounds like Dracula.

"Come now chiltren," she says, clapping her hands. "It is time to vash up for lunch. March, vun-two."

"And make sure you create a nice lather," my father adds. "You're wasting your time if you don't create a nice lather."

And so we bid a fond farewell to our grandparents and to the sanity they represent, and march single file into the house under the critical eye of Helga who, as it turns out, seems to share my father's obsession with sterilization. Now we have not one, but two people reminding us endlessly to create a nice lather. We might as well spend the entire day over the sink.

Much to our chagrin, both Phoebe and I are required to attend summer school to make up the five weeks of schoolwork we missed during our sojourn in Queens. We do not want to go, but Helga is adamant and, as we soon learn, there is little point in arguing with her about anything. She is a rock. Every morning she walks us to the local junior high school where the summer school classes are held and three hours later, right on the dot, she picks us up. We are told to march quietly and are not allowed to stray or lag behind during the long walk home. She is our own personal Master Sergeant. Another few weeks of Helga and we will both qualify for stripes in the Swedish Armed Forces.

My mother calls twice from New York during the first two weeks but she sounds weak and tired and so our conversations are short and to the point. We repeatedly ask her when she is coming home, we try to pin her down to an exact day, but she does not know when. She tells us to be good, to behave ourselves, to make her proud and then she hangs up. But we are growing impatient; we long for her to come home. At night, I can hear Phoebe sobbing into her pillow.

About a week later, the phone calls suddenly cease. One week passes, then two and we have not heard from her. I immediately assume the worst.

"Don't be silly, Martin," my father says. "Of course she hasn't died. Don't even say such a terrible thing."

"Then what's going on?" I say. "Why hasn't she called?"

"If you must know, she's gone to Germany with Opa and Oma," he says. "Just for a couple of weeks, to help her recuperate."

"Why didn't you tell us?" Phoebe asks.

"What does it matter?" my father replies. "If she's not here, what difference does it make where she is?"

"We miss her," Phoebe says, forlorn.

"Don't you think I miss her too?" my father asks.

This has not occurred to either of us. "How long will she be gone?" I ask.

"I told you. Two weeks."

"And then she's coming home?"

"And then she's coming home."

"Promise?"

"Promise."

But three weeks pass and then four and our mother still has not come home. By this time, Phoebe has thumbtacked a calendar to her wall and drawn a big heart on the day my mother is supposed to return to us. Each night she crosses off another day, but now she is fourteen boxes ahead of the one with the heart. We are both starting to lose hope that our mother will ever return to us. Phoebe continues to cry herself to sleep every night while I, the diehard stoic, the brave little soldier, maintain a stiff upper lip at all times. I am seven; Phoebe is five.

One night around midnight, I am awakened by the sound of coughing. I sit up in bed to listen for it again, but the next thing I hear is the sound of breaking glass. I pull the covers away and walk into the hall. Phoebe is already standing in her doorway, listening.

"Was that you coughing?" I whisper.

"No."

"Maybe it was Helga?"

Phoebe shrugs and we both tiptoe down the hallway and stand outside Helga's room, waiting for the coughing sounds to return. But nothing happens. Quietly, I open her door and peer inside the room. Helga is sound asleep, snoring like a congested plow horse. I look at Phoebe and shrug. And then we hear more noises, sobbing noises, coming from my father's attic studio. I put a finger to my lips and quietly, we pad up the stairs.

My father is sitting on the couch in his bathrobe, holding a piece of paper in one hand, a bottle of liquor in the other. A glass lies shattered at his feet. His hair is disheveled. We sneak up on him and he doesn't see us at first. When we are close enough to perceive that his eyes are red and his cheeks are streaked with tears, he becomes aware of us.

"Are you okay, Daddy?" Phoebe asks.

He looks up. "Go to bed."

"What's wrong?" I ask. "Is it something about Mommy?"

He does not answer at first. He blows his nose.

"What is it, Daddy?" Phoebe asks.

"I'll tell you what it is," my father says angrily. "It's your mother. She's staying in Germany. Indefinitely. How do you like that?"

"But you said she'd be back," Phoebe cries. "You promised us!"

Then my father starts to bawl. Great anguished, convulsive, choking sobs. Neither Phoebe nor I know what to do so we just stand there and watch. We are scared, both of us, paralyzed with terror. I glance across the room at the easel which holds another canvas of my father's horrible screaming man; the resemblance to his present state is uncanny.

Now my father, still wracked with emotion, tries to speak through his tears. "She's never coming back," he stammers. "Never!" He grabs me by the shoulders and shouts it in my face: "Do you understand me? She's never coming back. Never! Your mother is *never coming back*! She might as well be dead!" His face is bright red now and he is still shaking me. "It's your fault, Martin! It's all your fault! You're a nag and a whiner and your mother just couldn't stand it anymore!" And then he is once again overcome and buries his head in a throw pillow.

I am frozen in place as if someone had glued the feet of my Dr. Denton's to the floor. (Phoebe's exact words). Phoebe herself is in a state of shock, her hands clapped tightly over her ears. I put my arm around her but she pulls away and runs down the stairs to her bedroom. And suddenly, the obvious strikes me (or struck her and most likely occurred to me too), and that is this: if my mother never comes back, Phoebe and I will be stuck with *him* for the remainder of our childhoods. He will be our only parent. We will be brought up by this fruitcake and the Swedish meatball he has hired as a nanny. Within a week we find ourselves dreaming wistfully of orphanages and foster homes.

Finally, I pad back to my room. Phoebe is still bawling into her pillow. When she hears me at the door, she looks up. "It's not your fault, Martin," she says consolingly. Neither of us sleeps the rest of the night. Both of us stay in bed the next day with belly aches, which my father dutifully diagnoses as stomach cancer.

We do not hear from our mother for another six months. Six months! Then one day, a taxi pulls up in front of our house and she appears, tanned, rested, healthy and loaded down with luggage and gifts.

And so we are together again, one big, unhappy family.

✑

"That's it?" Nora asks.

"What were you expecting, a triple homicide?"

"I'm not belittling it," she explains. "I just wanted to know if you were finished."

"Oh," I say. "Well, yes I guess I am. At least that's everything Phoebe had to say on the subject."

"And she never asked your mother about it? Never confronted her and asked for an explanation?"

"No."

Nora nods thoughtfully and writes something down in her new notebook, a red loose-leaf binder with yellow alphabetical file separators. I have asked to see her notes, at least the parts that pertain to me, but she will not allow it. On the rare occasions when she must leave me alone in the office, when the doorbell rings or there's an emergency phone call she must take in another room, I have contemplated stealing a look, but have never actually found the nerve to try. For all I know, she's just doodling, drawing comical little caricatures of me as I fight to hold back anything resembling emotion.

"And you have no recollection of this at all?" she says, tapping her front teeth with her pencil eraser.

"None."

"Even when Phoebe was telling you the story? Nothing clicked?"

"Nothing."

"Wow."

"You're impressed?" I ask.

"Impressed? No. Amazed? Yes. We call it selective amnesia. In other words, you can't deal with it so you've completely blanked it out of your memory, assuming you're telling the truth."

"Of course I'm telling the truth," I say, stung by the accusation. "At ninety dollars an hour I'd have to be an idiot to lie."

"Or too terrified to tell the truth."

"I'm not terrified."

"That's right," she says. "I forgot. You're the brave little soldier."

Suddenly, out of nowhere, I feel a rush of emotion well up in me and I fight it back by looking away, folding my arms, crossing my legs, feigning interest in my shoes, my usual repertoire. I untie the shoe resting on my knee even though it does not need retying. I re-cross my legs and retie the other shoe. As usual, these little diversions succeed admirably and the emotional surge passes.

"So," Nora says. "As you were recounting this story to me, how did you feel?"

"I don't know."

"Of course you do. Think."

"Angry, I guess."

"Angry at who?"

"At my father for falling apart in front of us, for not keeping his anxieties to himself, for not protecting us, for being so self-indulgent. For BLAMING IT ALL ON ME! At my mother for staying away so long and not keeping in touch."

"And where do you feel this anger?"

"Guess."

"Show me."

"I feel it here," I say, pointing to my lower abdomen.

"Good," Nora says. "And did you feel anything else?"

"Sadness I suppose," I mutter

"Sadness for whom?"

"Sadness for Phoebe."

"Not for yourself?"

"No. Not really."

"Oh come on, Martin. You're seven years old, you've just been told your mother is never coming home and you don't feel even a little sad for yourself?"

"I suppose... I don't know... I felt... numb. I feel numb now. What does that mean?"

"What do you think it means?"

"That I've numbed myself."

"In a manner of speaking, yes. It means that you're doing your best to keep those feelings from surfacing. You've done that all your life and now forty years of repressed feelings are coming back to haunt you. They're having an effect on your health. They are making you sick, Martin."

"So now that I've uncovered this deep dark secret, I should be feeling okay again right?"

"Not necessarily."

"Not necessarily? Isn't that the whole point of all this?"

"It's not that cut and dried."

"What are you saying?"

"I'm saying you shouldn't expect immediate relief, just because you've confronted a painful episode from your past."

"So I could go on feeling sick forever, no matter what sludge I keep dragging up from my childhood? Is that it?"

"Maybe."

"Maybe? *Maybe*? MAYBE?? I don't want to hear maybe. I want to start feeling better godammit!"

"It's not an exact science, Martin."

"Now you're telling me this?"

"I thought you knew."

"All this could be for nothing?"

"Well... yes."

"I don't believe this! I've been hoodwinked! Bamboozled!"

I feel that awful rush again, but I manage to beat it back. Suddenly, I am so tired, tired of feeling sick day in and day out, tired of being sluggish and nauseous and detached, tired of the canceled dinners, tired of being a hermit, tired of therapy. It has been almost two whole years now and I have had enough. My throat constricts and I want to cry but I cannot. Nora looks at me, waiting for the catharsis that never comes. And then the numbness returns, the surge subsides. I take a deep breath, relax my facial muscles and steal a glance at her digital clock. My hour is over. Saved again. I leap to my feet.

"Aren't we in a big hurry," she says, tearing a sheet of paper out of her loose-leaf binder and handing it to me.

"What's this?"

"The name and number of a good psychopharmacologist."

"You're dropping me?"

"Don't be silly. We work in conjunction with one another."

"I don't get it. Why do I need to see a psychopharmacologist?"

"Because I think you've reached a point where you might benefit from medication."

"Medication? For what?"

"For anxiety-depression."

"But my symptoms are *physical*. I've told you that a million times. I'm not depressed."

"Let him be the judge of that," she says.

I fold the paper and put it in my wallet. "Fine," I say. "Is he expensive?"

"Yes, but your insurance should cover it."

"Good. A couple more months of these sessions and I'll be living out of a refrigerator box in front of Dupars."

"One more thing," she says as I am almost out the door. "I want you to talk frankly to your mother and find out exactly why she disappeared for six months. Her side of the story might be good to know for both you and Phoebe. You think you can do that?"

Needless to say, this is the last thing in the world I want to do. "Sure," I shrug blithely. "Why not?"

CHAPTER

M ost of the kids in my sixth grade class are embarrassed by their fathers, but none as much as I. The other dads wear baseball caps and talk about football and speak like Americans. They say "Yo" and "How's it going" and "You bet." They barbecue hot dogs on Saturday nights and go bowling once a week. They know about transmissions and knuckle balls and power tools. My father, on the other hand, carries himself with a stiff Prussian posture, wears an old fedora and speaks with a haughty German accent, his words punctuated by mispronunciations and incorrect inflections. He is neither gregarious nor personable. On the beach in Nantucket, he dresses like Nixon — dark socks, shined black shoes, Bermuda shorts and a tie. He wouldn't know a bowling ball from a Hostess Cupcake.

Fortunately, my father is kept so busy with hospital rounds and house calls that he has little occasion to run into any of my friends. And whenever he happens to be in the vicinity, whenever his Buick is in the driveway, I am adept at steering my friends clear of him. When, once a year, my school holds a Parent's Day, I feign an ambiguous stomach ailment and the enema my father administers is always preferable to the mortification I would suffer were he to visit Mrs. Schaffner's overheated schoolroom.

On spring afternoons, once the snow has melted and the ground

202 ᎔ John Blumenthal

has softened, a few of the neighborhood kids — Stewie Meyerson, Buzzy Tannenbaum, Kenny Fishbeck and I, among others — gather informally at the Liberty Street School playground and play baseball until dark. Usually there are six or seven of us, not enough to play a regulation nine-player game, but somehow we manage. The first baseman covers right field *and* first base, second baseman covers center field, shortstop and second base. Once in awhile, one of the dads comes home from work early and umps.

By the age of nine I have developed into a fairly competent baseball player. Not a prodigy, not a Hank Greenburg or a Mickey Mantle, but good enough to play Little League. Since I have a good throwing arm and can scoop up grounders with some ease, I generally end up playing third base, a position which, in our informal league, often includes left field and shortstop. No other position appeals to me — pitching is too much pressure, catching is too dangerous, particularly since none of us has a mask and because half the kids throw the bat after hitting. No one in our group wants to be catcher.

My hitting is erratic (infield grounders and the occasional pop fly) until one of the dads — Buzzy Tannenbaum's father, Gilbert, who once played on a high school varsity team — gives me a few tips on swinging and following through. After this informal instruction and a good deal of practice in the full-length mirror behind my mother's closet door, I can be depended upon to at least hit a single or better every time up at bat. In fact, it is Buzzy Tannenbaum's father who suggests I go out for Little League that summer. "You're good enough, kid," he tells me. "Better than most."

And so, with Gil Tannenbaum's complimentary words still ringing in my ears, I announce to my father that I am trying out for Little League that summer.

"Why?" he asks.

"Because I'm good," I say. "Gil Tannenbaum says I'm good."

"Gil Tannenbaum, the plumber? What does he know?"

"He knows baseball. He played on the Varsity. At… Princeton."

"Gilbert Tannenbaum went to Princeton? To study plumbing?"

"Yes. No. I don't know. What's the difference? I'm trying out and that's that."

"Not so fast, young man. You'll try out if I give my permission. I'm still the boss around here."

"Fine," I say grinding my teeth. "May I have your permission?"

"Tell me why this is so important to you."

"I don't know. It's fun. Besides, I might decide to become a baseball player when I grow up."

"You're not tall enough," he says.

"What?"

"You have to be tall. Baseball players are tall."

For a moment I do not know what he's talking about, but then it hits me. "That's *basketball*, Dad," I say rolling my eyes. "Baseball's the one with the bat. You hit the ball with a bat."

"And this is what you want to do when you grow up? Hit a ball with a bat?"

"Maybe."

"This is what you plan to do with your expensive education? Hit a ball with a bat?"

"I don't know. Maybe."

"Answer me this: What's the point?"

"Dad, it's a sport. What's the point of any sport?"

"You tell me."

"What's the point of anything?" I say angrily. "What's the point of your stupid old art?"

My father's eyes widen in shock. I have crossed the line here. I have kicked the rump of my father's one and only sacred cow. It is a given in my family that art is the single most important thing in life. For a moment, he is speechless.

"There is no comparison here, Martin. None at all."

"Oh yeah? Well, baseball might be hitting a ball with a bat, but what's art? All you do is smear paint on a piece of paper. Anybody can do that! Ever hear of finger painting? A two-year-old can do it! What's the big deal?"

"*What's the big deal*, Dr. Einstein? It just so happens that art is the culmination of centuries of civilization! And what is your precious baseball? Were they playing baseball during the Renaissance? I don't think so."

"That's ridiculous!" I say. "The Greeks had sports. The Romans had sports! The Romans were very big sportsmen."

"And look what happened to them!"

"What's that got to do with it?"

"Think about it," my father says.

As it turns out the whole question of my joining Little League is moot. We already have plans to spend the summer in Nantucket, just like we do every year. As a form of protest, I stop doing woodcuts forever.

Thirty-two years later, when I happen to mention in passing my dashed career as a baseball legend, my father waves his hand dismissively and says, "You were never *tall* enough Martin."

For weeks following Nora's admission that confronting my past may have absolutely no impact on my malaise, I am in a deep funk. Nora was my last hope and now, after thousands of dollars of therapy, I find out that she too is nothing but a fraud! All those hours of soul searching! All those hours mining every dull morsel of my past! And coming up with what? Fool's gold! I've been swindled, scammed, sold yet another bill of goods. So it is no surprise that the little piece of paper with Nora's psychopharmacologist's phone number on it remains in my wallet for weeks, hidden behind the bills and the receipts, becoming more wrinkled each time I sit down. I just haven't got the energy to subject myself to the hopeless panaceas of yet another quacksalver.

And so I suffer in silence. A few weeks pass without therapy and I am all right. No symptoms. Then, one morning, I wake up and...

You know the drill.

His name is Dr. Ferdinand Igor (he pronounces it "eye-gore") and in spite of a slight Eastern European accent, he is not, he assures me, from Transylvania. He is an American, born in New York City of Albanian and Portuguese parents, educated at Columbia University and the estimable Albert Einstein School of Medicine. He is a board certified Medical Doctor, and he teaches psychopharmacology to third year med students at USC Medical School. He is in his late-forties, a diminutive, soft-spoken man with a calming, almost soporific voice and a great deal of jet black hair everywhere but on his head.

His office is on the tenth floor of a high-rise office building in Encino, the bottom floor of which houses a bank and a pharmacy. The decor is contemporary but warm and unthreatening; peaceful harp music is piped in. One entire wall of the office is covered with various diplomas and awards, a testament to Dr. Igor's prolific achievements and a great savings on wallpaper.

"Very impressive," I say, nodding toward the wall.

"Yes thank you," Dr. Igor says.

"Where do you buy those?"

"Where do I—"

"A feeble attempt at humor," say I apologetically.

"Ah yes, I see," he says, displaying a perfect row of teeth. "Your therapist mentioned that you are a humorist by profession."

"Lately, it's more of a hobby," I say.

"It's nice to have a hobby," Dr. Igor expounds. "If everybody had a hobby, the world would be a better place."

"Hitler had a hobby," I point out. "He painted landscapes."

"There are always exceptions."

"Ain't that the truth?" I say, ogling the exits. This guy, I am thinking, is a fruitcake.

"Can you guess what my hobby is?" Dr. Igor inquires.

"Embalming?"

"No, in point of fact, I am writing a screenplay. It's all about a psychopharmacologist who solves crimes. Would you—"

"*Take a look at it?* No. I won't. Not for a million dollars. Not for TWO MILLION DOLLARS!" I scream. "And furthermore, answer me this: what ever happened to stamp collecting? Or numismatics? Whatever happened to TAXIDERMY? Or collecting string? Is everybody on this godforsaken planet writing a fucking SCREENPLAY?"

Dr. Igor recoils in his chair. "I seem to have struck a nerve. Do you wish to talk about it?"

"No thanks."

"Fine. Then shall we begin?" he asks, his voice cracking slightly.

"You're the boss," I say. "Fire away, but I must warn you this will probably be utterly futile. You see, there's nothing wrong with the old noggin. My symptoms are purely physical."

"Noggin?"

"Head. Brain. Gray matter."

"Of course. This is not unusual, Mr. Dorfman. Most of my patients suffer physical symptoms."

"But you're a *psychiatrist*."

"Yes," Dr. Igor says, "Thank you for enlightening me."

Touché.

And so, with no further ado, Dr. Igor fills me in on the nuances of his specialty, anxiety-depression. A more tedious soliloquy you'd be hard put to find. I am only half listening as he drones on about the differences between endogenous anxiety and exogenous anxiety. I hold back a yawn as he tells me that *exogenous* anxiety is the result of external difficulties and that it is considered normal. I nearly nod off as he explains that *endogenous* anxiety is the result of genetics and conditioning and biochemical aberrations in the brain and that it can cause a variety of unpleasant symptoms that occur randomly with no ostensible external provocation and so on and so forth...

"In other words," Dr. Igor clarifies, "any small malfunction in the chemistry of the brain can produce an infinite variety of physical symptoms."

"Sounds good to me," is my glib reply. "But I'm really not feeling all that much stress, Doc. I'm just a happy-go-lucky sort of guy."

"Oh really? Is that how you think of yourself?"

"Not even close."

"Not that it matters," Dr. Igor continues. "These episodes occur randomly and do not necessarily follow periods of stress."

Seductive as all this appears, I am still skeptical for I have heard variations on this song-and-dance before from all the other charlatans. Jaffe had his edema, Chung his winds, Guff her poisons. Why should I find Igor and his ridiculous chemical imbalances any more plausible? There's no blood test for anxiety-depression disease, no foolproof method of diagnosis. When I mention this, Dr. Igor explains that the only way to diagnose the disease accurately is for the doctor to ask the patient a number of questions. Said patient is encouraged to answer truthfully, regardless of the degree of embarrassment which, I assume, will be high. None of this strikes me as particularly scientific.

Nevertheless, we begin with my childhood, where else? To the best of my ability, I try to recreate for Dr. Igor the neurotic atmosphere of my youth. I tell him about my father's fluctuating moods, my mother's disdain for displays of emotion, my father's fears and anxieties about diseases and his obsession with germs and electricity. In other words, he gets an abridged version of what it has taken me many anguished weeks to divulge to Nora. As I speak, Dr. Igor quietly takes notes in a fancy leather-bound notebook. The tranquil harp music becomes a lively fugue for flute.

"Considering your childhood," Dr. Igor says, "and your father's compulsive fear of diseases, it is not surprising that your symptoms mimic those of other serious illnesses."

"Is that so?" I say.

"Has your father ever been diagnosed as obsessive-compulsive?"

"He doesn't really believe in psychiatry," I reply. "We've tried to get him to see a shrink for years but he thinks it's all just a bunch of hocus pocus. Poppycock. Balderdash. Stuff and nonsense. Drivel. Folderol. Piffle. Bilgewater. Fiddle-faddle. Tommy—"

"I get the picture," Dr. Igor says, a hint of annoyance in his tone. "And how do you feel about it?"

"I'm not sure," I say. "I find the whole business depressing."

After I have finished dredging up sludge from my childhood, Dr. Igor begins the quiz show segment of the process. He will ask me a series of specific questions that require simple yes or no answers. My score will determine whether I am a victim of anxiety-depression disease; if I am, he will prescribe medication to normalize the chemistry of my brain and, hopefully, alleviate my symptoms. And rainwater will turn to beer.

Do I sometimes feel woozy and off-balance?

Yes.

Are my legs rubbery and weak at times?

Yes.

Do I feel oddly detached, as if my surroundings are strange, unreal, foggy?

Yes.

Do I feel an overwhelming sense of gloom?

Yes.

Increased sensitivity to light?

Yes! Yes!

Frequent nausea? Yes Yes! A thousand times Yes!

After every new question, I feel myself becoming more and more excited. Incredibly, Dr. Igor is describing in perfect detail every last one of my symptoms! He is putting into words exactly how I have been feeling for the last two years! How can this be? How can he know? And then it hits me: Nora has told him everything; he has been briefed. He knows the answers before he asks the questions. This is nothing but a con game.

Not surprisingly, after I have completed the test, Dr. Igor concludes that I do indeed suffer from anxiety-depression. When we are finished with the session, I write him a check for $250 and he writes me a prescription. I give him paper, he gives me paper. Why do I feel that I am being bamboozled once again?

According to the literature, the Little Pink Pills cure by restoring the brain's malfunctioning biochemistry to its normal state. The most common side effects are weight gain, constipation, dry mouth and drowsiness. Less common are nausea, vomiting, blurred vision, muscle spasms and delusions. Maximum recommended dosage is 300 milligrams per day and operating dangerous machinery while on the medication is not advised. In most cases, the Little Pink Pills do not take effect for about two to four weeks. Dr. Igor counsels me not to be discouraged if the results are not instantaneous.

It is close to midnight and Ursula and the kids are asleep. The house is quiet. I am standing alone in the kitchen, holding one of the Little Pink Pills between my fingers, turning it, observing it, wondering if it really will be my magic bullet. Or if, like all the other cockamamie cures and nostrums and panaceas, it will go down in failure. Do I have faith in Dr. Igor? Frankly, no.

And so, I toss a couple of the Little Pink Pills back, chase them with a glass of orange juice and go to bed.

21
CHAPTER

Every Autumn, just before Yom Kippur, my parents close down our summer house for the winter. Cape Cod winters are notoriously harsh and blustery, and the house, a stately gray two-story that once belonged to an eccentric whaling captain named Jedediah Coffin, seems to be forever in need of repair. After every winter, siding and roof shingles must be replaced and the gray trim touched up with exterior semigloss. The offshore gales are so strong, they can crack windows, and the ancient plumbing requires at least one major repair every year. Pipes freeze, fuses blow, the roof leaks. The house, in short, is one big pain in the keester. So, my father putties and paints the windows and touches up the door trim and my mother cleans. Together, they put up the storm windows. On Yom Kippur they drop their work and attend Jewish services at a converted Quaker meeting house on Fair Street.

One night in the fall of 1991, shortly after The High Holidays, I am rousted out of bed by the ringing phone. It is Phoebe and she is beside herself. She is crying and blowing her nose and trying to speak all at the same time, and it is coming out garbled and unintelligible.

"Pull yourself together, stop sniffling and try to speak calmly," I say. "I can't understand a word."

She takes a deep breath and blows her nose. "It's Mom," she says. "She's been in a car accident."

"Oh God. She's not—"

"Dead? No, thank God."

I feel relief and anger well up in me at the same time. "It's four o'clock in the morning in the east, Phoebe. What the hell are they doing out driving at four o'clock in the morning?"

"It happened six or seven hours ago."

"And they just told you?"

"They airlifted her by helicopter from Nantucket. She's at Boston General. Dad didn't think the doctors in Nantucket were good enough to handle it so..."

"Oh my God, how bad is it?"

"She has a concussion, some broken ribs and her right leg is badly fractured."

"And Dad?"

"He's fine."

"How is that possible? Weren't they together?"

"I don't know. I didn't get all the details."

"What about the airbag?"

"What airbag? She was driving the Bug."

My parents maintain a Volkswagen at the summer house to save them the trouble and expense of ferrying over their Buick every year. The Bug can also maneuver more easily down Nantucket's narrow cobblestone streets, but it is old and rusty and unsafe.

"How many times have I told them to get rid of that car?" I say. "That car is a deathtrap. They might as well commit suicide!"

"You sound just like Dad," Phoebe observes.

An hour later, I am on the red-eye to Boston.

⁓⊙⁓

When I arrive at my mother's hospital room at 6:25 the next morning, I find her bed empty and stripped of its sheets. This is not a good sign. I have seen this scenario often enough on television to know that it can only mean one thing: the patient has been moved to the morgue. Suddenly, I am overcome with fear, choked up, barely able to speak, distraught. I have had no sleep in sixteen hours, I am a zombie, and I start madly searching the room for some sign that my mother was here. I look in the bathroom, I look behind the curtains, I yank open the shower door, the closet. I am temporarily insane. Until this moment, the possibility of death had not even entered my mind. But what if Phoebe's estimation of her injuries is wrong? What if the head injury is more serious than a concussion? Have I arrived too late? Are Phoebe and my father already at a funeral home, tearfully picking out a casket?

I step into the hallway. "Excuse me," I say, grabbing a passing intern in a green smock. "I'm looking for Mrs. Dorfman? Gloria Dorfman. From room 345?"

"Dorfman?" He is pale and unshaven and in the harsh fluorescent light I can see every hair stubble and blemish on his cheek.

"Broken leg, concussion…?"

"Oh yes. She's in surgery," the intern says. "Sixth floor."

"Thank you."

I dash for the nearest elevator and make it inside just before the doors close. The trip to the sixth floor is interminable. I pace. I bang the wall. I hit the button a few more times. Finally, when the elevator doors whoosh open I leap out into the waiting room where I immediately see Phoebe and my father sitting beside each other sipping coffee in Styrofoam cups.

"Martin!" they say simultaneously.

"How is she?"

"She's in surgery," Phoebe says. "What are you doing here?"

"You have to ask?"

"You didn't need to come," my father says. "We don't need you. We can handle it just fine ourselves."

"Well it's a little late for that," I say. "I'm here. I wanted to come."

"You took a plane?"

"No, Dad, I rode my bike."

"What if the plane had crashed?"

"It didn't. Can we drop this?"

My father shrugs.

"Is she going to be all right?" I ask.

"Of course," my father says. "Unless the doctors screw up, which is always a distinct possibility."

"What do you mean?"

"They won't listen to me," my father says. "They know everything better. Bunch of twenty-five-year-old know-it-alls, wet behind the ears To hear them talk you'd think they've been practicing medicine for thirty years. The medical profession is in a sorry state these days, I can tell you that."

I sit down and take a sip of Phoebe's coffee.

"Did you wash your hands?" my father asks.

"No."

"This is a hospital, Martin. It's crawling with bacteria. You should wash your hands if you're going to eat. By the way, you look like hell."

"Thanks."

"When was the last time you had a checkup?"

"Can we drop this line of questioning?" I say.

"No. How's your cholesterol?"

"Fine."

"Are you up-to-date on your tetanus shots?"

"Yes."

"One every ten years."

"I know, I know."

"While you're here, let's get a blood pressure reading."

"I don't think so."

"Your sister did."

I look at Phoebe in disbelief. She shrugs. She is more willing to humor him than I am. She gives in out of expediency while I stubbornly argue until I am blue in the face. Or until my blood pressure rises, which may explain why my blood pressure is so much higher than Phoebe's.

"My blood pressure is fine."

"Suit yourself," my father says. "You wouldn't be the first 42-year-old man to drop dead of a heart attack. Is that what you want?"

"Yeah Dad," I sigh. "That's what I want. I want to drop dead of a heart attack."

"Wise guy," my father says. "Always the wise guy. Always knows everything better. A regular Einstein."

I have heard this so many times, it no longer produces a reaction. Sighing, my father turns back to his newspaper. As far as he is concerned, our reunion is over. Phoebe stands up and signals me with a tilt of her head to accompany her to the vending machines. We amble across the room, out of earshot of my father. I maintain the charade by plunking a couple of quarters into one of the machines and pulling out a plastic-wrapped package of Ritz crackers. I am not hungry; I hand the crackers to Phoebe.

"I'm glad you're here," she says. "He's driving me nuts."

"I can imagine."

"I spent the night with him at the Ramada Inn. That was a real picnic."

"I'll bet."

"Not only does he snore, he gets up every hour to pee."

"He's an old man."

"Besides, there's something kind of weird about this whole accident thing." She whispers this, keeping a wary eye on my father across the room.

"Oh?"

"He doesn't want to talk about it. Every time I bring it up, he either leaves to go to the bathroom or goes outside to have a smoke."

"Maybe he was driving."

"But he doesn't have a single cut or a laceration or anything."

"So he was lucky."

"And another thing," Phoebe continues. "Mom doesn't have any cuts or lacerations either. How is that possible? She gets a concussion, breaks two ribs and her leg, but there's not a scratch on her."

"So?"

"You don't find that a little… odd?"

"What are you saying?" I ask. "Are you saying that Dad beats her?"

"I don't know what I'm saying," Phoebe says. "I just think something's weird. I asked Mom if the Bug got totaled and she says no, it's fine. They haven't even called their insurance company or anything and you know how anal they are about that kind of stuff. I told them I would take care of it and they said no."

I give this mystery some serious thought. "It was probably just a minor car accident and Dad was lucky, that's all."

"I don't know," Phoebe says.

And now we both look over at our father, an old man with white hair and a slight hunchback, a lonely, unhappy man, a man with scuffed shoes and a sprinkling of dandruff on his shoulders, and I suddenly feel an overpowering sadness, for I know that one day I will be that old man sitting alone on a plastic chair in a hospital lounge, while my own children secretly conspire about me in hushed tones across the room. And worst of all, I know this will happen in the blink of an eye.

⁓

Six hours later, we are still waiting. By now, the lounge is littered with the flotsam and jetsam of our long sojourn here: empty coffee cups and Coke cans, red plastic coffee stirrers, parts of uneaten ham and cheese sandwiches from the hospital cafeteria, Twinkie wrappers. I have tried ten times to concentrate on an article about the habitats of African lemurs in an old waiting room issue of *National Geographic*, but I cannot focus. I read the same paragraph over and over. Meanwhile, my father is pacing, his anger and anxiety growing with every moment that passes.

"She should have been out by now," he says. "It doesn't take this long to set a fracture. An hour or two tops! Unless they have some young inexperienced intern doing it."

"We went through that already, Dad," Phoebe says.

"Then what's wrong? Something's wrong. It shouldn't take this long. I'm a doctor. I know."

"Sit down, Dad," I say. "You're driving us nuts."

"I'm sure everything's fine," Phoebe adds.

Half an hour later, one of the rude, arrogant young doctors my father mentioned comes out to give us the news. He is a grave, humorless man in his late twenties with prematurely gray hair and cold light blue eyes.

"The leg is fine," he says, "but one of the broken ribs seems to have punctured a lung."

"Oh my God," my father says.

"We repaired the damage, but she lost consciousness in recovery and so far we've been unable to revive her."

"I knew it!" my father says. "I recommended a CAT scan but you wouldn't listen. You knew everything better!"

The doctor sighs. "I doubt it would have shown up on a CAT scan," he says. "She wasn't complaining of any pain and there wasn't any shortness of breath. No tests were indicated."

"What's the prognosis?" I ask.

"She's stable for now and her vital signs are fine, so we're not really worried. Frankly we don't really know why she's unconscious.

Unless she sustained some brain damage in the accident, but I doubt that. I'm sure she'll pull out of it."

"Hah!" my father says. "Didn't I say to do an MRI? Didn't I? Again you wouldn't listen. Imbeciles!"

"I really don't have time to listen to this," the doctor says wearily. "I have to get back."

"When will she be out of recovery?" Phoebe asks as he walks off.

"Not for another two hours or so."

As soon as the doctor wanders off, I turn angrily to my father. "You couldn't just keep your mouth shut could you?"

"Why should I? They're all idiots, all of them!"

"They're not idiots! You're the idiot!"

"Calm down, Martin," my sister says.

"It's always the same," I say to my father. "You have to express whatever you're feeling — anger, annoyance, hatred — no matter the consequences. The Great Felix Dorfman must be heard!"

"I'm entitled to express my feelings," my father says.

"Who entitles you? Don't you think in this case a little diplomacy might be in order? You think this doctor is going to want to hear your insults every time he comes around? No. So you know what he'll do? He won't come around anymore! He'll send a nurse, until you insult the nurse and then *nobody* will come around anymore. And Mom's condition might suffer from that. Mom might even die! Did that ever occur to you?"

"You're tired, Martin," he says. "From the plane trip. Take a little nap, you'll feel better."

"I AM NOT TIRED!" I yell.

I can feel my blood pressure rise. My hands are shaking. My face burns. Phoebe cowers a few feet away near the vending machines. My father, ignoring my anger, stands up and reaches into his pocket for a pouch of pipe tobacco. "I'm going out for a smoke," he says. And as I continue to fume, he strolls out of the room.

⊶

And so we wait. When they do finally roll my mother out of recovery, I am alone in the lounge, for my father has gone downstairs to the cafeteria for a pastry and Phoebe is in the bathroom. I follow the gurney into her room and watch as the orderlies lift her onto the bed. I barely recognize her. She is paler than I have ever seen her, paler than I have ever seen *anyone*, and her hair is flattened in the back and wet with perspiration in the front. A plastic oxygen mask covers her mouth and she is hooked up to a heart monitor on one side and an IV on the other. She looks awful. She looks like my grandmother before she died.

When my father returns and sees the condition my mother is in, he is beside himself with anger and fear. My outburst, from which I am still shaken, has had absolutely no impact on him, True to his usual form, he is unable to keep his anxieties to himself. The doctors are idiots, he raves. Morons! They botched it up. They did not give her the right tests, they made mistakes, they do not care, they are sloppy and lazy and incompetent. She is in a coma, he says. He insults the nurses and the orderlies who come around every hour to check my mother's vital signs. He is insolent to her doctors. He is, in short, a pest.

It falls to Phoebe and me to ease the situation. I suggest we steal some Demerol, shoot him up and send him off to a strip show downtown. More realistically, we conspire to lure him off the premises. We must, at all costs, keep him away from my mother's medical team, at least until she is well enough to dismiss him herself.

As it happens, my father departed Nantucket the night before with no luggage. The chopper pilot who airlifted my mother to Boston gave him a choice: either he could come along on the flight or his luggage could come along, but not both. Both would weigh too much. Both would be dangerous. And so my father hopped aboard and left his bags on the roof of the Nantucket Hospital which, presumably, is where they remain. He has been wearing the same clothes for two days and does not have a toothbrush or a razor.

And so, after much discussion, Phoebe and I are able to lure him to the Harvard Coop, which is just two blocks away, in search of fresh clothes and a new set of toiletries. The toiletries are a snap; the clothes prove nearly impossible. My father, it turns out, is more than a little neurotic about what he wears. You would not know this by looking at him, for his clothes always seem at least one size too big for him, the pants baggy and uncreased, the jackets formless. But after an hour, he has tried on every sweater in the place and still has not made a choice. And so we abandon sweaters and move on to an even greater challenge — underpants.

"What size do you wear?" Phoebe asks as the disgruntled clerk stands by, impatiently tapping her foot.

"I don't know," he says. "Mother buys my underwear."

"You've never bought underwear for yourself?" Phoebe asks, incredulous.

"No. Never."

"He looks like a medium to me," the clerk offers.

"No way," I say. "He doesn't even believe in the supernatural."

This pathetic attempt at humor leaves everybody looking blankly at me. "Never mind," I say. "Just a little play on words. Sorry."

"My son, the comedy writer," my father says sarcastically. "Now when he makes a joke, he has to explain it. Hah!"

"Can we get on with this?" I ask.

Phoebe picks up a package of boxer shorts and shows it to my father. He shrugs.

"If it doesn't fit perfectly," he says, "I'll return it."

"You have no idea what size you wear?" Phoebe asks, more than a little appalled.

"Not a clue."

"Dad, how can you go through life not knowing your size?"

He shrugs.

"We have to do something," Phoebe says to me. "He can't wear the same underwear every day."

"Okay," I say stepping forward. "I think I know how we can solve this problem. A little ingenuity is all it takes. Take off your coat Dad."

My father shrugs and removes his heavy corduroy jacket and hands it to the clerk. I step behind him and reach down into the back of his pants. With my fingers, I find the rim of his underpants and pull up on them until the tag shows. Phoebe starts to stifle a laugh and it suddenly hits me: I am standing in the middle of the Harvard Coop in broad daylight, giving my eighty-year-old father what amounts to an Atomic Wedgie. No matter. I proudly announce that he wears a size 36.

"Very clever, Martin," my father says. "You were always a very clever boy."

"Well thanks, Dad," I say, grateful for the praise.

"Not brilliant," he continues, suckering me once again, "not a genius. But clever."

An hour later we are still there, still unable to decide between the beige sweater and the gray sweater, the brown corduroy pants or the black wool pants, the boxers or the jockeys. Phoebe loses patience long before I do and moves off into the book section, which is downstairs. I stand doggedly in front of the dressing room, waiting for my father to try on the beige pants for the tenth time. It takes an eternity, for he is old; getting in and out of a pair of pants is not what it was for him thirty years ago.

"Are you almost done, Dad?" I ask.

But there is no answer, not even a grunt.

"Dad?" I ask again. "Are you okay?"

Again, only silence. Now I am worried.

"Dad, if you don't answer me right now, I'm coming in," I say. "I'm not kidding."

I listen for some sign, but I hear nothing. Not a peep. I fear the worst: a heart attack. Wouldn't that be a picnic — both my parents in intensive care at the same time? And so, I take a few steps forward and push back the changing room curtain.

My father is sitting on the wooden bench, half out of the beige pants, the zipper hopelessly stuck. He is sobbing quietly into a handkerchief. I don't know what to do. I stand there. He looks up at me, his eyes red and filled with tears. It is the look of a guilty child.

"It wasn't a car accident," he says, between sobs.

"What?"

"She fell down the stairs. Because there was no light on."

I can only stand there, staring fixedly, as he is again overcome by tears. The lights. Of course that is what happened. The electricity obsession. We should have figured that one out, Phoebe and I. But here's the kicker — he can't *blame* anybody for a change. It was his fault. No matter. As I look down at him, this profoundly unhappy, tormented old man, this man who creates ugly skeletal screamers for fun, I suddenly see how small he is, sitting almost fetus-like in the corner of that changing room. It's as if I am looking at him through the wrong end of a pair of binoculars.

And oddly, for one brief moment, I feel years of anger drain out of me.

◦◦◦

Phoebe, my father and I are sitting vigil in my mother's hospital room when she finally regains consciousness a little after midnight the next day. The three of us have been dozing, each of us contorted in a metal hospital chair that was not meant to provide a semblance of comfort even for plain unambitious sitting, let alone sleeping. Suddenly, my mother croaks something at us, her lips parched and dry, and when we realize that she is asking for water, the three of us leap up in unison and fall all over each other to get to the pitcher. All at once, she has three brimming Dixie cups thrust in her face. She takes one and gulps it down. The cool drink seems to invigorate her and she struggles to sit up in bed.

"Sleep well, Mom?" I say.

"Is that you, Martin?" she says groggily, trying to focus without her glasses as I fluff her pillow.

"In the flesh, Mom."

"What are you doing here?"

"I was in the neighborhood," I say.

"You took a plane?"

"Scottie beamed me up."

"What?"

"A joke. Never mind."

"My son, the comedy writer," my father says, shaking his head.

"You didn't need to come. Such a long trip. It must have cost a lot."

"Well, it's too late to worry about that now," I say. "Here I am, necessary or not."

"Well I'm glad to see you."

"I'm glad to see you too," I say.

She takes another sip of water and glances at my father. "Your father told you about the car accident?"

"We know what happened Mom," I say, taking her hand. "He told us the truth. It's okay."

This takes a moment to sink in. After all, she's been out cold for 36 hours. "It's a good thing he turned out those lights," she says.

"That dime we saved on the electricity is going to go a long way with these medical bills."

A second passes before we realize she is being facetious. My mother is not known to be the wit in the family. A day after surgery and she is cracking wise! We are all impressed and we laugh heartily, even my father. Suddenly, we are all a bit closer. We are momentarily united by laughter. We are the Waltons.

Phoebe leaves the next day but I end up staying on another full week, mainly to keep my mother company, but also to run errands and to make sure my father eats properly, bathes regularly and doesn't irrevocably alienate every member of the hospital staff with his endless reminders and accusations. Every other day, I bring take-out Chinese up to the hospital room and we eat together. We play Scrabble. We watch Masterpiece Theater. We read. Sometimes my mother and I talk about the good old days — whenever the hell they were supposed to be — or about my therapy. Although I have many opportunities to bring it up, I never ask about her unexplained six month absence following the hepatitis epidemic. I am tempted once or twice, but the words stick in my throat and so I let it pass. After all, what difference will it make now? It was a long time ago, a lifetime ago. Maybe she was tired of my father's neurotic idiosyncrasies and needed a long break. Maybe she had an affair. Maybe *he* had an affair and she found out about it. Maybe she was contemplating divorce. Who knows? Who cares?

By the end of the week, my mother is walking with a cane and the hospital officially discharges her. I arrange for them to take a hired car back to Highland Falls, for my father's driving ability is only considered legal in bumper cars. I also arrange for a housekeeper to help my mother clean and cook until she can manage for herself. My father is hopeless in this area and cannot even prepare toast. We part company in the hospital's underground parking garage where their driver waits.

"Thank you Martin, thank you for coming," my mother says. "I'm glad we had some time together."

"Me too," I say.

"I wish we got to see each other more often."

"Right."

"We'll send you a check for the airfare."

"Not necessary."

"Indulge me."

"Fine."

"Be a good boy, Martin," my father says, shaking my hand.

"You too, Dad."

"Remember to always wash your hands, Martin," my father advises as he climbs into the car. "And make a nice lather. You're wasting your time if you don't create a nice lather."

"Got it," I say, waving to their car as it moves slowly down the ramp and then disappears into the street.

CHAPTER

22

The effect of the Little Pink Pills is nothing short of miraculous. The morning after my first dose, I wake up feeling as if the last two years of misery and despair were nothing more than a bad dream. From the moment my eyes blink open, I am vigorous, energetic, invigorated, a soul yanked back from the abyss by a medicinal bungee cord. The world has gone from shades of gray to a palette of iridescent pastels. Birds tweet, grass grows and I am alive again. I can barely contain myself. I am exuberant, effusive. The endorphins have kicked it, the seratonin is flowing and I feel as potent as a teenager.

"This is most unusual indeed," Dr. Igor says cautiously when I call him that morning.

"What is?"

"That I got it right on the first try."

"That's encouraging."

"Sorry."

"Well I guess you lucked out this time," I say.

"Perhaps."

"Perhaps?"

"In my experience, it takes several weeks for the effects of the medication to be felt, but everybody reacts differently. You might very well be the exception. Still, we cannot rule out the placebo effect."

"Oh I think we can, Doc," I say. "This is not the first medication I've taken for this."

"Nor is it the first time your symptoms have disappeared," Igor points out.

"Thanks," I say. "Now I'm really depressed. I was fine before, now I'm depressed. Isn't it supposed to work the other way around with you guys?"

"Call me in a week," he says. "We'll see how things are progressing."

The very next day, I get a call from Ben Fogelman whom I have not heard from in almost a year. Icarus Films has officially given my script the green light. They have signed a director (a twenty-five-year-old Hungarian Orson Welles named Shmego Chacheszcow) and they are sending the script around to various actors. A production office has been set up in Vancouver, locations are being scouted, budgets drawn up, story boards drawn, crews assembled.

"In other words," Fogelman says, "the money train has left the depot."

"That's great, Ben," I say, truly delighted. "Have they scheduled principal photography yet?"

"Six months."

"Wow."

"So, *mazel tov* to both of us, especially me because, just between us, I've got more than a few of my own dollars invested in this particular project."

"Is that wise?" I ask. "To expose yourself that much?"

Before the words leave my mouth, I regret the wording of that question. But Fogelman doesn't seem to notice.

"Probably not. Most producers wouldn't invest a penny of their own, but I'm old-fashioned. If I believe in a project I put my money where my mouth is. If the picture does well, I'll be rolling in dough. That money bought me three gross points."

But I have more on my mind than Ben Fogelman's imminent

wealth. "About this director," I say. "I suppose he'll want to meet with me at some point, get my input…"

"Don't count on it," Fogelman says. "This guy, this Shmego is one of these *auteur* types. A prima donna. You didn't hear this from me Martin, but he's one arrogant prick."

"Oh?"

"Thinks he's a big genius. Thinks he's some kind of Slavic Frank Capra. What an ego on this guy. So don't expect much."

"Can I hang around on the set?"

"What for?"

"It's my baby they're shooting."

"You writers kill me," Ben says. "Take it from me, Martin. Film-making is boring. You sit around for hours watching the lighting guy and the makeup guy and the dialogue coach and all the other schleppers. You'd be wasting your time. My advice? Stay home, write another script."

I take this to mean that Shmego does not want to have anything to do with me. I have probably been banned from the set. No matter. My name will be immortalized on celluloid, right next to that of Larry Bud Pushkin. Unless the whole thing falls through.

Six months later, thanks to the Little Pink Pills, my physical condition continues to improve. My appetite for food returns and I quickly gain back every pound I lost over the last three years, and then some. The dark circles under my eyes disappear and my pallor gives way to a healthy pink coloring. My self-imposed hibernation comes to an end and Ursula and I resume our old stature in the social hierarchy. On my forty-third birthday, Ursula throws me a surprise party. After surviving the initial bout of angina when twelve of my closest friends pop unexpectedly out of a small bathroom, I actually manage to enjoy myself a little. I eat, I drink, I make merry. I blow out candles. My wish? Not fame nor fortune but the very basic plea that I feel well for the rest of the month. Lately, the glass is always half *full*. So what if I am one year closer to my death? Consider the alternative.

And then another miracle happens. Icarus actually manages to assemble a cast of B-list actors, and principal photography finally commences on June 3, 1993. Several months later I receive my half of the back-end check which, after deducting Gavin's 10% and all the taxes, comes to $65,459, not a fortune, but as Ursula reminds me on any number of occasions, it is preferable to a sharp stick in the eye. No argument there. We buy a new car, get the kids new bikes and have the kitchen cabinets refaced.

One year later, Icarus releases the film nationwide, but in only 540 theaters. It receives mostly tepid reviews, a few downright pans, and earns a pathetic $4,000,000 at the box office before it is pulled, after only three weeks, to make way for the summer blockbusters. It is, in other words, a huge flop. To add insult to injury, several critics put the film on their Ten Worst Lists at the end of the year. My only consolation is the fact that Shmego takes most of the blame. Gavin makes sure that Larry Bud Pushkin takes the rest.

But the film's impact does not end there. In 1995, it is mentioned in the Business Section of the *Los Angeles Times*. The context is an article about the recent bankruptcy of Ben Fogelman's production company. The failure of my film is cited as one of the primary causes of his financial ruin. Apparently, Ben's investment of his own personal income in the film was larger than I thought, and when his company goes belly-up Ben sinks with it. One year later, Ben Fogelman commits suicide by locking himself in a garage until he suffocates from the carbon monoxide fumes. My film is mentioned once again, this time in his obituary. Having been the catalyst in his bankruptcy, my film is now cited as one of the indirect causes of his suicide. I am aghast. I am appalled. I am also immediately reminded of the phrase that Ben Fogelman uttered to me so many times, a phrase that, in retrospect, sounds eerily prescient: *You writers kill me.* My God! Did he mean this *literally*? Had I known in advance that my script was going to end up *murdering the producer*, I might have thought twice before putting pen to paper. My purpose was to amuse, but I suppose one must never underestimate the power of the written word. I am not formally invited to Ben Fogelman's funeral, but I attend anyway and, as is the custom, I take up the shovel, say a prayer and throw a little dirt in the grave. It is a depressingly small gathering that has come to wish him adieu, mostly family members, very few Industry people. Jen and Ted are conspicuously absent. No matter. From that day on, whenever I see liver — goose, chicken, chopped, cooked or raw — I think fondly of Ben Fogelman.

⌘

And then one day the reality of it all finally strikes me. For until now it has not dawned on me that I am, technically speaking, *mentally ill*, that I am, as they say, loco, unhinged, daffy, dotty, balmy, bughouse, slaphappy, one taco short of a Combination Platter. If insanity is nothing more than a chemical imbalance, a slight misfiring of electrical sparks between the synapses, then I am as authentic a whacko as any garden variety paranoid-schizophrenic or manic-depressive. Four hundred years ago, they would have locked me in a drafty castle tower and thrown away the key.

And there's more: As a result of my unusually speedy reaction to the medication, Dr. Igor has included me in a case study, which he delivers once a year to his students and at conventions all over the world. Although I am still virtually unknown in the film industry, I am quite famous in the milieu of shrinkdom, although there are no royalties or residuals to be had, no film rights, no endorsements, no high-paid testimonials. To psychiatrists all over the world, I am the well-known crackpot Martin D.

But I have plenty of company — most of the human race for instance.

Sure, we're not *all* paranoid-schizophrenics or manic-depressives or obsessive-compulsives, and granted some of us are better at putting forth a convincing image of mental normality to the outside world, but underneath it all we are all a little crazy. There is no such thing as normal, you see; there are no *functional* families, the very term is an oxymoron. The normal condition of the human species is total raving insanity. Why? Because only lunatics would undertake the daunting task, generation after generation, of survival on this lonely, inhospitable planet, in the middle of a dark, unfathomable universe. Only a race of complete loonies could be able to live happily for eighty-odd years, knowing that, at any moment and without warning, death could end it all in an infinite assortment of utterly gruesome and horrific ways. Stomach cancer, Saturday night specials, arteriosclerosis, Buchenwald, quadriplegia, road rage, myesthenia gravis — it's a wonder any of us live past the age of two.

So what makes us get up every morning and *not* commit suicide? What makes us keep going? Chemicals. The very chemicals that my brain is somewhat lax in producing on its own. Serotonin, dopamine, endorphins, the *happy* chemicals. The chemicals that keep us from hanging ourselves out of total despair. The chemicals that have us grinning inanely through the most crushing, unimagineable human disasters. In other words, we are all *stoned* folks. Intoxicated. Plastered. Crocked, tanked, soused, stinko, strung out, blotto. Every last one of us.

Except the clinically depressed. We get to experience life stone cold sober. There's no fog on our mirrors, folks. What you see is what you get.

And so I muddle through. Nora's insightful words about my youth often echo in my mind, and I find myself reliving the childhood I was never really permitted to have through the shenanigans of my own children. And every day, I am aware that *these* are the best years of my life, these pleasant days that I spend navigating them through their childhoods. I surely do not want them to grow up too fast as I did. Life is short enough as it is and one day, sooner than I think, I will watch them move out of my life and into their own lives and I will be a lonely old fuddy-duddy surrounded by a thunderous silence where once there was childrens' laughter. Oh yes, that one will be a difficult good-bye, an occasion for the sunglasses if ever there was one. Even today, when I look at photos of them when they were two or three my eyes get damp. In the meantime, I like to think that I am doing my best to raise them in an enlightened way, but who knows? Maybe twenty years from now, they too will end up slouching sullenly on some therapist's couch, staring at a box of Kleenex, folding their arms defensively and talking about what a godawful mess Ursula and I made of their lives.

As for my parents, they continue their peculiar symbiosis. My father stares at a blank canvas every morning for three hours and wraps the blood pressure sleeve around my mother's arm three times a day. She fulfills her part of the bargain by keeping her blood pressure high, falling ill periodically and breaking a limb or spraining a muscle at least once a year. When they are well enough to travel, they come out to California to visit. My mother always brings a new deck of cards and, just as my grandparents did with me, plays endless games of gin rummy with the kids, letting them clobber her for nickels and dimes; my father sits alone in a corner smoking his pipe and contemplating his mortality; and somehow my daughters manage to learn about the importance of creating a nice lather, for this is knowledge which they will one day pass on to their children and to their children's children through the generations as part of the Dorfman clan's tribal folklore.

Continuity, as my father would say. Continuity.

ᕬ

And what of Delilah?

After I am certain that the Little Pink Pills have worked their magic, after I am convinced beyond any doubt that I am cured, I call her. And why not? I no longer feel the need to commiserate. Our mutual desperation society has folded up its tent. We are both veterans now, survivors of our own private hells, doughboys who lived through the trenches and so, for old times sake, I invite her to meet me at the soup joint one Sunday afternoon.

I am surprised at how terrific she looks. Gone are those deep, sickly gray shadows around her eyes. The face has filled out, her body borders on pudgy. Her cheeks are ruddy, her voice robust, her tone cheerful. I am sure she notices similar corporeal improvements in my own condition.

As afternoon turns to dusk, we catch up on each other's progress — she's up for a soft drink commercial and later this summer will play in a charity production of *Two Gentlemen of Verona* — but once we have explored this subject thoroughly, neither of us, it seems, has much more to say. And so, after I fill her in on my recent adventures in script development, we eat our watery soups in silence. I suppose all we ever really had in common was the illness. In health, we have little to say to one another. Apparently, Delilah feels this as strongly as I do.

"Well," she says.

"Well."

"So."

"So."

"I'll see you around."

"Yeah."

"Guess this is good-bye, then," she mutters.

"Guess so."

Then she takes my hand and gives it a little shake but does not let go. "Aren't you forgetting something?" she asks.

"Am I?"

"The rain check."

"The rain check?"

"You don't remember? The time you picked me up from Twain's? We were sitting in your car…"

The light dawns. "Oh yeah. Right. The rain check."

"We don't really have to if you don't want to."

"A deal's a deal. Go ahead. Give it your best shot."

I close my eyes and pucker up. Nothing happens for about two seconds. Then I hear Delilah scrape out of her director's chair. Another second passes and she pecks me lightly… on the cheek.

"That's your best shot?"

"Afraid so."

"Could use some work."

"I'll look into it."

"Right."

"Guess this really is good-bye then."

"Yup."

"It's been nice knowing you, Martin. Really."

I nod my head solemnly. "Stay well, Delilah."

"We'll always have Van Nuys," she says. "They can't take that away from us."

"No they can't," I agree, lifting my glass of water in a toast. "Toujours Van Nuys."

About The Author

J ohn Blumenthal was born in Middletown, New York and attended
Tufts College. His humorous essays have appeared in such publications as *Playboy* and *Punch*. In addition to several novels and
nonfiction books, he has also co-written the screenplays for the movies *Short Time* (20th Century Fox) and *Blue Streak* (Columbia Pictures). He lives in Southern California.

T o obtain additional copies of *What's Wrong With Dorfman?*, please contact your local bookstore or provide the following information:

Name _____

Address _____

City _____ State _____ Zip _____

____ copies @ $11.95 each $ _____

California residents, please add applicable sales tax $ _____

Shipping: $3.20/first copy; $1.60 each additional copy $ _____

Total enclosed $ _____

For more than 5 copies, please contact the publisher for quantity rates. Send completed order form and your check or money order to:

Farmer Street Press
2060-D Ave. De Los Arboles #497
Thousand Oaks, CA 91362

e-mail: FarmerStPress@aol.com
888-297-4498

or order via our Web Site at
http://www.WhatsWrongWithDorfman.com

International shipping is extra. Please contact us for the shipping rates to your location, if outside the United States.